SOUTHERN STORM

44 SOUTH, BOOK 2

NICOLA CLAIRE

ISBN: 978-0-473-38240-7

❀ Created with Vellum

ABOUT THE AUTHOR

Nicola Claire lives in beautiful Taupo, New Zealand with her husband and two young boys.

She's tried her hand at being a paramedic, bank teller and medical sales representative, (not all necessarily in that order), but her love of writing keeps calling her back.

She has a passion for all things suspenseful, spiced up with a good dollop of romance, as long as they include strong characters - alpha males and capable females - and worlds which although make-believe are really quite believable in the end.

There's nothing better than getting caught up in a compelling, intriguing and romantic book.

When she's not writing or reading, she's out on her family boat at Lake Taupo, teaching her young boys to fish, showing them the beauty that surrounds them in nature and catching some delicious trout for dinner.

Creating rich worlds with dynamic characters and unexpected twists that shock and awe has been pure bliss for this author. And just as well, because there's a lot more story yet to tell...

For more information:
www.nicolaclairebooks.com
nicola@nicolaclairebooks.com

ALSO BY NICOLA CLAIRE

Kindred Series

Kindred

Blood Life Seeker

Forbidden Drink

Giver of Light

Dancing Dragon

Shadow's Light

Entwined With The Dark

Kiss Of The Dragon

Dreaming Of A Blood Red Christmas (Novella)

Mixed Blessing Mystery Series

Mixed Blessing

Dark Shadow

Rogue Vampire (Coming Soon)

Sweet Seduction Series

Sweet Seduction Sacrifice

Sweet Seduction Serenade

Sweet Seduction Shadow

Sweet Seduction Surrender

Sweet Seduction Shield

Sweet Seduction Sabotage

Sweet Seduction Stripped

Sweet Seduction Secrets

Sweet Seduction Sayonara

Elemental Awakening Series

The Tempting Touch Of Fire

The Soothing Scent Of Earth

The Chilling Change Of Air

The Tantalising Taste Of Water

The Eternal Edge Of Aether (Novella)

H.E.A.T. Series

A Flare Of Heat

A Touch Of Heat

A Twist Of Heat (Novella)

A Lick Of Heat (Coming Soon)

Citizen Saga

Elite

Cardinal

Citizen

Masked (Novella)

Wiped

Scarlet Suffragette Series

Fearless

Breathless

Heartless (Coming Soon)

Blood Enchanted Series

Blood Enchanted

Blood Entwined

Blood Enthralled (Coming Soon)

---

44 South Series

Southern Sunset

Southern Storm

Southern Strike (Coming Soon)

DESCRIPTION

Sometimes life makes decisions for you. They're just not the decisions you would have made for yourself.

> *STALKER.*
> *KILLER.*
> *MOHAWK-WEARING BOY RACERS?*

Trouble seems to be following Olivia Logan. When she's forced to leave Auckland and move to Twizel, Olivia thinks her stalker problems have been left behind. But the small southern town of Twizel possesses its own threats. The people are strange. The community tight knit. The farmers...

Well, let's just say they leave other men for dead.

> *HANDSOME.*
> *DAMAGED.*
> *GOT A THING FOR DAMSELS IN DISTRESS?*

Matt Drake is one seriously messed up cop. And one very determined father. When he hires a new homeschool teacher for his traumatised twin daughters, he doesn't realise the woman who walks through his door is there for more than just his kids. Or that she's more than she appears. And he sure as hell doesn't realise she's bringing trouble with her. But trouble is something Matt is good at. Making it. Fixing it.

The type of trouble Olivia Logan brings, though, is dark and dangerous, and utterly addictive. No one's sure Matt is up to dealing with that. Not even him.

This sleepy hollow has just woken up and Twizel doesn't care if you were born here or born to live here. Sooner or later your secrets will come out.

This is the second book in the 44 South Series: 44° South of the Equator where things can get a little strange.

CHAPTER 1

ISN'T THAT WHAT THEY ALL SAY?

LIV

SOMETIMES LIFE MAKES DECISIONS FOR YOU. THEY'RE JUST NOT the decisions you would have made for yourself.

"This has to stop, Olivia," David murmured to my side.

I couldn't formulate an answer. My eyes were stuck fast on the four-foot tall picture pinned to my office wall.

"It's escalating," he added.

It was. There was no denying that now. The picture was of me. I had no recollection of it having been taken.

"He's getting bolder," David said. "As if he doesn't care if he's caught breaking and entering our building. You know as well as I what that means."

Yes, it meant his ASPD was advancing; the situations he placed himself in carried increasingly greater risk.

"Next he'll act on his aggressive impulses. He's already sacrificing animals for you. Soon it will progress to harming people."

The picture was painted in blood. The crime scene analysts had determined it was cat blood. Not human. But the implication was clear.

"This is a direct threat to your safety, Dr Logan," the police detective standing behind us said.

I didn't turn to look at him. I couldn't stop looking at my picture on the wall.

"Without knowing which one of your patients is doing this," the detective added, "we can't protect you adequately enough."

I blinked. Took in the carefully written words. Knew whoever had done this had taken his time. Spent more than a few hasty minutes in my office. Had possibly even been here all night.

"He bypassed the alarm system," the second detective said. He seemed very earnest and forthright. I liked him. He didn't sugar coat his words like the other officer did. "He's intelligent. Fearless. And fixated on you. I don't need a psychology degree to figure out he's crazy."

"Crazy's not a term we use lightly, Detective," I said.

"Olivia," David pleaded. "This can't go on. It's not safe. For you. For any of us."

What he didn't say, was it wasn't safe for our patients. For our business. For our bottom line.

I let out a sigh and glanced around my office. It had been my home away from home for eight years. I'd done some good in here. Reached a few people. Helped others.

My eyes were drawn back to the enlarged photo. Some people I apparently hadn't helped at all.

"We'll go through your client list again," the first detective said. Detective Stone, if I remembered correctly. "Try to single out a prime suspect. Someone saw something around here last night."

"But if they didn't," the other one added, Detective Sergeant Pierce, I reminded myself, "he'll return. Without a response from you, he'll be compelled to investigate. What did you say Antisocial Personality Disorder patients do? 'Do things - even though they may hurt people - to get what they want.' He wants you, doctor. He wants you to react. Don't give him that."

"Take a break," David said. "Just a month or two." He glanced at the detectives. Stone smiled; Pierce shrugged. David frowned and then turned his doctor face on me; the one that said he cared. "It won't take that long to find him."

"A month or two?" I said. "What am I supposed to do for a month or two?"

"Go to the beach. Get a suntan," David quipped.

I was lily white and proud of it.

My eyebrows drew together.

"I don't know, Olivia," he added, frustration marring his voice now. "But this can't go on."

I nodded my head. He was right, of course. I was just being stubborn. I didn't like the idea of one of my patients making me run. Running implied fear. I wasn't scared, per se. I was angry.

How dare someone chase me away? Even my education didn't help to dissuade the anger. I understood, on a purely academic level, that this person couldn't help his fixation.

On an entirely emotional one, an entirely human one, I wanted to rage.

This was so unfair.

"Two months," I said.

"Maybe three," Detective Stone said.

"Six at the most," Detective Sergeant Pierce corrected.

I looked at David. "We'll share your case load amongst us."

"And if one of those is the person in question?" I demanded.

"We'll be watching the office very closely, Dr Logan," Pierce offered.

"But not so closely we break your patient/doctor confidentiality agreements," Stone groused.

This was why they wanted me gone from here. We didn't know who was doing this. Every time I opened my door to a familiar face, a patient I had been treating for weeks, months, maybe years, we didn't know if this time would be the last time I opened my office door.

I stared up at the picture of me outside my home. *My home.* And allowed myself to read the words.

The knife was cold. You never said it would be so cold. The blood was warm. You were right.

Right about what? I'd been over my notes. Again and again and again. I hadn't talked about knives or blood or the obvious connection between them with any of my current patients. Nothing to indicate a ticking time bomb was hidden in Auckland City.

Was watching me get into my car outside of my home.

"We've got this, doc," Detective Pierce said. "We're watching your patients with criminal records. We're watching those without. We're watching the office and your home. But we need some space. We need to take out one of the variables to make it easier to watch them all at once."

He scratched his goatee beard.

"You're the obvious variable that needs to go."

"Go where?" I asked, shaking my head. I had no family to speak of. My friends all lived in and around the CBD. "Where?" I asked again, a smidgeon of panic entering my tone.

"Somewhere far enough away that he won't follow," Stone said. Pierce scowled at him and then settled hard eyes on me.

"Somewhere no one knows you," he added. "Somewhere you know no one, as well."

That could just about be anywhere outside of Auckland.

"Been to the South Island?" he asked. I shook my head. "Mackenzie Country?" I gave him a dumbfounded look. "Twizel," he finished, throwing a newspaper down on my desk.

"Twizel?" I asked, stepping forward and looking down at the Otago Times. "Where the hell is Twizel?"

"Good enough for me, doc," the detective said.

"We'll give you a false identity," Stone added.

"You can still do some good," Pierce said.

"Not exactly the sort of thing you were doing here."

"But close enough."

David reached forward and picked the paper up. "Homeschool teacher?"

Detective Sergeant Pierce shrugged. "Kids need someone who can handle their special needs."

"What sort of special needs?" I demanded.

David scanned the help wanted ad. His eyes came up to mine. "They're mute."

"Perfect if you ask me," Stone said, straightening his well-worn jacket. "If you slip up and tell them who you really are, they won't be able to give you away." He mimed zipping closed his lips.

"You have got to be kidding me," I muttered.

"Kids," David said. "You've always been so good with the littlies."

I glared at him. He smirked.

If there was one thing I was scared of, it was kids.

Fuck my life. Isn't that what they all say?

CHAPTER 2

THIS HAD TO FUCKING STOP

MATT

The souped-up Subaru spun its tyres and sprayed an arc of gravel up into the air. It fishtailed slightly, and then righted itself, the kid driving it waving his hand out the window in apology as he shot off down the highway. I closed my eyes and slowly shook my head.

This was Twizel. We didn't get boy racers.

His entourage pulled out from behind my police ute, hooting their horns in a chorus of ear-splitting tones, and then followed their counterpart in a vibrant line of pulsating neon blue LED underbody lights.

It was the middle of the day. What the fuck they thought those lights would do was anyone's guess.

I walked back to my truck scowling. It was a familiar sensation lately.

Pushing hooligans and the ever increasing vandalism in the township that seemed to come with them aside, I turned the ute towards Red Tussock. Coffee was in order. I had a feeling it was going to be a very long day.

A newly minted Red Tussock Ranger - RED 13 - was sitting in

the homestead's return, but Luke's car was missing. I stared at Zach's overly shiny ute and scowled further. Just what I didn't need. But I was here now, and he'd probably spotted me the moment I hit the tree line, so leaving would show my hand. Give him the upper one.

Zach had a tendency to pounce on weakness.

I pushed through the door to the kitchen and walked over to the coffee pot. It still looked fresh, so I poured myself a generous portion and leant back against the bench to take a sip.

"What are you doing here?" Zach asked from the kitchen table, his eyes on the newspaper spread before him and little else.

"I live here."

"Not in the homestead you don't."

I took another sip of my drink.

"Crime rate's up," he said when he didn't get a bite out of me.

"Nothing new there," I commented mildly.

"Someone graffitied the library building. Bet Helen chewed their balls off."

"Could have been a girl."

"Drawing a penis ejaculating?"

"It was a small penis."

Zach snorted.

"Found a job yet?" I asked.

"Doing some stuff around the place for Luke." He shut the paper with a disgruntled thump. "Might as well be cleaning the fucking latrines."

"You're the one who left the army."

His eyes finally met mine. "It seemed like the right time to come home."

He meant because of me. I stared down into my coffee and didn't comment.

"You just missed Luke."

"Where's he gone?" I forced myself to ask. Why was it so hard to talk to Zach?

Fuck. I knew why. So did he. Missy.

"Officially? Into town to pick up some shit from PGG Wrightson's. Unofficially? He's gone to see Maggie."

"Maggie's working the Pukaki stretch today," I pointed out.

"Luke knows how to drive," Zach shot back sarcastically.

I scrubbed a hand over my face and turned to rinse out my cup.

"I like her," my brother offered. "She's got spunk."

"She's Luke's."

Zach's chair pushed back with a piercing screech. I spun around and faced him. He looked riled.

"I know who she belongs to," he said between gritted teeth.

"You always know, Zach," I replied before I could stop myself. "But that doesn't mean you care."

"Fuck you."

He stormed out of the house and stalked to his Ranger. The engine revved loudly. Throwing it into gear, he shot out of the return, spraying gravel. Several pieces hit my police car. I leant against the kitchen bench, hands spread, fingers grasping granite, and lowered my head.

He hadn't deserved that. My body started to tremble. My throat felt bone dry. I pushed myself upright and walked into the lounge, opening up the drinks cabinet. I stood there for far too fucking long looking at the whisky. Staring the fucking thing down.

The trembling became a full body shake. Sweat rolled down under my shirt collar. I licked my lips, my hand reaching out before I could stop it. The bottle in my grip before I could think to shut the cabinet door.

I held it before me and read the label. Every single word. I read it again for good measure and then I slowly leant forward and placed the bottle back on the shelf, closing the door.

My cell phone ringing broke the heavy silence in the room, allowing me to draw breath for the first time in what had to have been minutes. I reached into my pocket and withdrew the phone, swiping the screen and bringing it to my ear.

"Drake," I said in way of greeting.

"Son, where are you?" Dad's voice came down the line. "It's almost one. She'll be here any minute."

I closed my eyes and tipped back my head, praying for this to be over.

"Work," I said, my voice sounding distant.

"Your mother and I are happy to keep her entertained, Matt," Dad offered. "But the woman really needs to see you before she accepts the position."

"She needs to see the girls," I countered. "I'm irrelevant."

"Hardly," Dad muttered. "Get your arse over here."

"Joshua!" Mum called out in the background. "Mind your tongue."

"Sorry, love," Dad mumbled. "Matt," he said, voice lowered. "If you don't pull your sh... self together and get involved in these girls' rehabilitation then I'll have you cut out of Red Tussock."

"You can't do that, Dad," I pointed out with forced patience.

"I am still the head of this family, Matt. I can and I will. Get over here."

The phone went dead, along with any hope of avoiding reality.

It wasn't that I didn't want to spend every second of every day with Rachel and Dani. It was just that they reminded me of her. And it's not as though they looked exactly like Missy. No. It was darker and more twisted than that.

The longer they didn't talk, the harder it was not to imagine what happened. Not to think up a multitude of reasons for them to have withdrawn into themselves. We still didn't know what Marinkovich did that day. We knew he'd been there; he admitted as much himself. But we didn't know why or what happened. How it had all happened.

But we did know, though, how it ended. Missy dead. The girls mute. And Ivan Fucking Marinkovich on a lynching.

If he weren't already dead, I'd kill him all over again. Those thoughts haunted me late at night, too. Darker than the others. More twisted. I imagined the knife I'd use. The rope. The bloody knuckles.

I could smell the taint of blood on the air. Feel the sting of each pummel. Taste his fear.

But in truth, I sometimes wondered if it was *my* fear I tasted in the middle of the night when I woke up sweating. The sheets tangled, my chest heaving. I'd wander down the hallway, trying to get my breaths to even, and peer into the girls' room.

Then I'd cross the hallway and peer into the master bedroom.

I hadn't slept in there since Missy died. Since it all came out and my life was torn apart like a piece of soggy paper. I hadn't crossed the threshold once. I'd stare at that bed and the throw pillows she loved so fucking much, and I'd wonder if I could ever get past this.

This hurt. This anger. This... devastation.

And then I'd remind myself I had two beautiful daughters and I'd face the day all over again.

What a hero. Breathing. Existing. Craving another mouthful of oblivion.

This had to fucking stop. *Please. Just let it stop.*

CHAPTER 3

I CAN DO THIS

LIV

THE PROPERTY WAS A GOOD HALF HOUR OUT OF TOWN. IF YOU could call Twizel a town, that is. I guess it was big enough. It had a supermarket. Kind of. A petrol station. A café and library.

A police station.

I'd made sure I knew where that was. The detectives in Auckland had told me to learn the lay of the land as soon as I got here. So, yesterday was spent driving down each street, surprisingly getting lost, and mapping out escape routes.

I laughed sharply at my life now as I slowed my car and parked it behind an oversized black ute in front of the small weatherboard house. It looked tidy and neat, the grass trimmed, the fence painted. A swing seat hanging under an old oak tree in the front yard. Rust-gold leaves offering up a canopy to sit under.

But there was something hopelessly sad about the picture before me. I couldn't quite place it at first. And then it came to me in a blinding flash of light.

There wasn't a single flower in the flower beds.

It was autumn. Flowers still bloomed in autumn. But every single flower bed in front of the house was barren. As if it had been dug over at the beginning of last winter and never tended to again. There were no weeds to be seen, so someone cared enough to stay on top of the gardening.

But there were no flowers and the absence of them said more than if they had been there.

I climbed out of the Volvo and looked up at the porch, the front screen opening as soon as I closed my car's door.

"Hello," I called out. "Is this the Drake house?"

"One of 'em," an older man said. "You must be Olivia Smith." Smith, it was cringeworthy. But the detectives assured me 'Smith' was a viable option. Changing my first name, they said, would be harder to remember.

They clearly didn't realise I held three degrees and a higher than average capacity for retaining information.

"Yes," I said. "I'm Olivia." I walked toward the older gentleman and offered my hand. He had to be in his seventies. I was sure the man I had spoken to on the telephone had been younger.

And then I remembered the girls.

"You must be Rachel and Dani's grandfather," I said.

"Guilty as charged," the man said. "Joshua Drake." He shook my hand with enthusiasm. I could feel the roughness to his palms, the callouses on his fingers. I glanced down at the barren garden beside us.

Thankfully, Joshua didn't see the question undoubtedly in my eyes.

"Come on inside," he said, jovially. "The wife's just pulling out some baking from the oven, and Rachel and Dani are keen as mustard to meet you."

"And their father?" I asked.

Joshua's shoulders hunched. Just slightly. You wouldn't have noticed if it wasn't your job to assess every little nuance of a person's behaviour.

"He's on his way. Had to work," Joshua offered. I wondered if 'work' was a euphemism for something else.

I followed the older man into a surprisingly feminine kitchen, noting the rooster theme interspersed with cherry blossoms on damn near every surface. The combination boggled the mind.

"There you are," a grandmotherly figure exclaimed. "Just in time for lunch."

The smell of bacon and egg pie met my nostrils, and I smiled. I'd always had a soft spot for pies.

"It smells delicious," I remarked.

"It is delicious," Joshua offered, smiling proudly at, I was guessing, his wife.

"Go get the girls, Joshua," the woman said, beaming back at him. "Mrs Smith, please sit down."

"It's Miss," I said, catching myself before I said 'doctor'. "Miss Smith," I added, to hear how it sounded.

Strangely, I didn't mind it. The absence of 'doctor' said a lot as well.

"Miss Smith," the woman said softly. "I'm Catherine Drake. Matt's mother."

Matt was the girls' father. The one 'working'.

"Nice to meet you," I said, just as two small girls entered the kitchen behind Joshua.

Their utter quiet stole all sound from the room. Not just the fact that they weren't talking - I'd expected that - but because they also didn't stomp as children so often do. Didn't take up space by simply breathing loudly. Didn't scrape the chairs or thump an elbow down on the table or sigh out loud.

They were a void in the air. An empty hollow of space where something once had existed.

I stared at them and felt a part of me crumble. These children needed help.

"Hello," I said, my voice neutral. "You must be Rachel and Dani."

Predictably, they said nothing.

"This is Rachel," Joshua started, placing a hand on the girl with slightly longer hair's shoulder.

I held my palm up to stall him. My eyes dragging off their emotionless faces to his startled one.

"Don't speak for them," I said.

"But they can't speak for themselves," Catherine argued; a little affronted, I think.

"They don't need to," I reassured her. "Not yet, anyhow. But they do need to know they are expected to answer."

Catherine glanced toward Joshua. He had a hard look in his eyes.

"Have you dealt with this sort of thing before, Miss Smith?" he asked.

I met his eyes and let him see the confidence in mine. "Yes, Mr Drake. I have."

"And your qualifications?" he pressed.

More than he knew. I reached into my handbag and pulled out the résumé the detectives had compiled. Heavy on education. Light on psychiatry. An exact opposite of my actual qualifications.

"If I'm to do this," I said softly, "I need to do this my way. You understand?"

"Not really," Catherine said from beside her husband. Beside the girls, too, I noted.

It was me against them. A table between us. I suddenly wanted this to work. For them to trust me. Which was ironic, considering I was here under false pretences, sporting a false identity and false qualifications, as well.

But I was *not* the wrong person for this job. Despite the lack of paediatric psychiatry to my credit, I did know a thing or two about post-traumatic stress.

"Who else have you interviewed?" I asked, going with my gut.

The adults looked uncomfortable. The children looked a million miles away, but I was betting they heard every word.

"What are your options?" I pressed. I thought they had very few. In bumfuck Twizel.

I needed them to know I was their best bet.

"Nothing is more important than these girls," I stressed. "Than allowing them to feel safe and nurtured, while addressing their illness."

"Illness?" Joshua demanded.

"What would you call it, Mr Drake? A phase?" I asked.

He shook his head. The movement looked uncertain.

I glanced toward Rachel and Dani, their eyes downcast, their bodies immobile.

"It's called a mental illness," I murmured. "A psychiatric disorder. It's a name, not a label. It represents a behavioural or mental pattern that may cause suffering or a poor ability to function in life. It's treatable," I added. "I can treat it," I promised, aware I might have been biting off more than I could chew.

"By using tough love?" Joshua asked.

"No," I said gently. "By setting some boundaries. Making sure the girls are aware of certain expectations."

"They can't talk," Catherine argued.

"From what their father said on the phone, there is no physical reason why not."

Both grandparents looked down at the girls.

"Then why haven't they yet?" Catherine asked, sadness lacing her tone.

"That's what I aim to find out, Mrs Drake," I offered in return. "I *can* do this," I said. "I'm very good at it in fact."

"And entirely too full of yourself," a gruff voice said from over my shoulder.

CHAPTER 4

HOW LONG'S A PIECE OF STRING?

MATT

Damn it, I didn't want to do this. I especially did not want to do this with an upstart JAFA. I had no idea if she was actually from Auckland, I think she mentioned Wellington on the phone. But Wellington, like Auckland, was in the North Island.

And she was in my territory now.

"Mr Drake?" she asked, moving to stand from her seat. I waved her back down and walked around the table, pressing a kiss to the head of both girls.

"Matt," I said. "If we're to do this," I added, using her turn of phrase, "then we do it my way. First name basis only."

She studied me for a long moment and then nodded her head. She had the most vibrant red hair I'd ever seen. Like a candle flame, flickering. It hung down her back in shiny waves. Bright blue eyes studied me out of a porcelain white face.

She was a china doll and wouldn't last five minutes in Mackenzie Country.

"Bacon and egg?" I said, taking a seat at the head of the table.

"Your favourite," Mum offered, fussing over the girls' plates like the mother hen that she was.

"So," I said, sitting back in my seat and studying the teacher in return. "You think you're the right one for the job." It wasn't a question. But most people answer when challenged.

She just smiled.

Interesting.

"Have you worked in someone's home before?" I asked, nodding my head in thanks to Mum as she served up a portion of pie on my plate.

"No," she said, succinctly.

"Does it bother you?" I asked, scooping salad out onto the side of the plate. "Driving out here every day?"

"Does it bother you driving into town every day?"

I smiled. Little doll had sharp teeth. I picked up the mayo and slathered my lettuce.

The teacher watched my every move.

"They've fallen behind a little in their studies," I said, forking a bite of pie and shoving it in my mouth. I chewed, waiting for her to comment. She said nothing.

I was getting a confused signal from this female. Was she or was she not interested?

"They're hard workers," I added. "Love reading stories. I like them to be outside at least part of the day."

"And their special needs?" she asked. "What cognitive therapy are you currently doing?"

"They visit a shrink once a month in Timaru," I said between mouthfuls. "His instructions are to act as if there's nothing wrong in their behaviour."

"Gareth Turner," the teacher said. "I'm familiar with his approach."

I blinked. Was she now? Outstanding.

I shrugged my shoulders. "What do you think you can bring to the equation?"

She paused as if weighing her words carefully, and then something flashed in her eyes. Determination. That's what it was. She had teeth, and she wanted to bite.

"Naturally, I'll focus on their studies," she said. She was lying. "I'm particularly well versed in tailoring my approach to the individual needs of my students. I've dealt with PTSD before, Mr Drake."

"Matt," I said, watching her lips as she talked.

"Matt," she said, and my mind stalled. "But," she added, making me force my attention up to her eyes, "the girls need to know they are expected to talk."

Hold on just a god damn minute.

"So, you think you know more than a psychiatrist?"

She smiled. Her lips were thin, and the smile forced.

"I think I can add an alternate perspective," she said slowly.

"We've managed OK with Turner's approach."

"Have you?" She purposely looked at Rachel and Dani. "Girls," she said. They both looked up at the sound of her authoritative voice. "Please bring me your workbooks."

"Which ones?" Mum asked. The teacher held up her palm to silence her.

I leant back in my seat and folded my arms across my chest and just watched.

"We'll start with writing. Show me your latest efforts." Rachel looked at Mum for guidance. Dani kept staring at the teacher. "Please," she added, her voice softening. "I'd like to see what you've written."

Dani pushed back her chair and left the room. Mum's mouth hung open as Rachel scurried to follow. Dad just watched the teacher with narrowed eyes.

"I realise," she started, "that you don't know me." She was looking at her plate of uneaten food. "And I realise these girls are precious to you. They're hurting," she said, and I felt my stomach drop. "They're frightened," she added. My heart pounded. "Post Traumatic Stress Disorder manifests itself in various ways. Flashbacks. Nightmares.

Severe anxiety. Uncontrolled thoughts about the event that triggered it." She lifted her eyes to mine.

I could barely breathe.

"They are living it daily. They will not stop living it daily until something is done about it. Acting as if everything is normal will not achieve this. In patients so young exposure therapy is ill advised. But cognitive therapy has proven to be successful."

She talked like Turner. Like a fucking psychiatrist.

"We start by giving them clear expectations of how they should behave. Including the expectation that they will answer each question we pose them. Closed questions are helpful when we need an immediate reply. But in the long-term ask only open-ended questions with the expectation they will be answered." She stared out of the kitchen window, watching the clouds roll past in the sky. "They're breathing too quickly," she said out of fucking nowhere. "For every breath we take, they take several. I'll need to teach them how to slow that down."

Her eyes landed back on me.

"Nothing I do will harm them," she said. "But it will force them to face whatever happened. Not directly, but through a series of cognitive tasks that will help make the memories less invasive."

She leant forward across the table. I noticed Mum and Dad leant toward her as well. I held my ground. It was difficult not to show how much she affected me. This woman who had turned up out of nowhere and now flipped my world on its arse.

"What do you do when you're faced with something stressful at work, Matt?" she asked.

"This isn't about me."

She smiled. Clearly, she was calling bullshit on that. "Humour me," she said.

I clenched my jaw, noticing the girls were standing out in the hallway, giving us time to finish our conversation. Or just observing the new person in their lives without the pressure of being caught.

"I take a step back from the situation," I offered.

"Physically or mentally?"

"Mentally," I offered. "I sing a few lines from a song in my head before I talk out loud."

She smiled. I could see her desire to know what song was my lifeline. She didn't ask. Her control was impressive.

"Cognitive therapy," she said. "Challenging a negative thought process with a course of action to prevent yourself from reacting inappropriately. You do it naturally every day in your life. The girls don't have that ability. They need it. I can give that to them. Trust me. I *am* very good at this."

Fuck. I believed her. She had me second guessing myself.

"How long?" I asked. She blinked. "How long do you think it will take?"

"How long's a piece of string?" she said... and Dani laughed.

CHAPTER 5

NARCISSIST

LIV

"Well, how's it going, then?" David asked over the telephone line.

"Good," I said, leaning back on the rental's couch. "As good as it can, I suppose, in the middle of nowhere."

"Do they even have power down there? Or are you reading by candlelight?"

"They have flushing loos, too, you know," I deadpanned.

"You just have to go out in the dark with the spiders to use them," David offered, laughing.

"Something like that," I said, picking at a loose thread on the sofa's sole cushion.

"You sound down, Olivia. I know it's hard, but it won't be forever."

I pushed thoughts of the twins and their father - the real reason for my distraction - out of my mind. "You're right. Has he done anything?"

There was shuffling in the background as if David was getting comfortable. As if talking about my stalker was a topic that elicited comfortable feelings.

"Everything's been quiet here," he finally admitted.

"Is that good or bad?"

David made a non-committal sound. "The cops think he may know."

"Know what?"

"That you've gone." I sucked in a breath. "The escalation in his behaviour would indicate he was gearing up for a major event. To have pulled back now is unusual."

"You agree with them?"

I heard him scratching his jaw. It was probably covered in dark stubble. David always looked better at night. Not so clean cut or proper. A bit like a certain farmer.

I shook my head as David said, "Yes, I do. Olivia," he added, "even if he's aware of your departure, he doesn't know where you've gone to."

"He seems to know an awful lot awfully quickly."

"But Twizel?" David said. "None of your clients have left the city."

"None of my current ones."

"You think he's a former client?"

"Limiting the suspects to my current patients is shortsighted."

"Even so," David soothed. "You're in Twizel. It's miles away. You're safe."

"I'm sure you're right," I said, wanting suddenly for this conversation to be over. "Listen, it's been a long day. I think I'll get some sleep."

"Have you taken anything to help?"

I scowled. "I don't need help sleeping."

"You said you were having difficulties just last week."

Damn him and his razor sharp memory. David was a lot like me in that regard.

"There's not as much noise down here," I offered as explanation.

"Not much electric light either," he said, chuckling.

"But there are spiders," we both said together. I smiled. "Go to bed," I mock ordered.

"But it's so lonely in there," he mock-whined.

"Stop bugging me," I added.

"Never," he said and hung up.

I smiled at the dial tone and swiped the phone closed. I'd known David since university. We'd dated for a while, but our personalities didn't quite mesh. Romantically, that is. He'd been a little too clingy for me. Professionally, though, I couldn't have wished for a more supportive partner. One who saw mental illness in the same light as I.

Worth the effort.

To David, mental health was a very personal crusade. His sister had committed suicide not long before I'd met him. He was the only other psychiatrist I'd ever worked with who put in the excessively long hours I did. Who made it his life's work to reach people.

I pushed the memories away and picked up the remote, turning off the TV, then straightened up the couch. Looking around the room, I realised there really wasn't anything else for me to do, but go to bed. It was only ten o'clock. I'd be running on the treadmill back home or watching a movie on Netflix.

I barely got free to air TV here.

How long? Matt Drake had asked.

Longer than I wanted to stay here.

I moved into the kitchen and opened the fridge. Great, I was comfort eating now. I was just about to close it when I heard a crash outside the window. The light was on in the kitchen, and it was pitch black outside so I couldn't see what had caused it. I stilled, like a possum in headlights. Then shut the fridge door and bolted to the light switch, flicking it off. Ambient light from the lounge spilt into the small area, but at least I wasn't backlit.

I crossed to the back door and flicked on the external light. My rubbish bin had been toppled over. It wasn't that full of trash, I'd only been here a couple of days. But the evidence of poor eating habits was on display for the entire neighbourhood. Ramen noodles and

Maggi soup. I cringed. I couldn't leave it like that. There were cats bordering on feral living across the street. Hence the toppled bin, at a guess.

I pulled an old cardigan off the back of a kitchen table chair, and shoved my arms into it, then tugged on my boots and unlocked the back door. I peered down the driveway, but couldn't spot the furry culprit, so grabbed a broom from the laundry and headed outside.

At the very least, I could chase the feline away like a fishwife.

It only took me a couple of steps out into the still night air to realise no cat had done this.

I stared up at the side of the rental house at what could dubiously be called an anatomically correct depiction of an erect penis. In lurid pink spray paint. My shoulders tensed. At least it wasn't written in cat blood.

I walked toward it, my eyes darting up and down the driveway, a spot between my scapulas itching, and swiped a finger through the still wet paint. The rubbish bin was toppled when they saw me go in the kitchen. They'd just been here.

I hightailed it inside the back door and bolted it closed, then pulled out my cell calling 111. I don't think I took a breath during the entire panicked conversation with the emergency operator. I stood with my back to the fridge and my eyes on the kitchen window, my cell phone in one hand and a blunt carving knife in the other, and waited for the police to arrive.

It didn't even cross my mind that it would be my new boss.

His face appeared in the kitchen window, a scowl claiming his lips. His eyes connected with mine immediately.

"You OK?" he asked. I nodded. "Wanna unlock the door?" he pressed. I nodded.

Then finally peeled myself off the fridge and crossed to the door.

Matt stood there staring down at me and frowned. He did that a lot, I realised. Then he reached out and slipped the knife from my claw-like grip.

"Bit overkill for kids, doll," he said.

"I didn't... I wasn't..."

"Take a seat," he said more softly, leading me by the shoulders to a chair at the breakfast table. "Heard the bin, did you?" he asked. I nodded.

He placed the knife back in the drawer as if he knew already where it would go. Then he proved how much he was aware of the layout of the kitchen by pulling out two mugs from the cabinet and starting the kettle boiling.

"Tea or coffee?" he asked. "No, wait. You've got hot chocolate here. That'll do. Fuck knows you won't sleep after this."

Speaking from experience?

"See anyone?" he asked conversationally, watching me from under a fall of messed up dark blond hair. He'd just been woken up, I realised. He'd been asleep on the job.

I scowled. His brow arched.

"Well?" he asked. "Did you see anyone? Outside the window," he added, nodding toward the thing for good measure.

He was also speaking decidedly slowly. Extremely slowly in fact. As if talking to an idiot.

I glared at him. He smirked back. Narcissist.

CHAPTER 6
WATCHED AND JUDGED

MATT

"I'm quite capable of understanding you, you know," Olivia said pointedly.

I smiled; the fire wasn't just in the colour of her hair, then. "Never doubted it. But did you see anyone?"

She shook her head.

I placed two mugs of hot chocolate down before her and took a seat across the table. It was tiny. Matched Maggie's to perfection, right down to the chipped Formica top. I had no doubt Maggie wasn't at home this evening. Otherwise, she would have come out of the flat next door, guns blazing. No, she'd be at Red Tussock. Helping Luke to sleep better.

What did I get? I got the 'shrink' doll. The 'psychiatrist' teacher. Little red fucking riding hood with a psychology diploma.

"They're getting better," I commented mildly, blowing on the hot chocolate to cool it.

"Who is?"

"The penis drawing vandals."

"You've had more penises pop up in Twizel?"

I tried not to laugh. She was so fucking serious. "You'd be surprised," I said. "Penises are a dime a dozen down here, Liv."

"Liv?" she sputtered.

"Olivia's too much of a mouthful," I explained. "What? No one ever called you Liv before?"

"Not really."

"Shame."

"They haven't called me 'Doll' either." Said in a dry tone of voice.

"Ah," I murmured, scratching my jaw. "Heard that, did you?"

"Yes."

I stared off into the far corner.

"Why?" she eventually asked.

"Why what?"

"Don't be obtuse, Matt. It doesn't suit you."

"Do you always call a spade a spade?"

"Honesty's essential in my profession."

"Teaching? I would have thought being too honest with kids is how penises come to pop up all over the place."

She blinked at me. The hackles on my back stood up. What was that? What triggered that reaction? My sense of humour? Maybe I was just rusty. I relaxed back into my chair again.

"Is it not the same for cops?" she finally said.

"Honesty?" I huffed out a breath. "Yeah, we're honest, too."

I don't think she believed me. Strange, because there was something about her I wasn't sure I believed, too.

"You think it's just kids?" she asked, nodding towards the kitchen window.

"They painted the same penis on the library wall yesterday."

The relief that briefly flashed across her face was alarming. I sat up straighter in my seat. Again. At this rate, I'd be accused of becoming a jack-in-the-box.

"Do you know who they are?" she asked.

"Got a good guess, but haven't caught them in the act, as yet. They'll trip up."

"I think they might have thought I saw them," she admitted, her bottom lip slipping between her teeth in consternation.

"Kids," I repeated, watching her reaction to my every word. "We had a bunch of spray cans stolen from the hardware store. And now this. Once school starts next week, the spraying will stop."

"Nothing on the CCTV cameras?" she pressed.

I smiled; more of a grimace really. She wasn't looking at me, so she missed it. "This is Twizel," I said carefully. Maggie always jumped down my throat when I said that.

"Oh," was all Olivia said.

"Do you need a hand cleaning up that mess out there?" I offered.

"No," she rushed to say and then laughed. It was self-deprecating. "I haven't been to the supermarket yet."

I raised an eyebrow. She flicked her gaze to my face, so caught it.

"I've been subsisting on packet food," she explained, blushing. Fuck, but that was a sexy colour on her cheeks. "You'd see exactly how far I have plummeted in my dietary habits."

"Dietary habits," I repeated. "You even sound like a teacher."

She looked up at me but just bit that lip. I expected her to say something along the lines of, 'that's because I am.' But she didn't. She just stared at me as I stared at her and the room got hotter.

I cleared my throat. "I better get going. Dad will want to get home to Mum."

"You're going home?" She didn't sound impressed.

"Unless you want me to spend the night." *Whoops. How did that slip out?*

Her eyes widened, and she sucked in a sharp breath.

"You know," I added. "For protection against spray can holding kids." Argh, now I sounded like a condescending prick.

"Yes," she muttered. "But I thought you must have come from the police station."

"The station's not manned at night."

"Everyone works from home?"

I nodded my head and then thought of Maggie. "Well, from a comfortable bed."

Her eyes darted toward the door that I knew led to the single bedroom in the house. Was she thinking about me in her bed?

Fucking hell, get a grip. She was my kids' brand spanking new teacher. *Not going there. Nah-uh. No way.*

"Anyway," I said, scrubbing a hand across the back of my neck. "I wasn't on call tonight, Mac was. He's been sent out to a traffic accident in Pukaki. So, I'm second tier. Not much happens in Twizel. Usually, I can get away with not leaving the kids with Mum and Dad." I shrugged my shoulders.

"But I called in about a bunch of spray can wielding kids." She looked chagrinned.

I smiled. Her eyes darted down to my mouth. My grin widened. "Yeah," I said, feeling a little bit too happy right then.

"Thanks, Matt," she said softly. And I felt something. Right there. Right in the pit of my stomach. Where all I'd felt lately was acid and bile and a whole lot of crud. But it was sweet and warm and downright unexpected.

Even my penis started to resemble the artwork outside.

I shifted on my feet and then strode to the door.

"You sure you don't need a hand cleaning this up?" I asked, looking down at the trash strewn across her driveway.

"No. Go home," she said. "I've got this."

"Doll," I said. "I don't doubt it." Then I walked down the driveway before she could offer a comment.

My cell phone buzzed when I reached the car. I swiped the screen and stared at the text. I'd given her my number, for the kids, of course. I just hadn't expected her to use it.

Olivia: Doll? I'm starting to wonder just what goes through your mind, Senior Sergeant.

I smiled. My thumbs about two sizes too big.

Me: Even ur txts sound like a teachr

I held my breath while I waited. I didn't have to wait long. Even typing long hand, the woman was faster than lightning.

Olivia: There is nothing wrong with correct grammar.

I chuckled to myself and then looked out of the windscreen to make sure I wasn't being watched.

Me: Its the fullstops tht make me :)

There was nothing for a long moment; long enough for me to start the car. Then just as I put it into drive, the phone buzzed again.

Olivia: Go. Home. To. Your. Girls.

My smile slowly fell as if peeled from my face by the weight of sadness. Dani had laughed today. At this woman. At this slightly uptight, highly intelligent, redheaded school ma'am.

I looked back down the driveway, but the house was in darkness. The rubbish already gone.

Who was she? Something told me she was a whole lot of trouble. But Dani had laughed.

And I'm a sucker for my daughters' laughter. I hadn't heard it in way too long.

I pulled out from the kerb checking the shadows. But no hooligan stared out at me with disgruntled teenaged eyeballs. All the way back to Red Tussock, though, it felt like I was being watched.

Watched and judged. I hoped Olivia Smith had some answers because I was fairly certain I'd be found wanting.

I'd been found wanting for the past twelve months.

CHAPTER 7

NOT THAT I WAS THINKING OF STAYING HERE

LIV

I stared up at the penis. It looked lurid in the light of day.

"Should have hosed it off last night," Maggie commented mildly. She'd driven into the driveway half an hour ago and knocked on my back door. Introducing herself as Sergeant Blackmore of the Twizel Police and my neighbour.

Apparently, she'd been at Red Tussock Station last night and missed all the action. She'd said that with a wry grin. I gathered she'd experienced some other form of action that she was unwilling to talk about.

"I didn't want to hang around outside in the dark," I explained.

Maggie made a non-committal sound and then said, "Didn't Matt offer to do it for you?"

"Ah, no." Maggie frowned. "But he did offer to pick up the rubbish."

"Chivalry isn't dead, then," she said dryly.

I smiled. I liked her. She was petite and at the same time a giant. Standing there in her blue police uniform, stab vest, and a gun holstered on her hip - a rarity for NZ cops - she seemed invincible. I decided I wanted to be her when I grew up.

"A scrubbing brush and some mineral turps should do it," Maggie advised. "Just swing by Wrightson's, they should have all you need."

Not that there was a lot else to do on a Sunday in Twizel.

I nodded my head but didn't shift from my observation of the penis.

"Why do kids draw genitalia anyway?" Maggie asked.

"It's to do with the pre-frontal cortex," I said before I could think better of it.

"The what now?" Maggie replied.

I suppressed the sigh that wanted out. Being a teacher and only a teacher was hard.

"Something I read once," I prefaced. "The PFC is in constant dialogue with the limbic part of the brain. That's the emotional part of the brain. In adults, this connection is in balance, each one inhibiting the other. But for teenagers, there's no inhibitor to stop them acting out. They think something will be exciting, dangerous or funny, and go straight ahead and do it without the PFC telling their limbic side of the brain to slow down. To stop and think before acting."

"Not sure all adults have that balance either," Maggie commented.

"Yes, well, that's where mental disorders come in. They upset the balance. But in theory for adults, the balance existed at one time, and the disorder just tripped it up. Unless, of course, the disorder is carried over since childhood."

Maggie stared at me for a long moment, and I thought perhaps I'd overdone it. It was a passion of mine, the brain. Not talking about it was harder than I had imagined.

"Bit of light reading was it?" Maggie asked, brow arched.

I forced myself to smile and then shrugged my shoulders. "It's how I branched into special needs education."

I didn't like lying to her. Aside from the fact that I immediately felt a kinship with the woman, she was also a police officer. Someone I should be able to trust. But if the Auckland detectives who had sent me down here to hide hadn't informed the local police station, then I could only assume the Twizel cops fell into the 'don't tell them anything' category.

Still, lying went against everything I stood for. Open communication leads to a healthy mental state of mind. I'd always believed that. I was in danger of coming away from Twizel fucked in the head.

"And that's a good thing," Maggie said, interrupting my train of thought and making me think she was reading my mind. For a second there, I thought she condoned mental instability. "Rachel and Dani need someone like you," she added, bringing me back on track.

"Twelve months is a long time to remain mute," I agreed.

"Try six years," Maggie said, her lips pursing.

I blinked at her. She offered a crooked smile. "My brother," she explained. "PTSD," she added. Then she looked back at the penis as if to indicate the topic was over.

"Wrightson's," she repeated. "Do you know where it is?"

"I have GPS in my car."

"Glad someone came here prepared," she muttered. "OK, good to meet you, Olivia. Welcome to the crazy world of Twizel."

She waved goodbye and jumped back into her police ute, leaving me staring at a florid pink penis dripping ejaculate down the side of my rental home's wall.

I'm sure I could think up a joke to that somehow.

I shook my head, locked up the house, and climbed into my car. PGG Wrightson's was on Main Street, so really didn't require a map to find it. I pulled into the parking lot, rolling the Volvo to a stop next to a beat up Toyota flatbed truck. There was a cow standing on the back of it, chewing its cud. It blinked down at me, swished its tail at a non-existent fly, and then started to pee. The spray of urine splashed over the side of the truck and onto the hood of my car.

I closed my eyes and tipped back my head, staring at the cloudless sky, praying for patience. How long, he had asked. Too long, was now my answer.

There was nowhere else to park; Wrightson's was popular. In a farming community, that made sense. So, I breathed steadily and headed into the store, locating what I needed within minutes. The young man who served me had a purple mohawk. I thought it a strange choice of decoration, but he'd also chosen to place a ring through his nose. Reminding me of the cow currently repainting my car out in the carpark.

"Visitor?" he asked.

"I just moved here," I explained handing over the cash required.

"To Twizel?"

"Yes."

"Why?"

Because I have a stalker back home, who has escalated his behaviour pattern and evidence suggests I may get hurt.

"Job," I said instead of all of that.

"In Twizel?" he repeated.

I smiled. "Yes."

He leant forward and rested his elbows on the counter. He looked about twenty. Fifteen years my junior. He still had the odd pimple on his freshly shaven face.

"Need a tour guide?" he enquired.

"In Twizel?" I asked, turning the tables on him. He didn't catch the irony.

"Yeah. Could show you where all the good spots are for parking."

Preferably not next to a flatbed truck with a pissing cow.

"You know, where it's cool for hook-ups and the like."

Oh, that kind of parking. Perhaps if I'd ever done 'parking' before, I would have caught that a lot sooner.

"Ah," I said, uncertainly.

"I drive a Subaru," he advised. "WRX. It's got an STI trim, loud exhaust tip, hellaflush, scoop, low-line stance and underbody LEDs. It's sweet-as. What do you drive?"

"Volvo," I said, feeling surreal.

"Volvo?"

"Yes. S60."

"Modified?"

Bloody hell. Couldn't the guy see he was way out of my league here? And that I'm way too old for parking of any kind. Let alone in a vehicle with after factory modifications.

"Ah, no. I just bought it."

"Can help you with that if you want."

"With what?"

"Tricking it out."

"Um, that won't be necessary. Thank you."

He shrugged and stood up from his lean against the counter. "You know where I am," he said, turning his attention to the next customer.

I slowly lifted the turps up off the counter and took a step away. My eyes stuck fast on the young man's mohawk and nose ring. I forced myself to start walking toward the door, but as it swooshed open, I heard the guy say to his next customer behind me, "Visitor?"

"I live here," the gruff farmer replied.

"In Twizel?"

"Yes."

"Why?"

I started laughing as the door closed behind me, the sight of the cow and the addition of a pile of shit on the flatbed not lessening my amusement.

Twizel was going to be interesting. Maybe they needed a permanent psychiatrist.

Not that I was thinking of staying here.

CHAPTER 8

LIFE JUST GOT INTERESTING

MATT

A black Volvo was parked in front of the house. When I climbed out of my ute and walked past it, I noticed the paint on the bonnet was dull. In every other respect, the car looked brand new. The hood was out of place, but I liked it.

I flicked a glance back at my Ford Ranger. Dirt splattered the sides and sheep shit coated the alloys. There were insects stuck all over the grille.

Next to the Volvo it looked like something from a post-apocalyptic movie. The Volvo had a long way to go.

I pushed open the front door and heard Mum in the kitchen talking to Dad. I headed toward there but stopped when I spotted movement in the lounge room off to the side. I poked my head inside and watched for a moment.

Dani was reading a book, and Rachel was scowling. Arms crossed over her chest, defiant look in her eyes, a stubborn set to her shoulders.

I'd seen that look a thousand times before.

Over twelve months ago was the last time I'd witnessed it.

I stood stock still, barely breathing. My heart ached. My chest burned. I didn't dare move, not that I could have. I didn't want to be seen.

"What's this word?" Liv was asking.

Rachel ground her teeth.

They stared at each other for a full minute.

"OK," Liv said, undeterred. "Tell me what you think they mean by this?" She pointed to a line in a book placed between them.

Rachel remained stubbornly still.

A full minute passed as if Liv was timing it to the second.

"Do you think it has something to do with Freddie and his dislike of Sally?" she asked.

Rachel looked down at the book and then nodded her head.

"Brilliant," Liv said. "That's exactly what it's about." Rachel relaxed slightly. "But why do you think he said that to her?"

Rachel blinked. Liv waited the full minute for a reply.

"And look here," she said enthusiastically. "He does it again on this page. Did you read that?"

Rachel took a second to comprehend this was a question not requiring a verbal answer and then nodded her head.

"Why do you think he repeats himself?"

Rachel blinked. Liv waited.

"You know what I think?" Liv asked after a minute of silence. Rachel slowly shook her head as if she thought the question was a trick of some sort. "I think you know the answer."

Rachel glared at her. And then holding Liv's gaze, reached down and picked up a pen from the table. Without breaking eye contact, she pulled a pad over and placed the nib of the pen to paper.

"You want to write your answer?" Liv asked softly.

Rachel nodded her head.

"Sweetheart," Liv said, and I sucked in a breath of air quietly. "I want to hear you say it."

Rachel shook her head.

"Why, Rachel?" Liv asked carefully. "Are you afraid of something?"

Rachel blinked.

"Of someone hearing you?"

Rachel just stood there.

"It's just us. You, me and Dani."

Rachel's eyes met mine. It took a second, but Liv slowly turned around and spotted me.

"Mr Drake," she said, voice devoid of emotion.

"Matt," I corrected. "It's time for lunch." I wasn't certain if it was, but I could smell something good wafting out of the kitchen. And I sure as shit wasn't going to admit to eavesdropping.

"OK," Liv said cheerfully. "We'll pick this up after lunch." That was addressed to Rachel, who promptly slammed her pen down on the table and ran toward me.

She wrapped her arms around my legs and buried her face in between my thighs. Like a limpet.

I stared down at her and then slowly placed my hand on top of her head. My fingers were shaking. Rachel didn't usually instigate contact.

"Lunch, girls," Mum called out from the kitchen. In the next moment, Rachel was gone. Dani chasing after her.

Slowly Liv got to her feet and faced me.

"You seem surprised," she said carefully. "Does Rachel not usually run to you for comfort?"

I shook my head.

"Does she cry?" What sort of question was that?

And then I thought about it. I shook my head.

"Does Dani?"

"Yes. Sometimes."

Liv smiled. It was full of understanding. "This is going to take time, Matt," she informed me. "But I can help them."

She kept saying that. But all I saw was my little girl in a battle of wills when she didn't need to be. Then running to me to make it all better afterwards.

As if she read my mind, Liv added, "Behaviour out of the norm -

the norm that the girls have established since becoming mute - is to be encouraged. Whether you believe that behaviour productive or not. I will never push them too far. But they need to be pushed."

She watched me, assessed me. Her eyes taking in every flinch that swept over my face.

"It's best if they don't get confused, though," she added. "I do one thing. You do another. That sort of thing. You need to encourage them to talk as well. Right now, for Rachel, I'm the dragon. You're the dragon slayer."

"You want me to be a dragon, too?" I demanded. Was she trying to turn my kids away from me when they were already almost too far out of reach?

"No. Not at all." She took a step closer. Then another. Until she was a mere couple feet away from me. "I want them to understand that the dragon is good. That the dragon is safe. That it'll help them."

"Not protect them."

She shook her head. "The type of protection they want is not the type of protection they need."

"That doesn't make any sense."

"On the contrary," she argued. "You're the parent. They're the kids. Six-year-old kids who have experienced a traumatic episode which has altered the way they see the world and react to it. Who should be leading whom in that scenario?"

She was right. But I was angry. I ran a hand through my hair and swallowed thickly. My throat was fucking dry. And for all the wrong reasons.

I wanted to hit something. I wanted to shout and rage. Fucking Marinkovich. I wished the fucker was still alive. Then I could make him pay.

I could kill him slower than I did the first time. Drag it out. Make it painful. As painful as my every single day.

A soft hand came down on my arm and rested there. My muscles bunched. My skin tingled. Liv's fingers squeezed tightly.

"It's OK to be angry," she murmured. "It's OK to feel that kind of rage."

"What would you know?" I growled.

"You think I don't get angry?"

I stared down at her. She laughed derisively.

"I didn't exactly pick Twizel because I wanted to live here," she said.

"Then why did you take the job?"

Her eyes flicked away. I reached up and gripped her chin, bringing those bright blues back to my face.

"Olivia?" I pressed. "Why did you take the job?"

"The girls..."

"Bullshit. You came all the way down here without having confirmed employment. Moved into the Harrisons' rental without a backwards glance. Why did you take the job?"

"You said it yourself, I came before the job was confirmed. I don't need to work. But it seemed fortuitous."

"Fortuitous? Is that what you're going with?"

"Yes." She looked furious. Furious and worried.

My fingers still gripped her chin, her cheeks flushed an inviting pink. She licked her lips.

I leant forward, let my breath brush over her moist skin, and said, "You're hiding something." She tried to shake her head. "You're hiding something, and I intend to discover what it is."

"Matt," she said. "There's nothing."

"Doll, you forget. I'm a cop. And I'm very good at it."

"Now look who's entirely too full of themselves," she muttered.

I smiled. My thumb stroking across her jaw. And then I let her go and walked toward the kitchen.

Life just got interesting.

CHAPTER 9

I WAS A GUPPY

LIV

It was Sunday again. A long weekend. Maggie was at the door. I'd spent Monday to Thursday driving back and forth to Red Tussock, trying to avoid Matt Drake, and making slow progress with Rachel and Dani. They still hadn't spoken. Not that I had expected them to at this early stage. But their behaviour *had* altered.

Which was causing friction between the Drakes and me. Rachel throwing tantrums was not an easy thing to witness. Their silent angel now made noise. Just not the verbal kind they wanted.

"It's Easter," Maggie said when I opened the door.

"Yes, it is," I agreed.

"What are your plans?"

"Washing."

"Washing? On Easter Sunday. Have you no shame?"

"I'm sure God doesn't mind," I said dryly.

"Ah, but He does. Just ask the motorbike riding Reverend."

"The what?"

"Never mind," Maggie said waving her hand between us in dismissal. "You'll meet him there."

"Where?" I asked, eyes narrowing.

"Red Tussock."

"Oh, no," I said, shaking my head. "I'm not going back there."

Maggie slowly smiled, her head tilted to the side, considering me.

"I see," she said.

"See what?" I demanded.

"It's like that, then." What? "I wondered what had got him so riled." Who? She reached forward and gripped my hand and then hauled me out of my door. "Nothing like a bit of fresh air to get the blood pumping."

"Maggie!" I said. "You're not making any sense."

"Egg hunt," she replied as if that explained everything.

"You're crazy," I said in all seriousness, as she bundled me into her police ute. "And I don't use that term lightly. Not in my profession. But you, Sergeant Blackmore, are certifiable."

"Whatever," was the intelligent answer she came up with.

"What egg hunt?" I demanded as she put the car in gear and rolled it down the driveway.

"Every Easter, Red Tussock throws an egg hunt. It's a little play on words as well as an opportunity to support the community. A bit of a Fair-like atmosphere, if you will."

"I'm still stuck on the play on words part."

"Oh, yeah. Well, the Drakes have been here in Mackenzie Country for one hundred and twenty years. Before then, they were in England. Farming. Hard to believe, I know. But farming is in their blood from way back." She winked at me and then turned her attention back to the road. "They used to hunt foxes in Kent or somewhere equally as English. Now they just hunt eggs."

I stared at her, my lips twitching. Then the laughter bubbled up and out of my mouth. I clutched my stomach as Maggie cackled beside me and tears started to stream down our faces.

"They hunt eggs," I said between hiccups.

"No foxes in New Zealand," Maggie explained and set me off all over again.

"Anyway," she said, watching me with a small smirk on her lips, "they hide a couple hundred chocolate eggs in one of their back paddocks that borders on the National Park, and Twizel comes out to find them."

"All for a bit of chocolate?"

"Well, no. There's also things wrapped up in the eggs. Vouchers and the like. And then there's the stalls local businesses set up selling their goods at flea market prices. Even Smokey's sets up a mobile tavern in the pasture. The Musterer's Hut," she scowled briefly and then went on, "has a stall full of coffee and cakes. It's fun. Or so I've been led to believe."

"You've never actually gone to one before?"

She shook her head. "First time. Virgin egg hunter here. That's why I'm bringing you."

"Me?"

"Moral support."

I snorted.

"And because everyone wants to know what's got Matt so frisky."

My eyes widened. "Frisky?"

"Lively. Bubbly. Perky."

"Please stop."

"Bouncy. Animated. Playful."

"No. No more. I can't take it."

She was laughing so much it was hard to tell what she was saying, but I was sure there was a 'Peppy', a 'Sparky', and a 'Zippy' in there somewhere.

"You're going to crash the car," I pointed out.

"Wouldn't be the first time," she quipped, entirely too relaxed about the idea of an accident.

"I'd like to remain in one piece, Sergeant."

"This is Twizel," Maggie said. "Anything could happen."

"Is that the local saying? 'Twizel. Where anything could happen.'"

"Don't forget the background music. Think *Twilight Zone* with a little *Twin Peaks* thrown in for good measure."

"There's a boy racer who served me at Wrightson's," I started; speaking of things weird and whacky.

"Derek Gribble."

"Gribble?"

"Yes. One of three boy racers currently causing all sorts of mayhem for us on the highways."

"He has a ring in his nose like a bull."

"Yeah. You should see what else he's got pierced."

"Have you?" I asked stunned.

"Picked him up drunken and disorderly the other night. He was peeing against the souvenir shop's front window. Everyone knows not to piss Alicia Parsons off. Excuse the pun." She chuckled at her own witticism. "She got it on camera," she added, "and then repeatedly played it on a big screen in her shop front window. Zoomed in on the adornment to his dick."

I stared at her, aware my mouth was hanging open.

"In Twizel?" I pressed, sounding like the dick-pierced-person in question.

"*Twin Peaks*," she said with a grin and pulled the ute into a gate I hadn't used before on Red Tussock.

The drive, if you could call it that, was rough. The ute bounced over it in an entirely too frisky manner. There was no way my Volvo would have managed. When she finally pulled to a stop beside a paddock full of vehicles, I noticed all of them were either trucks or utes or four-wheel drive SUVs. Maybe I'd been too quick to pick my Volvo out when I'd landed in Timaru.

Not that I intended on staying.

My door swung open as I reached for it, Maggie jumping out of her own side, meaning that someone else had beaten both of us to it. I ducked my head and peered up at the man before me.

Matt Drake peered back down at me, a slow smile curving his lips. Dani beamed at me from behind her father's jeans-clad legs, and Rachel looked off toward all the action, pretending I wasn't even there.

"You made it," Matt said.

"I didn't have much of a choice."

Matt grinned. "No one misses the egg hunt. Twizel will be empty."

"A bit of a worry if a tourist rolls into town, isn't it?"

"We left a note," he said dryly.

"What? 'Out for lunch?'"

He reached down and gripped my hand and then hauled me out of the car.

"Nah," he said, his eyes darting all over my face and then up to my tied back hair. I hadn't been planning on socialising. Washing had been on the agenda. So, I wasn't exactly dressed up.

How does one dress up for an egg hunt anyway?

"Gone fishing," he finally said and then smiled.

It was a mischievous smile. It was a sexy smile. No one had ever smiled at me before like that.

Matt Drake wasn't lying. He *had* gone fishing.

My mouth opened and then closed and then opened again.

Great. I was living up to my potential. No longer a psychiatrist. Not even a teacher.

I was a guppy.

"Salmon," Matt said as if he could read my mind. "We fish for salmon around here."

Yeah, right.

CHAPTER 10

LIFE WAS FULL OF LIES

MATT

I wasn't meant to be flirting with her. I wasn't meant to be flirting with anyone. But that smart mouth and bright eyes and fiery red hair just kept intruding on my thoughts. Invading my mind. Eroding my conviction.

I told myself that I'd kept an eye out for her arrival for the girls' sake. I told myself that I'd walked off in the middle of a conversation with Justin without a word because Dani had spotted her teacher. I told myself Rachel needed a wingman and the more she was around Liv, the easier it would get.

I told myself all of this, but I knew better.

I just didn't like it. Didn't like it one fucking bit.

"So," Liv said as we made our way through the parked cars toward the tents. "An egg hunt."

"You say that like it's a bad thing," I murmured. Rachel walked in front of us, back straight, chin lifted, eyes anywhere but on Liv. Dani skipped alongside her teacher. Not holding her hand, but I saw the way her eyes flicked to it.

How could one child act so differently from another?

"Not at all," Liv said. "Just unexpected."

"It was Justin's idea," I explained. "He's all about balancing the universe. Yin and yang. Paying it forward. He toyed with being a Buddhist once."

Liv smiled. I told myself I didn't like that, too.

"I'd like to meet him."

"You'll get your chance," I said. She'd be bombarded with my brothers and cousins shortly if I knew them.

We walked into the main 'thoroughfare', and Liv stopped dead in her tracks. Her eyes widened. Her mouth opened in a small round O. Her hand slipped into Dani's without realising.

I stared at where my daughter clasped her teacher's hand, where white skin met pale nutmeg. Liv didn't spend a lot of time outside in the sun, I realised. My eyes darted up to her face and spotted the tell-tale freckles dotted there.

"This is..." Liv said.

"Impressive?" I offered.

"Yes."

"Glad it meets with your approval," Justin drawled off to the side.

I glared at him, but he wasn't looking at me, his eyes were all for Liv.

"You must be the teacher," my numbskull brother said.

"You must be a brother," Liv shot back and smiled.

"The more handsome one," Justin offered, flashing her the smile he uses at Smokey's.

"But not the more humble one?" Liv guessed.

"Ouch," Zach said, strolling up to join in my nightmare. "She got you good, bro."

Zach offered Liv a casual grin; one that I was certain she'd fall for more than Justin's practised smile.

"Brother number two," Liv said.

"Depends on what you're grading us on," Zach replied. "I'm the capable one."

"Capable?" Justin demanded. "What, driving a tank and blending into the desert makes you capable?"

Zach arched an eyebrow at him and smiled.

"Captain Zach Drake," he said, offering his hand for Liv to shake.

She did, amusement in her eyes. She flicked her gaze back to Justin. "And you're what exactly? The charismatic one?"

"Absolutely," Justin said, grasping her outstretched hand. "And the intelligent one," he added. "I run the vineyard."

"You're Justin, then," Liv surmised.

"The one and only."

I rolled my eyes. Rachel sniggered. Then quickly looked away when I spotted her. Liv noticed as well.

"How do you put up with their egos, girls?" she said, squeezing Dani's hand lightly. Dani smiled. Rachel scowled and stared off into the distance.

"Gonna throw down at the dunk tank, Rach?" Justin asked.

She flicked her eyes towards him briefly but didn't smile.

"Who you gonna drop this year?" he pressed.

"I'm game," Zach offered. "Been a while since I last saw your skills in action, kid."

Rachel didn't blink. Didn't move. Didn't look at either man.

"How 'bout dunking your dad?" Justin asked.

"Or Uncle Luke?" Zach added.

"Dani?" Justin said. "You up for it?"

Dani shook her head, and Rachel turned and scowled at her.

"Hey," I said. "Enough of that, Rachel. Looks can hurt, too, sweetheart."

Especially when you used them instead of words.

Her eyes swept over me, and the scowl turned defiant.

I held her gaze, refusing to back down, realising I was having a staring match with a six-year-old. It was more interaction than I usually had with Rachel. But the reason behind her sudden bad behaviour wasn't lost on me.

I sighed. The sound weighted. Fuck, I needed a drink.

Running a hand through my hair, I turned to Liv. Aware that I'd lost that round by looking away before Rachel.

"Wanna grab a coffee?" I asked.

"Sure," she said, her gaze still caught on my daughter. Dani started dragging Liv toward the Musterer's Hut tent, the smell of caffeine and chocolate spilling out from under its coverings.

I started to follow and then stopped dead in my tracks. Rachel hadn't budged an inch. Arms crossed over her chest. Frown still in place. Eyes narrowed.

"She can stick with us, if you want," Zach said.

It would have been easy to give in. Hell, I'd been chasing the easy track for the past year. Most of it, I hadn't even been present. Possibly wouldn't have even noticed this crisis that Rachel was having.

I suddenly felt like an utter fucktard. A loser father who wallowed in self-pity. Who swam in a shit pile of guilt. It hurt. Reality fucking hurt.

Realising you'd let your daughters down in their hour of need gutted a man completely.

I stood there in the centre of Red Tussock's Annual Egg Hunt and stared down at half of the most precious thing to have entered my life. I felt sick with the guilt. Which wasn't new to me. I felt ill with the rage that always seemed to simmer just beneath the surface. I felt hollowed out with the hurt. Destroyed by the sense of abandonment.

Missy had left us all well before she'd even left her body.

I walked over toward Rachel and crouched down in front of her. Her eyes skipped off to the side. I reached up and cupped the back of her neck, then brought my forehead down to rest on my child's.

"It's gonna be OK," I whispered. "We're gonna be OK," I said. "We'll get through this, Rach. Together."

I told myself, as I slipped my hand into hers and led her towards a waiting - and watching - Liv and Dani, that I was right. That I hadn't lied.

I told myself that. But I didn't believe it.

Life was full of lies. I should know. Missy had told me the biggest lie of them all. And I'd fallen for it.

CHAPTER 11

SOMETIMES YOU JUST NEED TO LAUGH

LIV

He was drowning, I realised. He was weighed down by so much emotion it was killing him. Hurting him. Suffocating him. Dragging him under.

Matt had given me a brief written account of what had transpired - what they thought had transpired anyway - the day the girls' mother had been killed. The one-page document had mentioned the lover Missy Drake had taken. The fact that the girls had undoubtedly met the man on occasion. And had seen him on the day she had died.

It explained the trauma. The PTSD. It explained a lot. Not just where Rachel and Dani were concerned, either, but about this man, as well. This man who tried to appear strong and in control and utterly reliable, when in reality he was bowing under the pressure, losing himself in the process, and had undoubtedly been absent in his girls' lives.

I followed a now impassive looking Rachel and a heartbroken Matt into the Musterer's Hut tent. Dani subdued at my side. Zach and Justin had peeled off, gotten distracted, or just chosen to step back from their brother's heartache. Allowing him some dignity as he fell apart.

I wondered if I should step back, too. But Dani clung to me and ignoring what was happening to this family was not who I am. Not who I had trained to be.

They needed help. And I suddenly wanted desperately for that help to come from me.

A woman behind a makeshift counter smiled at Matt as he approached.

"Senior Sergeant!" she said, voice booming. She was stunning to look at, but also stunning in a way that simply took up space, demanded you notice her, and wouldn't let you look away. "Great day for a hunt," she remarked.

"It is," Matt managed. Drowning.

The woman's smile faltered slightly, but then she turned her attention to Rachel.

"Hot chocolate, Rach?" she asked. Rachel nodded. "Marshmallows in or out?"

Rachel bit her lip but didn't reply.

"Shall I surprise you?" the woman said. Rachel nodded.

I let out a slow breath of air and stepped forward.

"Hi," I said. "I'm Olivia Smith. The girls' teacher."

"Tanya Ruka," the woman said, shaking my offered hand.

"Please leave the marshmallows off," I said with a smile.

"Excuse me?" Tanya demanded.

"If Rachel would like marshmallows, she'll tell you if she wants them in or out of the hot chocolate."

It felt like the entire tent stopped talking, stopped breathing. Turned to stare. Silence that shouldn't have been possible in a paddock full of fairground stalls wrapped around us. Boiled in the air beside us. Brushed up against my clammy skin, pressing against my windpipe.

"Matt?" Tanya called, her hard eyes not straying from my face. "Who the hell is this?"

Matt stood stock still. Rachel glaring up at him. His hand shaking in her little grip.

Perhaps I shouldn't have pressed for this. Right here. Right now. But my gut told me this was important. Essential. Though if Matt didn't back me, treating these girls would become an impossibility.

I'd told him the importance of being united in their treatment. I'd told him why they needed that guidance, that hard but steady hand. I'd told him, but right now I was uncertain if he'd even remember the conversation. Remember what he was trying to achieve by having me here.

Matt was a million miles away. Lost to his grief and heartache and anger.

This could go one of two ways.

I turned my attention to my employer and waited. For a second, I thought he'd leave us all hanging.

But then he blinked, his hand jerking in Rachel's hold, and said, voice loud enough to carry, "Rachel will ask for the marshmallows if she wants them."

Tanya pulled back, a surprised look on her face. And then her steely eyes drifted to me.

"OK," she said, not giving away what she was thinking. "Just let me know, Rach," she said, "and you've got 'em. Dani?" Her eyes darted down to the girl at my side. Her gaze not missing the way Dani's hand gripped mine.

"Hot chocolate?" Dani nodded. Tanya sighed. "Marshmallows in or out?"

Dani bit her lip. Her eyes darting to the jar of marshmallows on the counter. Her little hand shook with the desire to speak, to answer, to get what she wanted.

Tear filled eyes came up to mine, pleading.

All over marshmallows. My throat constricted. My chest was too tight. I'd felt things while treating patients before; it's impossible sometimes not to. But I'd never felt so conflicted, so torn apart by my desires to protect as well as help.

"Go on," I said, my voice thick. "You can do it."

Dani's eyes darted to the left. To her sister. And then she slowly shook her head and looked at the ground.

"I sure hope you know what you're doing, Ms Hotshot," Tanya muttered. "You fuck 'em up anymore, and the whole town will have your arse."

"Tanya," Matt said. "Enough."

"Don't tell me how to act in my own shop, Matt Drake," Tanya snapped back.

"I'll tell you how to act in front of minors if your actions are inappropriate," Matt said calmly. I gathered this was his police voice.

Tanya glared at him.

Matt stared impassively back. That's where Rachel got it from, I realised. Her father. She was watching him now. Every nuance. Every tick. Every muscle twitching.

And then her eyes moved to mine. They were hollow. Absent of emotion. A child her age needed an outlet. Her tantrums were a start. But her go-to reaction was to tamp everything down. Just like her father.

I wondered if Dani was more like Missy. More capable of showing her hurt and longing.

I wondered if Rachel held that against her.

We took our hot chocolates - minus marshmallows - from a still fuming Tanya and settled into a seat outside the tent itself. Watching the world go by. There were dogs on leads and sheep on leads and a little pink pig following its owner. I was sure I saw a hamster in a rainbow coloured tutu. People were laughing and shouting and, across the way in what had to be the mobile tavern, clashing plastic cups full of foaming beer together. Two uniformed cops strolled past and nodded to Matt, making me realise he wasn't. In uniform, that is. The man and woman cop stopped and spoke to the public, one smiling, the other frowning behind mirrored sunglasses.

I spotted Matt's brothers watching them, another couple of guys having joined them, all eyes on the female cop. Justin was ribbing

Zach, elbowing him in the side and leaning into no doubt offer salacious commentary as the female cop looked up and smiled.

Maggie was standing over by a stall full of farm equipment, a man standing beside her that had to be another Drake brother. Luke, at a guess. He was deep in conversation with the owner of the stall, but his palm kept rubbing absently along the back of Maggie's neck in a soothing and proprietary manner.

Everywhere I looked there was a Drake or someone who looked like a Drake; cousins? The entire town seemed to be here, but making up an important, an integral part of it, was the Red Tussock farmers. The Drake family were rooted in this land, and it showed. They cared.

I looked across the table at Matt, who was staring at nothing, nursing an untouched hot chocolate. My eyes scanned Rachel's and Dani's blank faces.

And then a familiar mohawk, nose ring wearing young man stopped in his tracks and beamed at me.

"Hey," he said, his mates stopping beside him. All three of them wore baggy, ripped jeans, and sported unique and colourful hairstyles. "How's it going, S60?"

I smiled and lifted my cup up in greeting. "Great," I said.

Mohawk smirked. "Been meaning to ask you," he said, taking a step closer. "Can I test drive your Volvo?"

His mates started laughing their arses off, and it wasn't until Matt stood up that I got it.

"Easy, Sarge," the kid said. "Talking about her car, not her... you know what."

"Although *I'd* fancy test driving her vulv..." one of his mates started.

Matt took a menacing step towards them, cutting the jokester's words off, and making them scatter. The two uniformed cops perked up across the way and then followed behind the boys at a rapid pace.

"Tell me they won't get arrested for making a joke," I said.

Matt stared across the table at me, still standing, and said, "Some jokes need to be silenced."

I looked at the girls who had watched the entire episode and not shown an ounce of amusement or shock or any kind of emotion.

"Sometimes you just need to laugh," I countered, feeling like crying.

CHAPTER 12

I DON'T KISS AND TELL

MATT

WHAT WAS I DOING HERE? I DIDN'T FUCKING KNOW. PART OF ME wanted to shout at the woman for making me out to be the bad guy. Part of me wanted to protect her from over opinionated baristas.

The whole fucking town had watched. Tanya facing off against Liv.

I'm not one to worry about public opinion. Not anymore. Too much had happened to ruin my standing in Twizel. Too much shame to crawl out from under.

I once would have said I was a good cop.

Now I'd killed a man and would do it all over again. Slower. Harder. With more blood spilling. Coating my hands. Running down my throat. Painting the world red.

I wanted this to stop. This... storm of emotions. I wanted to not feel anything anymore like I did when I got drunk. But I hadn't touched whisky in well over four months. And I knew if I started it now, there'd be no stopping.

Rachel needed me. Dani needed me. I needed my girls.

"Come on," I said, not bothering to sit back down again or finish my untouched hot chocolate. "Let's go get ready for the hunt."

"What do we have to do?" Liv asked, assuming she was coming with us. For a moment I was tempted to tell her this was family business. She wasn't a Drake.

But then I saw Dani's hand in hers and the way my girl looked up at her teacher, and I knew there was no separating them now. No getting Olivia Smith to extricate herself from my life.

I stared at the redheaded she-devil before me, having a strange desire to run my fingers through the strands of her shiny, fiery hair; as if desperate to be burned by fire.

Which was ridiculous. I'd only just been thinking about not feeling and here I was aching to feel more.

"The girls like to go in the hunt, but they can't keep the eggs," I said, forcing myself to answer. "Defeats the whole purpose of giving something to the community. So, we trail behind them and replace the ones they find with plain chocolate ones. They get their eggs, someone else gets their voucher to Wrightson's."

Liv laughed, startling a breath out of me.

"I still can't believe you hunt Easter eggs. I half expect to see a hound dog baying as it sniffs out the chocolate. The townsfolk chasing after it with wicker baskets in hand."

I smiled at the imagery. It did seem strange for a bunch of hard-edged Mackenzie Country locals to traipse around a field in search of artificial eggs.

"You'll get used to it," I said. "First time's always the hardest."

"For many things," Liv said, looking down at Rachel.

I swung by my ute and grabbed the plastic bag of eggs, stuffing them in the back of my jeans before the girls could start bugging me. I pointed off to the paddock, and they went running.

"They know what you're doing," Liv said dryly.

"They've known from the age of three."

"You've done this every year?"

I thought back to last year. To how we'd done it as a family. Missy beside me, carrying the plastic bag in her oversized handbag. Smiling after the girls as she watched them 'hunt' out their treats.

She'd been happy then, hadn't she?

She'd been happy because I wasn't working. I never work on Easter Sunday. It belongs to Red Tussock. It hadn't even really belonged to Missy.

I swallowed thickly, cursing my ignorance and blindness. Cursing the clarity of vision I seemed to have nowadays.

"What's put that scowl on your face, Matt?" Liv asked quietly.

"Nothing," I said out of habit. I'd said that a lot to Missy as well, I think.

Missy always let me have my peace.

Liv didn't. "Is it that boy? Gribble?"

"The boy racer?" I said bemusedly. I shook my head.

"Then what?" I saw what she was doing. I'd done it many times when interviewing a reluctant suspect.

"It's not important, Liv."

"Anything that makes you unhappy is important."

I wondered why that sounded so good.

"The past," I said shortly. "We've all got one."

"You, the girls, and Missy," Liv said, unafraid of calling my bluff.

I closed my eyes, feeling Missy walk beside me. Feeling like I was being dragged back into a world that hadn't been real.

"She loved them," I said, opening my eyes and staring out across a now packed paddock.

"Are you angry with her?" Liv asked.

"What sort of question is that?"

"A reasonable one," Liv countered. "She loved them. You loved her. And now she's gone."

"It wasn't her fault." Marinkovich was to blame even if I could no longer prove it; I'd killed him before he'd had a chance to confess all his sins.

Liv said nothing for a moment and then clapped her hands in delight when Dani came running over holding an egg.

"I'll look after it for you, baby-girl," I said, taking the egg and waiting for her to turn around. I twisted slightly and chucked the egg over toward Alan Bennet, the local chemist. He nodded his head and swept up the offering.

"They're all in on it," Liv said.

"Yep."

She smiled. I let out a soft breath of air.

Then sucked it back in again when she said, "Are you angry with her, Matt?"

"Liv," I warned.

"Sometimes talking about it can help."

"You're a teacher not a psychiatrist," I pointed out.

She ducked her head and looked out toward Mount Glenmary. "I dated one once," she said.

"And that makes you an expert on psychology?"

"He talked a lot. I listened."

"Was he a jerk?" I asked, amused despite myself.

"We're still friends."

I shook my head and accepted an egg from Dani, throwing it toward Alicia Parsons this time. She saluted me and handed it off to someone else.

"I don't know how to do that," I admitted. "Be friends with an ex."

"You must have exes still living around here," Liv said. "Twizel's a small place, you'd run into them frequently."

"There was only ever Missy."

I regretted the words as soon as they were out of my mouth.

"Ah," she said, but she didn't say anymore. I wasn't sure if I should have been relieved or disappointed. I'd wanted the line of questioning to stop. But I hadn't wanted to stop listening to Liv.

"Fifteen," I said to the girls when they gathered around us half an hour later. "That's one more than last year."

Rachel held out her hand. "You got seven," I said. She crossed her arms over her chest and scowled. "Dani got eight." Dani beamed. "You can have one now and one after supper."

Rachel stomped her foot.

"Hey!" I said. "None of that. You want the egg or not?"

She frowned and then slowly held out her hand.

"Will you girls share with Liv and me?" I asked, handing over the first of their bounty.

Dani nodded her head. Rachel turned away in a huff.

"Rach..." I started, and Liv's small, soft hand landed on my arm to still me.

"You know what," she announced, "I haven't seen this dunk tank yet."

Rachel spun back around and cocked her head. Then a calculating look crossed her eyes.

She flounced away, and Dani started to follow. "I'm not sure this is a good idea," I admitted.

"It's a terrible idea," Liv agreed. "But laughter is the best medicine."

"Your shrink boyfriend teach you that?"

Liv arched her brow at me. "I don't kiss and tell."

And now I couldn't get the picture of her lips out of my head. Specifically, her lips and me kissing them. The guilt made me stumble.

If it hadn't have been for the small, soft hand that reached out to catch me, stopping my fall, I would have hit the ground.

CHAPTER 13

SO BRAVE

LIV

It took Dani three goes to dunk her father. Rachel dunked Zach in one and Justin in two. Luke laughed at them all but said he had important station business to attend to. Maggie laughed at Luke and simply pushed him into the tank using feminine wiles and a well-placed-kiss-to-the-side-of-the-neck distracting technique.

The girls shook with giggles, their faces flushed, their eyes alive and real.

"Not a bad idea after all," Matt said, towelling off his hair. His t-shirt clung to his chest, accentuating every dip and curve and hard muscle. For a moment I couldn't look elsewhere and then Rachel tapped me on my arm.

I stared down at her, and she blinked up at me and then looked toward the dunk tank.

Matt stilled. Zach and Justin stopped joking with each other. Even Luke watched on with a silent Maggie.

"What is it, sweetheart?" I asked.

She pointed at the tank and then gripped the hem of my shirt and tugged.

"Revenge is sweet," Matt muttered under his breath only loud enough for me to hear him.

"Yes," I agreed, allowing Rachel to drag me toward the tank.

We stopped just shy of the ladder leading up to the drop seat. Rachel pointed at the seat and then pointed at me.

There was a conflicting look in her eyes; defiance mixed with insecurity.

I crouched down in front of her, like her father had, and said, "Would this make you feel better?"

She nodded.

"Would this make you happy?"

She nodded again.

"Like it makes you happy dunking your uncles?"

She bit her lip.

"Not like that?" I guessed.

She shook her head.

"I see," I said, looking back at the tank.

"Are you too chicken?" Justin called out.

"Come on, teach," Zach added. "Be a good sport and take one for the team."

But I wasn't part of the team. Not in Rachel's eyes. I looked toward Dani, who was biting her bottom lip. She knew her sister well.

"Tell you what," I said to Rachel. She waited, a guarded expression on her face. For a six-year-old, she was smart. "I'll let you try to dunk me." Her brow arched. "You might miss," I pointed out. She rolled her eyes incredulously. I stifled a laugh. "I'll let you dunk me," I corrected and she smiled. "If you whisper something in my ear."

She took an immediate step back.

"She doesn't give up, does she?" I heard Justin murmur softly.

I didn't take my eyes off Rachel.

"Only fair," I said. "You want something. Something I can give you. But I want something in return."

How badly did Rachel want to humiliate me? Make me pay for making her remember?

"The first one's the hardest," I whispered. "You think you can't do it, but you can. Nothing will change, Rachel. I promise. Just one word in my ear. Just you and me. And then you can dunk me in a tank of bone-chilling water."

"It's not *that* bad," Zach muttered behind me.

"What do you say?" I asked the little girl in front of me.

She blinked back at me. I shuffled closer.

"He doesn't deserve your words, Rachel," I whispered. "He's taken so much. Don't let him have those forever."

It was a risk. I knew it. And I half expected her to turn tail and run. In an adult, it was justified treatment. In a child, I wasn't so sure.

I suddenly realised how precarious this all was. How ill equipped I was at handling children. The brain is still developing in a six-year-old. There are still so many neural pathways to be connected and strengthened. When people come to me, their cerebral development has been completed on a physical level. I just have to retrain them to what once was.

In children, you're attempting to forge new connections. Wipe out old ones which shouldn't have been formed at all. I'd done my research; I wasn't entirely ill-prepared. I'd read up on the twins' condition, on currently favoured treatment options, on the appropriate cognitive therapy; play therapy, art therapy, animal-assisted therapy, applied behaviour analysis.

I was attempting to bring each one into their daily school routine. Even the suggestion of the dunk tank had been made in that vein. But as I crouched here and looked into the eyes of this young person, I wondered if I'd got it all wrong. If I'd allowed my previous success with adults to cloud my judgement with this child. Rachel was reacting differently to her sister; to be expected, no two patients are alike, despite experiencing the same traumatic episode. Had I got it wrong? Had I made a mistake? Would Rachel pay for my ineptitude?

"It's OK," I said, beginning to stand. "If you don't want to. I won't make you. But I also won't climb that ladder."

If there's one thing you're taught in medical school, it's to be consistent in your treatment of a psychiatric patient.

"I've had fun today," I said. "This was fun." I was scrabbling, and every adult here knew it.

"Rach," Matt said, stepping forward. "Let's go find Gramps and Grandma, eh?"

She tugged her hand free of his. Then stomped her foot hard.

"Rachel," he said sterner.

She offered him a glare and crossed the short distance to me, then she waved me down to her height.

I knew what was happening was important. For so many reasons. I knew I'd engaged her, even if I'd almost pushed too far. I knew this was progress of a sort. Indication she was responding to treatment, as harsh as it had seemed.

I knew it, but I dreaded it. Rachel had so much anger inside her, this was not going to go smoothly.

My eyes met Matt's. His were wide and fearful. I crouched down and lifted my face to Rachel.

She stepped closer, her sister hovering in the background, one of her uncle's hands on her shoulders, grounding her. I'd thank him later. If I still had a job and hadn't been marched off Red Tussock for trespassing.

"What is it, Rachel?" I asked, my voice soft and inviting. "What would you like to say?"

She stalled. She couldn't do it. A part of me that had no right existing was relieved.

Sometimes I hated my job. Sometimes I felt their pain along with them. Sometimes reaching a patient, helping them, would make them fall apart. It was my job to put them back together again afterwards. In the right order. In the right way. Correcting what had been mixed up or switched off or hurt beyond their recognition.

I told myself this is what I do. I'm good at it.

I told myself I was ready. This was good. We were making progress.

I ducked my head down and caught Rachel's gaze.

"You are not alone," I murmured. "You're safe," I added. "Give me some of your pain, sweetheart. Put your hand in mine and let some of it go. I can take it. I'll always take it. Whatever you want to give me, Rachel, I'll take it with open arms."

I waited. She licked her lips. Darted her eyes towards the dunk tank. But we all knew the tank held no meaning anymore. It wasn't about dunking me. Seeking her revenge. We'd moved past that.

It was Rachel and her demons and the dragon who was prepared to slay them.

"I'm here," I whispered.

She looked at me, such hurt and anger and confusion in her eyes.

"It's OK," I said. "I've got this." *I've got you, darling.*

She leant forward, a small hand coming up to cup my cheek, her hot breath coming out in rapid stutters against my earlobe. Her body trembled.

My hands landed on her tiny waist. She leant into me as if offering some of her weight.

"He..." she said, her voice fracturing. If it were all she managed to say, I'd crow with delight. But Rachel was braver than me. "He made us watch," she whispered.

And the world ceased to exist. The smell of grass and the faint hint of manure and the sounds of the Fair winding up and the harsh breaths of those standing around us in a tight circle. It all disappeared.

Just me and this child. This fragile, broken, courageous child.

I wrapped my arms around her and held her close. I didn't ever want to release her.

So brave.

So beautiful.

So broken.

CHAPTER 14

BY TOMORROW MORNING, I'D REMEMBER WHY NOT

MATT

Shit. What the fuck? OK. I could handle this. I could still breathe. I could still stand. Fuck! What just happened?

Rachel spoke. I didn't hear the words. But I saw her throat move and her lips open and the shock that thrummed through Liv's body.

Fuck. I wasn't sure what I was meant to be feeling. Elated that she'd done it? Proud that she'd met Liv head on? Scared to death that what she'd said would break me.

It looked like it might have broken Liv.

My girl's arms were wrapped around Liv's neck, her body clinging to the woman as if she was her lifeline. The same woman who had repeatedly pushed and pushed my little girl until she'd cracked. And spoken.

Liv was saying something. I couldn't hear her; a ringing had started up inside my ears. Rachel was nodding her head. Clinging tighter. I wanted to demand to know what was being said, being shared between them. But I couldn't move, couldn't make my fucking legs move an inch. Couldn't do a thing but stand there and stare.

Fuck. What was happening?

A small hand slipped into mine, and I jerked. My eyes dipping down and spotting Dani. I scooped her up and clung to her as if the child should be comforting the parent. As if by hugging one daughter I wouldn't feel so lost to the other.

A small hand reached up and swiped away a tear. A fucking tear. On my cheek.

"Dani," I said, holding her tighter. Pressing my cheek to her cheek, breathing the same air as each other. "Baby-girl," I murmured, wanting to hold Rachel, too. To talk to Rachel, too. To hear her talk back.

I staggered over to Liv and collapsed on the ground beside her. My knees sinking into the soft dirt. Dani clung tighter. Rachel didn't even see me. And then Liv shifted, bringing my little girl into my arms. Allowing me to touch her her, hold her, while she clung to Rachel, too.

We ended up in a pile of limbs and wet cheeks and soft words; Liv's and mine. Rachel had fallen back into silence.

I could hear Liv now; hear what she was saying.

"You're so brave," she whispered. "So brave. They're yours now, darling," she said, not making any sense. "All yours, you brave, beautiful girl."

I shuddered as a sob racked my frame.

"We have you," Liv was saying. "We're right here. We're not going anywhere, you understand? You can give us all the hurt, sweetheart. We've got this."

Rachel nodded. And I couldn't stop the hiccuped sound that spilt out.

Liv's hand slipped into mine, gripping it tightly, squeezing it reassuringly. When she let me go and started to untangle herself from Rachel's arms, I almost choked on the words. *Don't go.* Rachel did make a sound of protest. Not words, but more than she would have done previously.

But Liv just laughed shakily, pushed up to her feet, her hands trembling slightly and then brushed down her hair. It was a tangled mess of red curls, bits sticking up here and there from Rachel's grasping fingers. She looked pale and beautiful; an avenging angel. Then she smiled wryly and started toward the ladder into the dunk tank.

Rachel pulled back and blinked, tears streaming down her cheeks. Tears I hadn't seen in twelve long months. She stood up. Took a step toward Liv. Her little body trembling as she sucked in breath after breath after breath.

Liv slowly climbed the ladder, looking more and more beautiful as the setting sun caught her hair, flared in her vibrant blue eyes.

"A deal's a deal, Rachel," she called down, settling herself precariously on the seat. She glanced down into the water and grimaced. "Although, it does look icy, indeed."

I stifled a laugh. Dani looked up at me and smiled.

Rachel cocked her head to the side.

"Come on, then," Liv called down to her. "You can't back out now. Your audience is waiting."

Rachel turned around slowly and spotted her family. Uncles, grandparents, cousins, great aunts. A few locals who'd eschewed good manners and stayed for the show.

She blinked and then looked back at Liv.

Liv smiled down at her. Then raised her fisted hand, punching the air, and shouted, "I'll meet my fate head on!"

Zach and Justin burst out laughing. Maggie was shaking her head. Luke just looked bemused.

Rachel let out a huff of breath, then slowly walked toward the box of balls on the stall table.

"I dare you to take me on!" Liv shouted to everyone and no one. And to Rachel. "You can't beat me!"

"Someone shut her up," Zach drawled.

"Quick, Rachel," Justin added. "Before she starts campaigning for supporters."

Dani slipped out of my lap and ran over to her sister. Rachel looked at her. They stared at each other, faces devoid of emotion.

It wasn't over, I realised. *It wasn't over.* Not by a long shot. My eyes met Liv's. She smiled softly. She knew it wasn't over either.

And she was honouring her word. The word she'd given Rachel when she'd pushed her into speaking. I bet there wasn't much Liv did that wasn't honest. She spoke her mind. She did whatever she set out to do. And she honoured any bargains she had with children.

"Get her, Rach!" I called out. "Make her fall!"

"Hey!" Liv shouted back. "Quiet in the cheap seats."

"Come on, Rach," Luke urged. "Let's show the out-of-towner just how good we are at dunking."

"Make her wet!" Maggie shouted.

"She's wearing white," Justin called out, and Zach whacked him over the back of the head. He met my narrowed eyes and nodded his head. I nodded back.

But Liv *was* wearing white, so I made my way over to the stack of towels and grabbed one, determined to cover her up as soon as she climbed out.

"Rachel! Rachel! Rachel!" the cousins called out enthusiastically.

"Down with the teacher!" Justin shouted, sidestepping Zach's long arms.

Rachel picked up a ball and hefted it in her palm, testing its weight like a fucking professional.

"That's my girl," I murmured, pride making me smile.

"You owe me a drink after this, Matt Drake," Liv whispered from her seat above the tank of water.

"How about dinner?" I replied, offering her a wink, just as Rachel threw the ball.

Liv opened her mouth to respond and the ball connected. In the next second she was falling, arms up above her head, breasts bouncing delightfully, as she screamed and fell into the water.

She came up laughing and spluttering and pushing strands of dark red hair off her face.

"One shot!' she shouted, lifting her fist and punching the air above her head, like a prize fighter.

And I swear I fell a little for her then. For this woman who seemed so strict, so uptight, so full of passion. For this stranger who had walked into our lives and challenged everything we'd come to think of as 'normal.' Who'd taken one look at my girls and decided she'd help. Decided to push. Decided to take the time to work us all out.

I wasn't sure if she had all the answers, but Olivia Smith had some, of that I was certain. And right then, I'd take her branch of quack psychiatry over the Timaru doctor who hadn't done a thing for Rachel in twelve long months.

Right then, I allowed myself to believe I deserved her.

By tomorrow morning, I'd remember why not.

CHAPTER 15

THE LINES WERE BLURRING

LIV

MATT WAS QUIET IN THE CAR ON THE WAY BACK TO TOWN. THE girls had fallen back into eerie silence, but Dani had held on to one of my hands while Rachel had grasped the other. I'd walked them to their grandfather's car and helped them climb inside of it. Rachel had wrapped her tiny arms around my neck and breathed against my skin in a stuttering rhythm.

"Count, sweetheart," I'd whispered to her, reminding her how to slow her breathing down. She'd nodded her head and let me go, staring off out of the opposite window.

It would take time. I'd known it. Realistically one successful therapy session rarely solved anything long term. I'd need to build on this development. And there was no telling what Rachel's progress would do to Dani.

I still had a lot of work cut out for me.

But I'd be lying if I said I wasn't disappointed. I wanted an easy solution for everyone.

"What did she say?" Matt asked as Twizel township came into view. His voice was rough, his throat raw from emotion.

There was just so much damn emotion in this family.

As her parent, I was legally obligated to tell him. As my... friend, I wanted to spare him the pain of knowing.

"She told me, he made them watch," I said. Sugar coating it would only make him angry.

Hearing it would probably make him rage.

It was a lose-lose situation.

Matt's fingers clutched the steering wheel with white knuckle precision. His breaths sped up, his chest rising and falling dramatically. His face paled, and I wondered if it had been wrong to tell him this while he was driving.

But driving gave him something to focus on. Other than what those words could actually mean.

"I want to kill him again," he said, making me let loose a harsh breath of air.

Apparently, I didn't know the full story. Reacting to his statement, though, was not an option, so I calmly said, "That's understandable."

He made a non-committal sound and stretched his neck.

The heavy weight of silence in the car felt stifling.

"Did it help?" I asked. "When you killed him?" *How* had he killed him? How was he still walking the streets now?

"Is this where you tell me revenge is not sweet?" he shot back.

"Was it sweet? Did it make the pain easier?"

"I felt... justified. He was trying to take out my entire family. The girls. He held a knife to Dad's throat and a deadman's switch that led to a bomb. We would have all died.'

I studied his profile. Obviously, things had come to an explosive head, and he'd done what he'd had to do to save lives.

How much guilt did he carry?

"Did it ease the pain?" I asked.

He let out an unamused huff of laughter. "You don't ever give up, do you?" he said.

"It's not in my nature," I agreed with a small smile.

"You missed your calling," he said, as he pulled the ute into the street that led to my rental. "You should have been a shrink, not a teacher."

And now the guilt weighed heavily on me.

The ute rolled to a stop in my driveway, and we both stared at the now nondescript brick wall of my flat. No graffiti to mar its dull appearance. Just red brick and grey grout and concrete walls.

"Sometimes I don't think about her," Matt suddenly said. "Sometimes I forget that my wife cheated and broke up our family. Sometimes I laugh, and I realise I shouldn't. And it tears me up."

"Why can't you laugh? Who says laughter is reserved for everyone else but you?"

"She's dead," he said simply.

"You didn't kill her."

"But I didn't love her the way she needed it either."

He climbed out of the car and came 'round to my door. I just sat there. A tumult of thoughts rioting through my head. My body numb with emotion.

I wasn't meant to care for these people like this.

My door opened, and Matt reached in, holding out his hand. It was the simplest thing to reach out and take it. To let him help me from the car. I stood up, and he looked at me. Both of us saying nothing for a moment, and then he ducked his head, leant forward, and kissed me chastely on the cheek.

"Thank you, Olivia," he said rather formally. "Thank you so much."

I watched him walk back around to his side of the car and then forced myself to step away as he started it up. He offered a wave, his eyes connecting with mine briefly, and then he was gone.

"What am I doing?" I muttered to myself, staring at where the vehicle had been. "What the hell am I doing here?"

With a shaking hand, I pulled out my cell phone, finding David's number and starting the call. He answered on the third ring. He always answers on the third ring. That's why I could count on David.

"How's the deep, dark south?" he asked in way of greeting.

Dark, I wanted to reply. But instead said, "Interesting."

"Interesting? What could be interesting in Twizel?"

"And here I thought you were jealous of my sabbatical."

"Hey, I suggested somewhere you could relax and get a tan. It was Policeman Plod who went all boondocks on you."

I smiled. "It's not that bad. I went to a Fair today."

"A Fair? What did you do? Take a ride on a tractor? Shear a sheep?"

I chuckled, feeling better already. "Hunted for eggs."

He burst out laughing. "Well, that does kind of make sense. Happy Easter, by the way."

"You too."

I shivered, realising I was standing outside in my still damp clothing. I fished around in my pocket for my key and unlocked the front door.

"Anything new to tell me?" I asked.

"Olivia," David said. "It's not healthy to fixate."

"What else am I supposed to do, David? This needs to be resolved so I can come back home quickly."

"So, they haven't converted you completely, then?" he asked in a drawl.

"You think a couple of weeks in Canterbury is going to make me move to Christchurch?"

"I know you better than that. You've barely stepped foot out of Auckland." His voice softened. "And I also know this is a challenge for you, Olivia. I know you're out of your comfort zone, right now. But it won't be forever."

It felt like it. It felt like I had been here for years. I sat down on my rented couch and stared at my rented TV. Then closed my eyes.

"It's fucked up," I whispered.

David was silent. Then he let out a soft breath of air. "Tell me."

"The girls. They need better help than me."

"You're a highly educated and accomplished psychiatrist. Who else could be better for their treatment? Turner? We all know his approach to cognitive therapy."

I smiled, rolling my head back on the sofa.

"It's not just them. Their father. He's..."

"He's what?"

"Complicated."

"I see." Did he? I doubted it.

"The lines are blurring," I admitted so quietly, I hoped David hadn't heard.

"Oh," he murmured, dashing that fantasy. "*That* sort of complicated."

"No," I rushed to say. "I just can't seem to separate myself from their pain."

"Not good." He wasn't telling me anything I didn't know.

"I feel like I can barely breathe, David. They're decent people. They don't deserve this agony."

"No one does, Olivia. Not even you."

"Not even?" I demanded.

"That came out wrong."

"Tell yourself that, but I think you're jealous I'm taking a break and you're not."

"Yes, that's right," he deadpanned. "I always wanted to spend time in Twizel."

"Hey! It's not that bad," I complained on a smile. "There's fishing."

"Yes, and I know how much you love getting down and dirty with nature."

My smile slowly fell as I looked down at my crumpled t-shirt. It hadn't been that bad. Traipsing around in a paddock. Hunting for eggs. Being dunked in a dunk tank by a little girl who had stolen my heart completely.

"They're decent people," I said softly.

David laughed. It was derisive, insomuch as David could be.

"Good God," he said. "I'm calling Detective Pierce. We need to send out a rescue party."

I smiled. "While you're at it, find out what's happening with my case."

"Yes, ma'am," he said, and I could picture him saluting. "I'll get right on that. And your assignment for the day is to have a bath, do whatever it is women do at a spa and make yourself presentable." I stared down at my entirely unpresentable appearance and grimaced. "Can't have you going all native on me," he said.

"Yes, sir," I said smiling.

"Oh, that gives me the shivers, that does," he growled and ended the call.

I stared at the blank screen of the TV and then got up off my butt, heading towards the bathroom. Maybe David was right. I wasn't a country bumpkin. I was letting myself go. Blurring the lines completely. A bath and a manicure would go a long way towards correcting that.

As the water started running and the smell of the oil I'd tipped into it began to waft on the air, I realised I was kidding myself. It didn't matter what I looked like, how I dressed, what nail polish I painted my nails. It didn't matter at all.

All I could see was Matt Drake when I closed my eyes.

The lines were blurring.

CHAPTER 16

LETTING THE STORM SWELL INSIDE ME

MATT

FIVE DAYS IS ALL IT TAKES FOR YOUR HOPES TO BE DASHED completely. Less than a week. Longer than a fractured heartbeat. Five days to realise Rachel wouldn't speak to me. She'd only speak to Liv. If you could call whispering in her teacher's ear speaking.

"Of course, you can," Liv was saying, as Rachel pulled back from her latest whispered conversation. "But I'd like you to tell Dani."

Liv was trying. I could see that. Using every persuasive skill the woman had to get Rachel to branch out from her whispering. It wasn't working.

I wondered if Liv's hopes had been dashed, too.

I scrubbed the back of my neck as Rachel walked over to where Dani was painting. My eyes stuck fast on the girls' teacher. Her hair was so shiny today that it looked more like a piece of bronzed sheet metal. What the hell did the woman wash it with?

And why couldn't I stop staring at it?

My eyes darted to Rachel and Dani as they started to have one of their silent arguments. Dani shook her head. Rachel stomped her foot. And then she reached out and grabbed the piece of paper that Dani had been painting.

"Rachel!" Liv growled. But it was too late. The painting tore down the middle, two determined little hands holding it aloft for her sister to see. "Oh, Rachel," Liv murmured as Dani started to cry silent tears. "Go and sit on the naughty stool."

Rachel gave Liv a look as if she'd betrayed her and then stomped across the room to the stool in the corner clearly reserved for such things. Liv lowered her head and let out a sigh. I hadn't seen the girls' teacher this despondent. I almost revealed myself, but something held me back.

Maybe it was Dani. She walked over to Liv and laid a hand on her shoulder, her tears forgotten at the appearance of her teacher's distress.

"It was a pretty picture," Liv said. "Who was in it?"

Dani leant forward and said something into Liv's ear.

I stood upright, took a step toward them, my heartbeat thundering inside my chest.

Had Liv been holding out on me?

And then I looked at her and noticed she was crying. Diamond-like tears streaming down porcelain cheeks.

"Sweetheart," Liv said, an obvious lump in her throat. "You did it."

Dani nodded. Then leant forward and repeated the whispering act.

Liv laughed, and the sound of it - deep and throaty and real - sent a shiver down my body centring in my crotch. Fuck but that was a sexy laugh. I shook myself, trying to focus on Dani. Fantasising about the girls' teacher was not on the agenda.

"Me?" Liv said. "I thought it might be your mummy."

My heart stopped beating completely.

Dani shook her head adamantly.

"Why did you paint me, darling?" Liv asked. Dani leant forward and answered her.

I would have traded all my wealth to hear what my daughter said.

Liv paused when Dani pulled back and then reached forward and gripped both of her hands, looking her in the eye solemnly.

"That's not true, Dani," she said, voice a little sterner. "Your mummy loved you very much."

It was too much. I couldn't do this. I couldn't fucking do this anymore.

I turned around and stormed out of the house, coming to rest on the porch. I knew I was breathing too quickly. I knew the dizziness was because I couldn't catch my breath. I knew it would pass like everything passes. But while it was here it hurt.

"Son," Dad said quietly from off to the side. I spun around and spotted him smoking a cigar on the bench seat.

"Since when did you start smoking again?" I asked.

He grimaced and held the cigar out, staring at the glowing tip. "I don't know," he said, seeming amused at the answer. "Maybe Finn's wedding? Maybe before that?"

I ran a hand through my hair and turned toward the driveway. Leaning my hip against the porch railing, I stared off over the brown and green grass. My eyes landed on the flower bed at the base of the porch. At the turned earth and absence of flowers.

"Dani talked," I said into the silence.

"Did she now? Well, it was only time before she caught up with Rachel. Never did like her sister getting the better of her."

"Whispered in Liv's ear."

"Just like Rachel."

I nodded.

"It's progress," Dad said.

I nodded again.

"What's on your mind, son?" he asked.

I scrubbed my face and turned my back on the flower bed, looking Dad in the eyes.

"Do you ever think back and ask yourself 'did I miss something?'"

"No. And you shouldn't either. There's no good to be had living in the past."

"I can't let it go," I admitted. Dad frowned but didn't comment. "She was unhappy, Dad."

"You can't be held responsible for someone's happiness, Matt. Not when they don't tell you they're sad."

"Why didn't she?" I asked, desperate for answers.

"I don't know, son. Missy..." He looked out over the fields and then took a slow drag on his cigar. Once he'd blown the smoke out, he said, "That girl, she never could sit still for long. Always moving. Always talking. Never spent a moment just breathing, letting it all sink in. You walked at a different pace to her, son. You always did. Missy would run. You would meander."

"Why didn't you say something?"

"What was there to say?" he said, shrugging his shoulders. "You were determined to save her. Protected her like she was a princess. What girl wouldn't fall for that?"

"I didn't protect her from him."

Dad pushed up from the bench seat, his old bones creaking, and then walked over to the railing. A large, work-roughened hand landed on my shoulder.

"She didn't ask," he said and turned toward the door.

That was Dad's answer to everything. Ask, and ye shall receive. But I didn't work like that. Not everyone was capable of speaking. Of asking. Missy sure as shit hadn't felt she was capable of asking me.

I'd let my wife down. I'd ultimately let my children down. There was no one else to blame for what had happened to Missy. Marinkovich might have lost the plot and pushed her over the edge, but I'd let her run to him in the first place.

I kicked the porch railing and stalked down the steps, opening up the door to my ute and sliding inside it. It started with a roar that matched the noise inside my head. I didn't have a destination in mind when I turned out of my driveway. But somehow the ute remembered the way as if it had just been there yesterday.

I pulled up outside of Smokey's and walked directly up to the bar. Ordering a whisky. Tom stood in front of me, arms crossed, hook dangerously close to gutting his belly. He stared me down and didn't say a word.

Daring me.

"Fuck off," I said and lifted the glass to my lips.

"Didn't say nothin'," he muttered, sounding disappointed.

Sod him. Sod him and everyone else in this busybody town.

And sod Missy.

I downed the whisky in one swallow and slammed the glass back on the counter.

"Another," I said, letting the storm swell inside me.

CHAPTER 17

AND WAY TOO FAR UNDER MY SKIN

LIV

I watched as Matt drove off down the driveway, dust flying up behind him. I stood there, as if by waiting, the pain I'd seen etched on his face would simply disappear. But there was no wishing that sort of pain away. That soul deep, dark and twisted agony.

I could feel it. I could taste it. Every breath I took was full of Matt Drake.

This was a fucked up mess. A psychiatrist's worst nightmare. I was too close to my patients.

Not that Matt was a patient, per se, but he was tied up in his daughters' distress. He was part of the overall picture. His pain was their pain. Their pain was his pain. And I felt it all as if it were my own.

"He'll calm down," Mr Drake suddenly said from the doorway.

I turned and looked at him. He seemed older than he had this morning.

"I'm not so sure," I whispered.

"Oh, don't worry about him, Olivia. Matt's got a temper on him, sure. He feels things keenly. Always did. But he's also the most practical of my sons. The most logical. He'll wake up soon and realise none of it makes sense. The guilt. The heartache. Carrying that sort of blame."

"Will he?" I didn't think it was that simple. "He hasn't in the past twelve months."

Mr Drake looked toward where the girls were working. Finally having made up as if nothing had happened at all. I guessed you stuck together when it was just the two of you in your silent little world.

He sighed. "They're talking."

"Whispered words, but they are vocalising."

"That's good, huh?"

"It's excellent." I hesitated, then added, "Matt feels isolated from them."

He blinked.

"What?" he said.

"They're only whispering to me and," I turned and looked at them, smiling to myself, "each other. They haven't spoken to their father."

"He's jealous?"

"I didn't say that," I said, shaking my head. "It's more complicated than simple jealousy." He looked doubtful. "It's mixed up with his sense of guilt over Missy's death. His self-worth at having failed as a husband. And now as a father. I wouldn't be too hard on him, Mr Drake. Right now, your son is scared his world is about to fall down around him."

"Worse than when Missy died?"

I shrugged. "How much he loved his wife is relevant. But how much he loves his girls is the key."

"He adores them."

"That's what I'm afraid of."

"Shit," Mr Drake muttered. "Sorry," he immediately said. "Not right to swear in front of a lady." He looked at the girls again. "Or the kids." He smiled a crooked smile. Then looked out the front window. "Wife's got the car," he said out of nowhere. "Can't go after him."

His eyes met mine.

"I'm not sure I'm the right person," I hedged.

"Olivia," the old man said steadily, "I couldn't think of anyone better."

Why? I wanted to ask. Why not one of his brothers? Why me? A practical stranger.

I might have just answered my own question there.

And that was the predicament; I didn't *want* to be a stranger. I was neck deep in this family's problems. Their emotions swallowing me up whole. I couldn't separate myself from them now.

I didn't want to.

And what did that say about me? A doctor falling in love with her patients. With two little girls so traumatised they couldn't speak.

"Mr Drake," I started.

"The best place to check first would be Smokey's."

"The tavern?"

"If his head is where you say it is right now, then Smokey's will be where he's gone running."

"To drink?"

He looked sad. "He'd been doing so well," he said. But for Matt, this was a crisis.

"Smokey's," I said looking at the girls.

"I've got 'em, love," he said, walking towards his granddaughters. "Best you hurry. More than six whiskies and Matt's a goner."

Jesus, anyone would be.

He was sitting at the bar when I got there, exactly where his father said he would be. A glass of what had to be whisky was in front of him; it looked like it hadn't been touched at all. The place was worn, but welcoming. A little rough around the edges. A small group of rowdy young men sat in a huddle over jugs of beer at one table. A lone tourist at another, I ♥ NZ t-shirt announcing his status, talking to the town's pharmacist, their conversation drowned out by the cheering youths. I was pleased to see no mohawks.

I walked across the pitted wooden floor and took the stool beside Matt, grabbing the attention of the barman.

"Gin and tonic, please," I said, waking Matt up from whatever stupor he'd been stewing in.

"What are you doing here, Liv?" he asked. It was crisp and clear, not a slur in sight.

I glanced at his glass and then watched the barman, realising he had a hook for a hand. I stared a little too long at the prosthesis and then looked into the mirror behind the bar at Matt. He was watching me, his face tipped down, a small scowl on his lips. I could feel the heat of his gaze as if a brand on my cheek.

"You said dinner," I told him. "But I'll take a drink instead."

He huffed out a breath and turned back to his whisky. But he didn't pick it up. "I'm not good company right now."

"Me neither," I said, accepting the drink from Hook and taking a healthy swallow. I saw Matt arch his brow in the mirror.

Then he scowled at his drink and in a frustrated voice said, "OK, I'll bite. What's wrong?"

I smiled into my glass, and he cocked an eyebrow at me.

"You're good at it, you know," I said softly.

"At what?" he snapped back.

"Helping people. It comes naturally."

"Fuck no," he said, standing up and pulling his wallet from his back pocket. He dug out a twenty and slammed it down on the bar. Hook lifted his chin in acknowledgement but carried on with whatever task he was doing.

"I didn't take you for a runner, though," I murmured.

Matt stalled a couple of feet away and then tipped his head back and stared at the ceiling.

"Dinner, huh?" he said.

I held up the gin. He shook his head. "Given that shit up," he said. "Come on. I'll buy you dinner. Won't be flash, of course. This is Twizel, after all. But it'll feed whatever's eating you."

Strange choice of words, I thought. But then Matt was more astute than most people realised. Even his father.

My bet, he'd stared at his whisky and done little more.

But when he leant over and pushed open the door to Smokey's, letting me duck under his arm and walk through, I smelled it. Smoke and wood, and a rich, dark malt whisky.

Matt was a complicated man, I realised.

And then his hand landed at the base of my spine as he led me to his car.

Make that an intriguing man, I corrected. Complex. Confusing. And way too far under my skin.

As David would say, this was not good.

CHAPTER 18

LIFE IS A TRAGEDY

MATT

THERE WAS TOO MUCH CORIANDER IN MY GARLIC CHICKEN. Maybe I should have been worried about the garlic and not the coriander. But it was the coriander I picked out of the dish and placed on the side of my plate with a grimace.

"Why did you suggest Thai if you don't like coriander?" Liv asked with unveiled amusement.

It was the fanciest restaurant in Twizel, but I didn't tell her that.

"You said you liked it."

"I like fish and chips, too."

I stared at her. She shrugged.

"You didn't ask," she said with a grin.

My eyes darted down to her mouth and got stuck there. She had red lips that complemented her hair. Her skin. Her very blue gaze. The pert little nose with six freckles.

I blinked. "They over seasoned the meal," I said, sounding disgruntled.

"Swap," she announced, moving to place her pad Thai before me. "No coriander in this one."

She took my garlic chicken and placed it down in front of her and then began to eat. As if it was perfectly reasonable to swap our meals. I watched her for a long moment, feeling something deep inside I didn't want to identify, and then I picked my fork up and shovelled a mouthful of Pad Thai into my gob.

I grunted in appreciation. No coriander.

"You drive a Volvo," I said several minutes later; my stomach full, my body relaxed, the taste of coriander washed from my gullet.

"I didn't use to. I used to drive a BMW. But somehow I couldn't picture a BMW in Mackenzie Country."

I huffed out a laugh. "Not so sure a Volvo fits in either."

Liv offered a self-deprecating laugh back.

"Yes, well, I'd never been here before. Google isn't as accurate as they think."

"You Googled us? Is that how you picked Twizel? I thought it might have been more of a dart thrown at a map kind of thing."

"Now, now, Senior Sergeant," Liv teased, "not all of us have the good fortune of being raised on 50,000 hectares where we can spread our wings."

"Wellington a bit stifling?" I asked, and she paused. It wasn't the usual type of pause you get while someone thinks up a witty come-back, either. It was a possum-caught-in-headlights pause. An oh-fuck-what-do-I-do-now pause.

I smiled and wiped my lips with the napkin.

"Why Twizel?" I said.

"Why not?" she answered.

Liv was hiding something.

"They're talking to each other now," she suddenly said. I would have been angry at the abrupt change of topic if it hadn't concerned my girls.

"Yeah?"

"Whispering, but still," she said. "It's marvellous progress. The worst is over, Matt." She said it like she wanted to convince me. As if she was trying to tell me something important. Something even more important than the fact my girls were no longer mute.

"Why the whispering?" I asked, studying her carefully.

"It affords a level of protection they still believe they need."

"Where did you teach before?" I asked. I'd read the details in her CV. I'd even phoned someone for a reference. 'Brilliant teacher,' the guy had enthused. 'Very focused on the children,' he'd added. 'You won't regret hiring her.'

"A family in Newtown," she muttered, not meeting my eyes.

I'm not sure why I was disappointed. Liv could have her secrets. They weren't mine to pry into. But there was a seething pit of something dark and sluggish inside that hated that she'd just lied to me.

Silence fell over our little corner of the restaurant. Thick and real and coated in disenchantment.

I realised, I'd begun to see Liv as someone I *could* trust. The thought that she wasn't was damn near crippling.

"Where will you go after us?" I asked, forcing myself to face reality. Liv wasn't cut out for Mackenzie Country. She was here for a reason, and it had nothing to do with Rachel or Dani. Or me.

And everything to do with whatever she was running from. In my experience, running never achieved a damn thing.

"I have no plans to leave," she said lifting her eyes to mine finally.

And I could almost believe she meant it.

"You've got a life somewhere else, Liv," I said softly. She shook her head, but I leant forward to make my point. "You live in a rental and have made no effort to bring your own home's contents down here. You bought a new car, but you're not attached to it. The bonnet would have been repainted by now if you were. You talk about Wellington as if it's off limits to you. But I can see the hunger in your eyes to return."

"You're wrong."

"Am I? What are you running from?"

"Nothing."

"I don't believe you."

"You don't have to. It is what it is."

Not *it's the truth.*

I leant back in my seat and stared at her. It wasn't hard to do. She looked petite and fragile and lost, but underneath that vulnerability was an intelligent mind, a sharp wit, and a strong woman. I could see it in the way she interacted with Rachel and Dani. In the way she held her own with my brothers. In the way she made my heart beat too hard.

In the way she looked at me now, challenging me.

"I'm here now," she said. "And that's all that matters. Rachel and Dani need me."

"A teacher. Why you and not some other tutor?"

"It's not the subject matter that counts," she said. "It's the girls and their state of mind."

No other teacher would have looked at it like that. I knew the girls were behind in their studies. Desperately so. *That* would have been what a teacher focused on. That's what we had been doing; trying to get them to catch up in their own non-communicative way.

But Liv barged on in here and forced the real issue, barely glancing at the curriculum.

"And you've done what you set out to do," I agreed. "So, I ask again, where will go after us?"

She stared at me and then looked away, her fingers toying with the tablecloth before her.

"There is nowhere for me to go right now," she said softly.

What had she left behind in Wellington? A man? A death? A crime? What?

"Please," she whispered. "Don't ask me." Don't ask me to lie, she was saying. Don't ask me to lie to you.

I tossed the napkin down on the table and stood from my seat.

Then reached out my hand towards her. Maybe I should have walked away; I had enough shit in my life to contend with. But there was something about this woman. Something that spoke to me in a way no woman had for years.

I didn't want that attraction. I didn't want to add to my guilt. But

Dad was right; I can't stop myself. I see a woman in trouble, and I want to help. I want to be their knight in shining armour.

I didn't know if Liv was in trouble, but I did know that I hadn't stopped thinking about her every second of every day since she'd got here.

I'd even stopped having nightmares. Instead, the images that plagued me at night were far more dangerous. They involved red lips and redder hair and soft skin and freckles.

And the most beguiling blue eyes I'd ever seen.

So help me God, I wanted to save her.

When would I learn there're no such things as fairy tales? Life is a tragedy.

CHAPTER 19

IT WAS ONLY NATURAL I SCREAMED

LIV

He held my hand all the way to the car. His fingers laced in mine as if he was staking a claim to me. Making sure the world saw I was his.

In what capacity I was his, I didn't yet know. But Matt's whole demeanour had changed in that restaurant. After he'd asked me questions and I'd been forced to lie.

Most men would be running; I was sure Matt had figured out there were gaps in my story. He's a cop. He's apparently good at it. But instead of dusting his hands clean of me, he reached out and took hold.

Matt Drake ran towards trouble not away from it. And that filled me with such longing I could barely stop myself from reaching for him in return.

He stopped at the side of his police ute. Even out of uniform he favoured the official vehicle over his Red Tussock Ranger. It said something about the man. Off duty or on, he was there for the public. A part of me wanted him to be there for me, as well.

He turned to look down at me, a grim expression on his face. I traced the small laugh lines that spread out from around his eyes with my gaze. The stubble that graced his cheeks. The hard edge of his jaw as he ground his teeth.

He didn't look angry. He looked magnificent. Annoyance gave Matt a presence to take note of. Made him untouchable and conversely irresistible. Placed him on a pedestal and mocked all those beneath.

"You're trouble, doll," he said, voice deep and smooth like fine whisky. "You make me want to break the rules."

"What rules?" I said before I could stop myself.

"Life's rules," he replied immediately. "You make me want to break them all."

"Would it be so bad to break them?" I wanted to close my eyes and pretend I hadn't just said that.

And I also wanted to pat myself on the back for being so brave.

His hand came up and cupped my cheek. His dark eyes staring into mine as if he could reach the very heart of me.

"I could hurt you," he whispered.

I could be good for you, I thought. He made a sound. I realised I wasn't shielding my emotions. Whatever he'd seen on my face had him stepping closer and not farther away.

His chest brushed up against mine. His breaths quickened. His thumb swept over my cheek, dangerously close to the corner of my lips. And then he leant down.

"I'm going straight to hell anyway," he muttered and kissed me.

It was slow and deep as if we had all the time in the world. Or as if Matt wanted to savour every drop of me. He couldn't be rushed, I realised. He wouldn't be rushed. He'd taken a step over some invisible line, and he was damn well going to enjoy it.

Matt committed to an endeavour completely.

My hands came up and wrapped around the back of his neck, my feet stretching, up on the very tip of my toes to reach him. I tilted my head, opened my mouth wider, and invited him in. Enticed him to break every rule he thought he should follow.

He moaned. The sound sending shivers throughout my body. His hands clutched me, drew me closer. Made me feel like I was his saviour. His angel come to bless him. He tasted of tamarind and chives, seduction and longing. His body felt hard, and his lips felt soft, his tongue tangling with mine, making me dizzy.

Matt was everything I thought he would be and so much more. I revelled in his touch, in his kiss, in his heat. In this moment where he forgot his worries and allowed himself to breathe. This was why I let him kiss me, I told myself. Because he needed it. Because I could give him that brief reprieve.

Then I felt his erection pressed into my stomach, the world outside of *this* vanishing, and I kissed him back; hard, desperate, completely.

A laugh bubbled up and out of my mouth making Matt pull away. But only slightly. He started laying kisses over my jaw and down my neck as if he couldn't get enough of me.

"What's so funny, doll?" he murmured against a sensitive spot beside my ear. My back arched, my breasts pressed up against the broad expanse of his chest, his arms tightened around me, and then he kissed me right there, beneath my ear, with renewed intention. With focused intensity. Stealing all thought. Stealing all sanity.

Me, I wanted to say. *I'm funny*. Pretending I was in his arms for his benefit... and not mine. Completely.

I clutched him tighter. He kissed me long and soft and deliciously. Who knew the neck could be so sinful? Or maybe it was Matt's sinful lips that did it. That turned me into a pool of want and desire at his feet.

My fingers scrabbled for a hold in his hair. My breaths stuttered out of my mouth frosting the air. His hips rocked against me in a promise as old as time.

Then a loud exhaust backfired on the street, and a series of irritatingly tuneful horns blasted our world back into clarity. I blinked back the haze of desire and watched as three souped-up Subarus screamed past in a flash of blue LED lights underneath.

"Bet you wish you'd taken me up on that tour, S60," Gribble the purple mohawk wearing boy racer called out. "Drop the cop, and I'll show you how to really park!"

The car fishtailed out of Main Street and gunned it with its cohorts towards what I thought was Lake Ruataniwha. No doubt an ideal spot for parking.

I groaned and tried to step back out of Matt's grasp. He wouldn't release me.

"I'm fifteen years his senior, and he still insists on flirting," I complained.

Matt looked down at me with barely contained amusement.

"You're a shiny new toy," he said matter of factly. "In a place that rarely changes. Age has nothing to do with it. You're sexy as hell and leave every other woman in this town for dead."

He stilled. A horrible wash of mortification replacing the soft look of before. And then he abruptly stepped back.

I felt cold and desperate and utterly awful immediately.

"Fuck," Matt said and spun towards the ute.

"Matt..."

"No. Don't. Please."

He walked around to his driver's side and slipped into the car. I stood on the sidewalk and wondered if I should just walk back to my Volvo outside of Smokey's. It wasn't far. But it also wasn't how I'd envisaged the evening ending.

The passenger door opened, Matt leaning across the vehicle to peer up at me. "Get in, Liv," he ordered.

Not 'Doll.' 'Liv.' He'd pulled away. He'd withdrawn into himself again. Into a world where Missy deserved his loyalty and fathers of mute children should not laugh.

I took a slow, deep breath in and slid into the car. Matt started it without another word. In seconds we were outside my rental. A place I had barely put my mark on. A bolthole if ever there was one.

I turned to look at him in the dim light of the dashboard. He wouldn't spare me a glance.

"Thank you for dinner," I said.

"You're welcome," he replied.

Nothing had ever sounded so forlorn.

"OK," I said, as much for myself as him. I opened the door and slid out.

Turning back to look at the one man I wished to be honest with more than I wished for my own safety, I realised I'd made the biggest mistake of my life. Of my career. I'd fallen not only for the parent of two of my patients. I'd fallen for a man who was not free to fall for me.

I walked away from him, knowing I had to walk away from Twizel. From it all.

If I didn't, I'd end up breaking.

With a stuttered breath in I stepped toward my back door, the automatic security light the landlord had recently put in at Maggie's insistence blinding me for a split second.

And then I saw the cat. It was only natural I screamed.

CHAPTER 20

A STORM TWISTING HIGHER
AND HIGHER

MATT

"A cat," I said, desperately wanting to comfort Liv. She looked shaken. More shaken than a dead cat on your doorstep should mean. "It's probably been hit by a car and crawled here to die," I added, not making a blind bit of difference to her trembling.

When I'd heard her scream pierce the still of night I'd panicked. I'd damn near hit a rubbish bin when I u-turned and gunned it back to her flat. She'd been standing there in a pool of artificial light, staring down at the mangled body of the feline, face ashen, body tight, as if it was about to spring back to life and in a move worthy of a zombie thriller flick jump up and eat her brains out.

"Liv?" I said. "It's just a cat."

"Yes," she said. "A cat." As if that was significant.

"Is it yours?" I asked. I didn't think she'd brought anything from Wellington with her.

She shook her head, eyes still locked on the dead cat. "Across the road," she mumbled, then stepped over the cat and unlocked her back door.

I watched her move inside, flicking on first the kitchen light and then as I followed her, the lounge, the laundry, the bedroom and bathroom lights.

She was terrified.

Over a dead cat.

"What's going on, Liv?" I asked as she came back into the lounge and stared at nothing.

"It's just a cat," she said. "You're right. Just a cat."

"Liv, you're repeating yourself." I crossed my arms over my chest to stop myself reaching for her. Holding her. Protecting her.

I had no right.

She let out a shaking breath of air.

Fuck.

"Liv," I said, my body wanting one thing, my heart asking for another, my mind telling me to hold tight. Don't move. Don't touch. Don't want with every fibre of my being. "What does the cat mean to you?"

She blinked and then slowly looked up at me. Eyes brighter than the sky on a summer's day over Red Tussock.

"Nothing," she said on a blatant lie.

"Olivia," I snapped. "What does the cat mean to you?"

Her breath rushed out of her in a sound of surprise. Did she think I was just a country copper? Not as switched on as the city slicker boys?

"Damn it," she said and started to pace.

I waited. This was her secret to tell.

"I'm not from Wellington," she finally said, making me rock back on my heels and widen my eyes.

"OK," I said. "Where are you from?"

"Auckland."

I started laughing. Of course she was from Auckland. Can't keep the bloody JAFAs away. I glanced at the wall that separated Liv's flat from Maggie's. Aware my former *Auckland*-based sergeant hadn't run in here guns blazing. Fucking Luke.

"What else?" I asked.

She looked at me as if she thought I might attack. I suddenly had a very bad feeling about this.

"Tell me," I said softly.

"It wasn't my idea," she rushed to say. I didn't reply. "Twizel was chosen for me. Somewhere far away. Somewhere I didn't know anyone. Somewhere I wasn't known either."

"Witness protection," I said stunned. That was the exact criteria for witness protection.

But Liv shook her head. "They never called it anything like that. I'm not a witness."

"Then what are you?"

She bit her lip. "I'm a psychiatrist," she said, and I felt my knees buckle. My bum hit the wilted padding of her couch. "One of my patients, we're not sure which one, has been stalking me."

Fuck.

"The Auckland CIB detectives assigned to my case decided the patient's actions had reached a tipping point and my safety was compromised."

Fuck.

"He used cat blood," she said, my ears ringing. "Took pictures of me outside my house in Auckland and broke into my office in Grafton Road, pinning the photo to my wall with a message."

Fuck.

"In cat blood," she said, her voice small.

"You came here," I rasped. "To my home," I added. "To my girls."

"Matt."

I shook my head and held up a hand to stop her. "To my girls," I repeated.

"I didn't know."

"Know about my girls?"

"That he'd find me. I'm so far away. No one knows I'm here."

"Someone must do. The cops."

"They're good cops, Matt."

"What are their names?" I demanded.

"Harvey Stone and Ryan Pierce," she immediately replied. As if answering my questions now would stop me from exploding.

I stared at the far wall, trying to breathe. And then I got mad.

"What was the message?" I growled.

Liv jumped slightly but put on a brave face.

"'The knife was cold,'" she said. "'You never said it would be so cold,'" she added. "'The blood was warm. You were right.'"

Fuck me.

I stood up and marched to the back door, stepping over the cat, and walking down the driveway.

I'd made it to the ute before she caught up to me.

"You're leaving?"

"I'm checking on my girls."

"What about...?"

"You?" I said, rounding on her. "You're coming with me." It was out before I could stop it. Understand it. Think about it. I opened the door to the car and pointed inside. "Get in."

She stilled. I growled. She ducked her head, scrambled to get in the car, and then slipped on her seatbelt.

"Keys," I said, holding out my hand. She reached up and placed the house keys in it. "Lock this door," I snapped, stalking back up the drive.

I checked the flat over. Nothing appeared out of the ordinary. Grabbing a bag from the closet, I stuffed some of Liv's clothes inside and then stalked to the bathroom, shoving her entire cabinet's contents onto the top. Zipping it up, I turned off all the lights, checked the locks on all the doors and windows, and then closed and secured the back door. I stared down at the cat on the doorstep and then pulled out my phone.

It rang five times before Luke answered.

"You better have a good reason for disturbing me," he growled down the line. "Maggie is naked, and I intend to take advantage."

"Too much info, bro," I said, my voice sounding like gravel getting crunched by a car.

"What's wrong? The girls? Mum and Dad?"

"They're fine." I'd bloody make sure they were. "It's Maggie."

"What about her?" Luke demanded, sounding like a fucking bull on a rampage.

"Her flat's off limits. Keep her at Red Tussock."

"What the fuck?"

"I'll tell you all about it tomorrow."

"The homestead. Breakfast," Luke snapped. "And you better be talking."

He hung up, and I adjusted the phone, then took several pictures of the cat. There's no veterinary forensics in Twizel. I could have got the vet to check it out, but I was pretty fucking sure that the cat had been run over. Of course, with four severely fractured legs and a head caved in completely on one side, there was no fucking way it crawled to Liv's back door.

I chucked it in the rubbish bin. Washed my hands at the hose attached to the wall. And strode back toward my ute.

A stalker... in my town. Scaring my kid's teacher. Fucking *psychiatrist* teacher. Fucking scaring what was mine.

I was beyond mad. I was raging. A storm twisting higher and higher.

CHAPTER 21

I SHOOK MY HEAD

LIV

I woke with a start. There was a cartoon blaring out of the TV, not six feet from where I'd been sleeping. I blinked back the fugue of sleep and took stock of my surroundings. When my eyes landed on Rachel and Dani in their Tinkerbell PJs kneeling before the big flat screen, I bit my lip. If they were surprised to see their teacher sleeping on their couch, they didn't show it.

I rolled onto my back and stared up at the ceiling. I wasn't in any hurry to get up. Which said something about how comfortable the sofa was or how much in denial I was about what had happened last evening.

Matt had kissed me.

And a dead cat had been placed on my doorstep.

For a second, I couldn't decide which should worry me more.

The man of the moment appeared in the doorway, dressed in uniform, fresh-faced, and holding a coffee cup in one hand. He flicked a gaze over the girls and then dark eyes landed on me.

"You're awake," he said quietly.

"Yes," I said, suddenly feeling uncomfortable. I sat upright and checked I was presentable, then started to fold up the blankets and sheets.

"Leave that," Matt instructed. "Grab a shower, and then we're heading over to the homestead."

"We are?"

He nodded and then turned from the room, walking away without another word. I sat there for a while longer, contemplating what that meant, then let out a sigh and headed toward the bathroom. On the way past the master bedroom, I couldn't resist peeking inside. It looked like it always looked. Immaculate. Too feminine for the senior sergeant. A shrine.

I swallowed thickly and glanced into the girls' room, spotting the blankets in a pile on the floor in the corner under the window sill. I stood there for a long time wanting to cry.

He gave me his couch. Pretended it was nothing. Then slept on his daughters' floor.

Because he couldn't sleep in the master bedroom. *Wouldn't* sleep in the master bedroom.

This family was a morass of emotions. Bogged down in their heartache.

I turned away from the girls' room and met Matt's eyes. He was standing at the end of the hallway watching me. A sad expression on his face that vanished the moment he realised I'd seen him.

"You sleep on the couch," I said. He nodded. "You gave me your bed." He didn't reply. "Why don't you sleep in your bedroom?" I asked because that's what I do. I ask the hard questions. The ones that make people address their issues and get through to the other side.

But I wasn't sure this was an issue I could address. Or one that I should address. I waited for an answer I hoped would not arrive. Then when it didn't, I felt... lost. Shattered. I felt what Matt felt. I felt what I could see in his eyes; an overwhelming sense of ruin.

How did you fix this? How did you help someone whose pain

you keenly felt? I'd never been so in tune with a patient before. I'd never not known how to help.

Matt slowly walked toward me, his steps measured, his face impassive. He had coping mechanisms I'd seen a thousand times before. He had a shell that he wrapped around himself. Hugged a little too tightly.

He stopped before me and reached up and cupped my cheek with one hand. His eyes locked on my eyes, his face expressionless.

"I'm a mess, Liv," he whispered. "I'm a wreck. There's no denying. She did a number on me. Broke my heart. Fucked my life. You should leave."

I didn't want to leave. I had nowhere to go, granted. But that wasn't why I didn't want to leave.

I shook my head.

"I'm not healthy," he said, ignoring me. "I have nightmares," he added, making my heart fracture inside. "I don't trust myself. You shouldn't either."

I looked up at this man who was good to the very heart of him. Who thought he hid that broken part of himself from everyone. Dressed it up in a uniform and pretended to the world that he was fine. That he was OK.

I saw him, though. I saw him, and I wanted to see more.

I shook my head. Matt stepped closer.

"I drink too much," he said with a soft growl. "Fight too much. I want to punch holes in walls and smash everything. I'm full of anger and bitterness that tears at me. It'll tear at you, too."

I stared him in the eyes and willed him to see me.

I'm not going anywhere.

"I'm broken," he whispered. "I'm fucked in the head. I can't be who you want me to be."

I stood stock still and silent. My eyes imploring him to see.

"Liv," he groaned. "Leave."

I shook my head.

"I can't do this." I held my breath. "I want you," he said on a rasp of air. "I want you so much I can barely breathe. You make me feel something again. But I'm not ready. You *need* to leave."

"I won't."

He looked down at me, a confused look crossing this features. His hand still cupping my cheek trembled.

"I could hurt you," he pleaded.

"I could be good for you," I replied steadily.

Silence. Then, "I don't even know your real name."

For some reason that made me smile.

"Damn it, woman!" he swore. "What are you doing to me?"

I shook my head. I didn't have an answer. What was *he* doing to *me*?

"Stubborn, idiotic, brave, crazy girl," he growled. "Last chance," he snapped. "You should leave."

"No."

"Is it the stalker?" I flinched. It had nothing to do with that. "I'll talk to the Auckland boys. Get them looking into another place for you. Sort out what the hell they're doing. If they're CIB, they'll be good. Maggie probably knows them. I'll ask Maggie..."

"Matt. It's not the stalker."

He blinked.

"Then why won't you leave?" It was almost a plea.

"There's nowhere else I want to be," I said quietly. "No one else I want to be with. I'm not leaving."

"Liv," he said softly. Sadly. "I'm not ready."

And that was that. He felt something for me. He wanted me. He just wasn't in the right place to make that a reality.

"It's OK," I said reassuringly. "It's OK," I repeated, for me as well as him. "I'll keep teaching the girls. You keep doing what it is you're doing. We'll get through this. I'm not asking for anything you're not prepared to give. Just..."

"Just what?"

"Don't expect me to leave."

"Why? Why damn it?"

Why indeed?

"Well," I said. "I don't run from things." Auckland and the stalker aside. "I'm not a quitter. I started something here with Rachel and Dani, and I intend to see it through."

"You're mad."

I laughed. "That's not a term I use lightly. But maybe I am. I've certainly never behaved like this before; stayed where I'm not welcome. But I can't…"

"You're welcome. Very much welcome."

"Then why are you asking me to leave?"

Matt looked down at me with such a strange expression on his face; part frightened, part angry, part resigned.

"I'm not strong enough," he muttered. "Not against you. Not against this. God help me," he rasped.

Then his free hand came up and cupped my other cheek, his palms holding me still, face tipped up as he looked down at me.

"You're beautiful," he whispered. "The most beautiful woman I've ever seen. I'm dark and twisted and so not worth your effort." I opened my mouth to speak, and his thumb swept over my lips, resting there; telling me to remain quiet. I blinked. "I'm not finished." My body trembled. He growled, "If you stay…" But he *didn't* finish. He couldn't finish.

Matt had no idea what he would do if I stayed.

"It's OK," I said softly. "It's OK."

He looked lost. Afraid. Achingly in turmoil. Perhaps I should be leaving. Perhaps staying was selfish. But there was more to my refusing to leave than just him. There was Rachel and Dani. There was this family that needed help.

There was this strange, fervent part of me that somehow knew leaving would be the greatest regret of my life.

"What's your name?" he said, jerking me out of my disquieting musings.

I sucked in a breath of air but couldn't speak. Saying my name made my decision to stay real.

"If you're taking on my life and my problems, then I need to know the name of the person I could be hurting."

"You won't hurt me," I said, not entirely sure I believed that.

"Liv," Matt whispered. "I already am."

I smiled softly. Didn't he realise it was because he was who he was, now and then and in the future, that I stayed? I was already in love with him. I was already on his side. No matter what. I was already prepared to walk through hell to get him to heaven.

I reached up and cupped his cheeks in return, stubble scratching my fingers and making me want to rub my jaw against his like a cat.

"Olivia Hope Logan," I said. "Doctor of Psychiatry."

"Huh," Matt said on a breath of air. "Dr Logan. I like it."

I smiled.

"You should still leave," he added.

I shook my head. There was no way I was leaving.

CHAPTER 22

I COULD HURT YOU

MATT

Stubborn, infuriating woman. I wanted to hold her tight and never let her go. But I also wanted her far away from me.

I was going to hurt her. I knew it. I hurt Missy. I hurt my girls. I was going to hurt Olivia Logan.

I stared down at her, wanting to taste and bite and lick and feel. I stared down at her, shaking.

I couldn't do it.

I leant forward and placed my forehead on hers. Two steps away was Missy's and my old bedroom. Just down the hall were my daughters, who had only just started to talk again after their mother's death.

Standing before me was the woman who could be my salvation or my eventual ruin.

I felt too much. Hurt. Anger. Longing. Guilt.

I lifted my chin and laid a soft kiss on her forehead. Then stepped away.

"Shower," I said, then immediately wished I hadn't. All I could think of now was Olivia in my shower, naked and wet and slippery.

I ran a hand over my mouth and stared at her, dared her to make a comment, to challenge me. I wasn't sure I could step away if she did.

To hell with the girls in the lounge watching TV. To hell with Missy's memory across the hallway.

Invite me, my dick urged.

Leave while you still can, my head pleaded.

Save me, my heart begged, mercilessly.

"One step at a time, huh?" Liv said, smirking. Then she stretched up and kissed me chastely on the lips. Just like that.

I was reaching for her before she'd made it a step away. And hauling her back into my arms in the next heartbeat.

Damn her. Damn Missy. Damn my libido.

I kissed her with care. I kissed her as though she would fracture beneath me. I kissed her the way she deserved to be kissed. Long, slow, attentively.

I licked the inside of her mouth in hungry but methodical strokes. Wrapped our tongues around each other. Sucked hers in between my teeth in a rhythmic pulse. Pressed our lips together. My arms snaked around her small frame, one hand cupping the back of her head softly, the other, splayed flat against the base of her spine.

I devoured her with tenderness.

I consumed her with devotion.

I showed her how careful I could be.

I created a false sense of security.

I could hurt you.

Groaning, I pressed her up against the wall, then thought better of it and lifted her off the floor, carrying her the few steps needed to reach the bathroom. The door was kicked closed behind me. My hand fumbled with the lock. And then she was up on the bench, her legs wrapped around my hips... and I was lost.

Stop me, I thought. *Save yourself*, I pleaded silently. *Don't leave.*

"Liv, please," I whispered against the skin on the side of her neck. She said nothing. I wasn't sure whether to be happy or sad.

But I did know I loved tasting her. Licking her just there. Sucking on her tender skin and feeling her writhe beneath me. Eliciting little moans and sharp gasps and desperate fingers gripping. She was so responsive. Every touch of my lips or tongue or teeth made her back arch, her body shudder, her breaths rush out on a little sound of air.

She was a drug to me. Better than whisky. I would become addicted, I knew it. I would crave this reaction. Search out more until we were both weak-kneed. Make us addicts to each other.

The sounds she made would haunt me. Would fuel my dreams and chase away the·shadows. Would tempt me, and tug at me and make me crazy.

I was already half out of my mind for Liv.

"Make me stop," I begged, my lips on her collarbone, my tongue licking softly.

My hand swept up under her pyjama top and cupped a swollen breast, finger and thumb rubbing the nipple.

Fuck me. She exploded beneath me. From my simple touch and careful kisses and hard cock pressed against her centre. Her body bowed tight, her breaths all but ceased, her head arched back and she shuddered. The sound of her climaxing sent a thrill of ecstasy through me.

"You beautiful girl," I breathed, kissing across her throat and up to her earlobe. "You liked that, didn't you?" I pinched her tender nipple again, making her moan out loud. "How else can I get you to come?" She shuddered, her nails digging into my back and making me hungry.

I pulled her closer, bringing her arse to the edge of the bench, pressing my stiff cock harder against her.

Her eyes fluttered closed, and her face flushed, and her hands trembled. I rocked, watching her bite her lip, a tongue flicking out drawing me closer. I leant down and kissed her. Slow. Deep. Consuming. Rocking and kissing and kneading her breast, flicking her nipple.

I got lost in her moans and shudders and grasping fingers.

"Fuck," I groaned against her lips. "Such fire."

My fingers came up and stroked her hair; copper and reds and so shiny. I brushed the strands off her face and ran my hands down her body, savouring every dip and curve and soft, soft inch of skin. Gripping the t-shirt at the hem, I lifted it up and over her head.

Baring her to me.

Fuck. She was beautiful. Pale, pale skin. Creamy breasts rising and falling. Pink nipples begging for my kiss.

Still rocking against her, I lowered my head, eyes on her face, watching every reaction. Then licked across the nipple I'd been steadily pinching.

She came apart in my arms, under my lips, shaking against my erection.

Jesus fuck, but she was beautiful.

I sucked on her nipple, rocked into her mound, and waited for her to fall down from heaven.

"Again," I said, shifting to the other breast and wrapping my lips around it.

My arms tightened around her lower back, making her body arch and her head rest against the mirror. She was moaning and whispering my name and begging for more and that glorious cream skin was flushed pink, and I couldn't take it.

I couldn't stop.

I was addicted.

A third orgasm had her slumping against the mirror, breaths heaving in and out of her mouth, her eyelids shuttered, a drowsy satiated look in amongst the swirling blue of her heavy gaze.

I stared at her and felt the world shift. Felt my body jerk as if it had just woken. I licked my lips. Reached up and cupped her cheek with one hand, while the other softly squeezed her tit. I could feel how wet she was through our clothing. I could smell her arousal. My dick was aching, a wet spot staining my trousers.

I realised I was dressed in uniform. Completely clothed while the goddess before me was topless. It was strange to realise how much I liked that dichotomy. How much being dressed when Liv was nude made me ache to come.

I ran my hands over her sides, cupping her tiny waist, and then letting my fingers find the edge of her pyjama bottoms. Then I slowly rolled them down her legs as if revealing a prize.

I stood there staring at the vision of beauty before me. Smooth skin. Pale flesh. Not a blemish in sight. She was perfection. Utter perfection.

I could hurt you.

I could be good for you.

My eyes met Liv's. She didn't look away. I slowly undid my belt.

CHAPTER 23
MORE FOOL YOU

LIV

He didn't undress. He simply undid his trousers, pulling himself free, and rolling on a condom. He was big. The broad tip of his penis flaring wide. Moisture running down the long length, making me lick my lips hungrily. His eyes never left mine, as if he needed the anchor. Or was waiting for me to tell him to stop.

They begged me for something.

I remained silent. Maybe I should have stopped this. Maybe I should have heeded everything he'd said. I definitely should have taken a moment and thought of the children.

But I was lost.

To his need. To his heartache. To his desire.

To him.

His free hand reached forward and cupped my centre, a long finger dipping inside. I was wet and swollen and so sensitive. My body jerked. My back arched. I moaned.

"I could make you come like this," he said with dawning realisation. "Stroke you until you cream my fingers. You're so sensitive. So responsive. Fuck, Liv. What would you do if I fucked you with my tongue?"

I made a small sound of distress, riding his finger, shuddering so close to the edge.

"Fuck," he said again, slipping a second finger inside. "You are so fucking beautiful."

I came in an embarrassing rush of wetness, my vagina contracting and sucking his fingers in deep.

"Oh, yes," Matt growled. "You are so hot for this. So fucking hot for my touch. Liv," he said on a groan. "I can't stop."

That was my cue, I realised. That was my signal to slow things down. To let Matt breathe a little before he made the plunge. We stood on a precipice, and I'm ashamed to say I forgot everything I'd been taught. I stopped thinking like a shrink and acted like a woman.

A woman who was hot and horny and falling in love.

"Matt," I pleaded.

He kissed me. That slow, heady kiss he did. The one where I couldn't think, couldn't breathe, couldn't imagine living without this. He kissed me long and soft and with such utter care and attention. His fingers pumping slowly inside me, his condom-wrapped dick pressing against my mons, his lips and tongue making me moan and writhe and beg.

He kissed me like that for minutes. I came again. I'd lost count how many times now. He never paused. But every touch, every stroke, every lick and kiss and rock was delivered with such tenderness. Such infinite care it made my eyes burn.

It would have been easy to misinterpret Matt's soft, careful ministrations as something they were not. Matt Drake was just a caring lover. A gentle man. Trapped in a tortured soul.

"I can't wait," he said against my neck, his breath hot, his tongue hotter, his lips utter bliss. "I need to feel you around me. I need to be inside you. I need to know there's nothing between us."

I spread my legs wider, tipped my pelvis back, and opened myself up. His fingers slipped out, making me feel hollow, and then the broad head of his penis pressed against my entrance.

"You're so hot," he said. "Like fire." He rocked forward, entering me an inch. "So fucking tight," he groaned, his breaths coming swiftly. "Oh, Christ, Liv. I can't stop."

"You don't need to stop," I assured him, stroking a hand down his back and rocking my hips up to meet him.

"Liv," he moaned. "I don't want to stop." And with that, he pushed forward until the very end of me.

We both stilled, our breaths heaving, his eyes a little wild as they looked down into the very heart of me.

"Sweet Jesus," he said. "Why do you feel so good? So right?"

I reached up and cupped his cheeks, then pulled him down to kiss me. Against his lips, I said, "This is good. This is right. You don't need to stop."

He made a sound, and his hips jerked, as if involuntarily. And then he was kissing me and rocking into me, and moaning when I moaned, and sighing when I sighed, and letting go when I let go. Meeting me in paradise.

No beginning or end to either of us. Just two people, two bodies, two hearts and souls entwined. And two extraordinary climaxes.

His breaths stuttered out of him as his body weight pressed against mine. It wasn't the best of positions, my back had started to ache as soon as the euphoria had passed. The bench was hard, and the mirror was cold and clammy, and Matt was still fully dressed as if he could protect himself by remaining covered.

My heart ached. I pushed the useless emotion aside. Matt needed me.

"Next time, I want you naked," I said into the side of his head. His face was cradled on my shoulder, his lips pressed against the skin on my neck. His hands holding me as if he feared to let go. Feared what would happen, what reality would return to him when he did.

"Next time, huh?" he said.

"And I want your tongue," I whispered. "Right there."

"Where?" he asked on a reluctant chuckle.

"You know where."

"No. Tell me."

"Between my legs," I said, my muscles contracting, squeezing his still semi-hard cock.

He laughed harder. More naturally. If I could have seen his beautiful, soulful eyes, the laugh, I was sure, would have reached them.

"I bet I could make you come by just being inside you, like this," he said on a rumble. "Whispering how much I want to lick you out. Taste your wetness. Suck on your clit."

I shuddered. My sensitive insides trembling.

"Squeeze me again, Liv," he ordered. I did. "Fuck. Will you squeeze my tongue?" I moaned. He chuckled. "Will you suck it inside your pussy like you're hungrily sucking my cock?"

I started panting.

He rocked his penis into me just once. Pressing the base right up against my clitoris.

"What do you taste like, doll? Sweet or spicy? I want to lick you right now. Knowing you've had my dick inside you. Knowing you've already come a half dozen times. I want to drown in you. In your tight little channel. Lap you up, bite your clit, make you come."

The orgasm was no less impressive than previous ones, despite my body protesting the strength to endure it. I shuddered in Matt's arms, my chest aching as breaths streamed in and out. His cock jerked as I stroked it, covering it again in my release.

"Fuck," he whispered. "Fuck," he said again. "You are magnificent."

"So are you," I said, sounding beyond exhausted.

He laughed. His fingers smoothing my hair back as he looked down into my face.

"Thank you," he said with meaning.

"Well, you *are* magnificent," I offered, still a little stunned.

"Not for the compliment," he said. I stilled. "For not allowing me to freak out."

"Matt," I said, and he shushed me.

"I might still do it, so don't get cocky." He rocked his hips again

on the reminder of his own 'cockiness.' "But know if I do, I appreci-
ated your efforts."

My heart bled for this man.

"I'm not sure what this means," he admitted. "But I know I can't
let you go any longer. You had your shot. You chose to stay. And
now... Now, for better or worse, Olivia Logan, you are mine." Such an
old-fashioned perspective.

Such a turn on.

I huffed out a breath.

"More fool you," he added quietly. I held his steady gaze and
didn't back down. "Stubborn woman," he muttered.

"Silly man," I said, and he smiled.

There was still darkness there, a haunted look to his eyes that
made me want to weep with heartache for him. But he didn't pull
away until he'd kissed me thoroughly. And he didn't turn away as I
slipped into the shower.

But he also didn't get undressed and join me, either.

CHAPTER 24

ONLY IF I CAN RIP THE FUCKING ROOSTERS OFF THE WALL

MATT

I stood outside the bathroom and listened to the water running. I couldn't seem to walk away. I ran a hand over my face, covering my mouth. Tried to catch my breath, knowing the breathlessness I felt had nothing to do with physical exertion. I could still taste her.

Fuck.

My eyes drifted across the hallway until they found our bedroom. Missy's and my bedroom. My back hit the wall, and my legs gave way. I slowly slid down until my arse hit the carpet, my knees bent, my chest aching.

Thirty years I'd been faithful to Missy. Thirty years I'd barely looked at another woman. From the age of fourteen, Missy had been mine. It hadn't been planned. It just happened. I saw her getting teased one day, her glasses knocked off her rosy cheeks, and I'd stepped up. Stepped in. Laid a claim.

I wasn't sure what I was supposed to be feeling. Missy was dead. She was no longer mine. But thirty years is a long time to belong to someone. To be theirs in every possible way.

I stared at the pale pink and chocolate brown throw cushions up on our king sized bed. At the complementary quilt she'd made when she'd been pregnant. *Pink?* I'd asked her. *Pink for me, brown for you,* she'd replied. I'd shrugged my shoulders. Because it was Missy. Because I gave her everything she asked for. Because she was mine.

I tipped my head back and looked at the ceiling, realising I was rubbing my chest. I clenched my fingers and then forced myself to open them. I stared at my knuckles, at the hand that had fired the gun. The finger that had pulled the trigger.

I'd thought she'd been happy. I'd thought the throw pillows and the pinks and the browns and the roosters and the cherry blossoms meant that she was happy. I'd done my part. I'd married her. Given her a home. Never strayed.

And she'd run into the arms of a psychotic killer.

A harsh bark of laughter left me. Marinkovich was not alone on the murder front. I'd fired the gun that had killed him.

"What the fuck, Missy?" I whispered.

The shower turned off. I needed to get up, get away. Not be found here, broken on the floor of my hallway. I couldn't seem to move. Stuck in a horror movie. Stuck in the memories.

Dancing with Missy in the kitchen. Catching her smiling at herself in the mirror of our bedroom. Her singing to our girls as they fell asleep. Walking in on her while she was on the phone; her easy dismissal of the caller. The way she made me feel like I was more important than whoever it had been.

How quickly she'd picked up the telephone again afterwards when she thought I had left the building.

How long had she been seeing him? Months, the photos we found in his house suggested. Longer? Thirty years I'd been hers. Or so it had seemed.

I heard Liv talking. Her voice muffled behind the bathroom door. I realised she must have had her cell phone with her. Who was she calling?

My hand found my chest again. I was on a merry-go-round from hell.

The door opened. Liv stepped out, blinking down at me. No cell phone in her hand. She'd been talking to herself, I realised. For some reason that made me smile. Did she do that often? Mumble away quietly, ask herself questions, sort things out aloud?

"What are you doing, Matt?" she asked.

"I'm not sure," I admitted. Why was I still on the fucking floor?

Liv slid down the wall beside me and stretched out her legs. Both of us stared at the bedroom.

"Pink and brown," she said.

"I hated them," I muttered, glaring at the throw pillows.

"And the roosters?"

"Fucking birds."

"Cherry blossoms are OK."

"Don't even think about it."

"So redecorate."

Was it that simple?

I don't want to live here anymore. Why were we still living here? Fucking Missy. Even from the grave, she owned me.

Not anymore.

"Can you check on the girls?" I asked Liv. She stared at me for a long time and then slowly nodded her head. She made the motion of rising to her feet seem elegant. No one should be able to get up off the floor and look so stunning.

She took a step away and then looked back down at me.

"And you?" she asked. Such restraint.

I was sitting on the fucking floor outside of the bathroom where I'd just fucked her staring at my dead wife's decor. There was a hell of a lot more Liv wanted to say.

"Organising a sledgehammer," I said, pulling out my cell phone.

She laughed. It was beautiful. This woman was beautiful. So patient. So understanding. So unbelievably real.

I watched her walk back down the hallway towards the lounge and then made my call. Zach answered on the fourth ring.

"You running late?" he said.

"What?"

"Breakfast. Luke's pacing. Way to get him riled, Matthew."

"Fuck off!"

"Well, you're the one who told him Maggie's flat was off limits. Is it still off limits? Do I have to listen to them bumping uglies again tonight?"

"You could move out," I suggested.

"Where to?"

"The guest cottage."

"That's not even got a TV."

"So buy one."

"No internet either."

"Pay for the connection."

"Screw you!"

"You could move in here."

Silence. Not how I'd planned to persuade my fucked-in-the-head brother to take on my haunted house.

"It'll be vacant by the end of the day," I added. In for a penny, in for a pound.

"No shit," he said softly. "Where're you going?"

"The guest house."

"It's not got a TV."

I started to laugh. He joined me, chuckling down the line.

"Good for you, bro," he whispered.

Was it? I wasn't sure. Would this hurt Rachel and Dani? Would it stunt the progress Liv had made? Was I being selfish?

"Sometimes," Zach said down the line, "you have to fix yourself before you can fix anyone else."

"They teach you that in the army?" I asked.

"Nah, read it in a book at Justin's."

"New age shit."

"Got that right."

I let out a sigh.

"She didn't deserve you," Zach said. Fuck.

"Zach..."

"I know I made a fuss of you getting together. Thought she could do better than my straight-laced older brother. But here's the thing. I was wrong. I was fucking wrong, Matt. You deserved better than Missy."

"Don't say that," I whispered, tears stinging my eyes.

"I won't say it again," he promised. "But it needed to be said once."

"Zach."

"Want help shifting out?" He was moving on. Changing the subject. Clumsily, like a stampeding rhino. But that was Zach. Lacked all finesse when it came to conversation.

"You gonna move in here?" I demanded.

"Only if I can rip the fucking roosters off the wall."

I chuckled, just as Rachel and Dani came running down the hallway, bits of toast and jam on their PJs, Liv chasing them with grasping, claw-like hands. Rachel shrieked, throwing back her head and laughing. Dani joined her, squealing with delight as Liv caught her 'round the middle.

"Rip them off," I said. "Paint over them. It doesn't matter. This isn't my home anymore."

Rachel threw herself into my arms, as Dani cried out for me to 'rescue' her. I ended the call and grabbed my daughter. Tickling her where I knew she liked it.

"No, no!" Rachel giggled.

"Daddy, do me!" Dani demanded.

My eyes caught Liv's. She smiled.

It *was* that simple, I realised. It still fucking hurt, but it was that simple to start a new life.

CHAPTER 25

JUST WHAT MATT NEEDED

LIV

"WHY AREN'T YOU AT YOUR FLAT?" DAVID ASKED. I SHIFTED THE phone to my other ear and started the swing seat swinging, while the girls chased butterflies around the front yard of Red Tussock's homestead.

"There was a cat," I murmured, smiling at the sound of the twins laughing. They had their moments. Times when they went quiet. This, thankfully, wasn't one of them.

"A cat?" David queried, drawing my attention back to the call.

"A dead cat."

"Bloody hell, Olivia. You don't think...?"

"I don't know." I sighed and pushed my foot against the porch flooring to make the swing move more violently. "What have the detectives found out?"

David was silent for a moment and then he said, "Tell me about the cat. How did you find it?"

He was hedging. I let him. I wanted to hedge myself.

"I came home, and it was on my back doorstep."

"Jesus, Olivia. Are you all right?"

No. But there were more important issues to contend with. Like where I would sleep tonight. Matt and his brothers were packing up his house. Missy's grip was loosening.

What did that mean for me?

"I'm fine," I said. "What have the detectives found out?"

"You're not going to like it," David grumbled.

"Tell me."

"One of your former clients is missing."

I closed my eyes and let the swing soothe me.

"It might be nothing," David rushed to say. "His family says he disappears for days at a time often. He took his medication with him. Hasn't missed a dose in five years."

"What's his name?"

The sound of paper being shuffled filled the line, then David cleared his throat, preparing to read. "Callum Wilkes. Do you remember him?"

"Depression and anxiety," I said, picturing his face in my mind. "He wasn't violent."

"I checked your files, you haven't seen him in three years."

"He was doing well. The medication we'd finally got him on was working. He seemed fine."

"Fine. Is that your professional opinion, doctor?"

"You know what I mean."

"I do. And just because he's gone walkabout doesn't mean he's the one painting your office in cat blood."

"Or putting a dead cat on my doorstep."

"Fuck, Olivia! Maybe you should just come back."

"You've changed your tune. What happened to 'it's just a few months?'"

"A dead cat fucking happened." David didn't usually swear. He was too refined for that. Swearing now, and so frequently, meant he was worried. For me.

"I've got protection."

"What do you mean? You haven't invested in a shotgun, have you?"

I blinked. "No, nothing like that."

"Good, because you know if you have a weapon, it can always be used against you just as easily."

"And there aren't knives in my kitchen drawer?"

"That's different. A gun is something else."

I pictured Maggie this morning, as she walked out of the homestead's front door and got in her police ute. Pistol strapped to her hip. Maggie wouldn't let anyone disarm her. Cat killing stalker or not.

"I haven't got any weapons," I said, in a bid to relax him. "But the local cops are aware of my situation now."

Silence. "What have you done? Olivia, CIB wanted this kept quiet."

"They're cops! It's their job to protect the public."

"Has this got something to do with your new boss?"

"It has nothing to do with him."

"Are you sure? Pillow talk can be deadly." Melodramatic much?

"David, what's got into you? This isn't like you, at all."

"You're being stalked, Olivia! Do you really think fucking a patient right now is the right thing to do?"

My turn for silence.

"Olivia?"

"That was uncalled for," I murmured.

"I'm sorry," he rushed to say. "I'm just so worried about you. Can he be trusted?"

"Matt is the Senior Sergeant of Twizel Police, he can certainly be trusted."

"Then why didn't Detectives Pierce and Stone contact him?" David sighed. "I've heard things, Olivia. Cops talk. Matt Drake killed a man, you know. Shot him in cold blood."

"It wasn't in cold blood."

"Fucking hell! You know about it? And you still confided in the man?"

"It wasn't in cold blood," I insisted.

"He killed a man," David said very slowly. "It doesn't matter how he did it, he's capable of taking a person's life."

Something cracked in the background. Possibly the cell phone casing or maybe something on David's desk. I knew he was at work. I knew where he'd be sitting. Behind his big mahogany desk, Tiffany-esque lamp shining brightly, silk tie gleaming in the glow it cast.

"Olivia," he said earnestly. "You need to come home."

"No."

"What do you mean 'no'?"

"Actually, I wanted to talk to you about this." No time like the present. "I'm reconsidering my life goals. Readjusting my outlook. I think I might stay down here for a while."

"Are you serious?" he whispered. "What about the firm?"

"You've been saying you wanted to bring on some more psychiatrists. Some new blood, isn't that what you called it? Well, now's the time."

"And your patients?" That was a dilemma, but not an impossibility, either.

"They've already been spread out between the partners. Changing them back again now could cause more harm than good."

"You don't believe that."

"You do, otherwise you wouldn't have suggested I take two months off, and taken over their care so readily."

"That was before."

"Before what?"

"Before... before I knew it would be for good."

I let out a soft breath of air. "David." He was hurting. He didn't want me to go. How long had we been together? Working side by side, sharing the load? Eight years in Grafton Road alone, more in various smaller clinics. David had always been there. And likewise, I'd always been there for him, as well.

Right from the beginning.

"I don't know what to say," he whispered. "Just promise me one thing."

"Sure," I said, feeling cowardly. I just wanted this conversation to end.

"Don't make any firm decisions. Not yet, at least. It's only been a month. You're going through a tremendous amount of stress. It's not the time to change your life around so drastically." Seemed like he did know what to say, after all. "I've got a weekend off soon. I'll come down, and we'll catch up."

"The detectives said that wouldn't be a good idea. You might lead the stalker to me."

"I'll travel under a false name. No one will know."

"David..."

"Olivia, please. You can't just drop this on me and expect me to let you go."

Oh, damn. This wasn't how I'd wanted this to unfold.

"We're friends," I started.

"Olivia, we are far more than just friends."

He disconnected the call before I could argue. I stared off over the pastures of Red Tussock and felt a wealth of emotions stir up from down deep. Rachel and Dani had fallen silent some time ago, watching a butterfly in one of their traps. I forced myself to get to my feet, and shakily took a step toward them.

I was some distance away when I realised the butterfly was dead. Such a simple thing. A fragile creature with a short life span. But the twins had retreated into their heads again, their faces shut down, the front yard in utter silence.

I knelt down beside them and looked at the Monarch.

"I'm sorry," I said. "Sometimes that just happens."

Rachel looked up at me, tears brimming her eyelashes.

"That's what *he* said," she whispered and then pushed to her feet and started running.

"Rachel!" I yelled out, but she was already around the house and out of sight. I got up, took a step after her, and then looked back down at Dani.

Her face was completely white.

"Dani," I whispered, wanting to chase after Rachel, but not daring to leave Dani alone when she looked so fragile. "God damn it," I muttered, pulling my cell phone out and making the call.

Just what Matt needed.

CHAPTER 26

AND THE GROUND FELL OUT FROM BENEATH ME

MATT

Of all the people to find Rachel, it had to be Charlie Davis. The one man who reminded the girls of Ivan Marinkovich the most. Similar builds. Similar colouring. Similar tattoos covering similar muscles.

Rachel hadn't uttered a word since.

Dani had sat beside her sister on the bed in their new bedroom in the guest house. Silent. Stoic. United. Looking at them both had hurt. Maybe it was the fact we'd seen progress and were now being knocked back. Maybe it was plain and simple guilt.

Maybe it was karma, paying me back for my recent transgressions.

Thank fuck they were now both asleep.

"It was a mistake moving here," I said into the silence surrounding me.

"Bad timing is all," Dad muttered.

"Small things will set them off," Liv announced from her perch across the kitchen table. "Something which might seem inconsequential to us has significance to them. This would have happened even if you hadn't decided to move house."

"Bad timing," Dad repeated as if that was that. Nothing more to be said about it.

"And it won't be permanent," Luke offered. He pulled a map out of his back pocket and laid it out on the small kitchen table. He tapped a spot with his finger and then stood back and waited for something to happen.

"Is that supposed to mean something to me?" I asked.

"Zach found it," Luke explained. "Got Justin to take some pictures." He pulled some photos out of his jacket then and placed them on the table too. Liv leant over and sucked in a breath of air.

"That's gorgeous," she breathed, genuinely awed at Justin's talent. Or the stunning view of Red Tussock Station living up to its namesake in autumn.

"Can see all of Red Tussock from up there," Luke added as I reluctantly leant closer to look. "Bit hard to get to it right now, of course, but if we grade an access way, make a new road, you could take the twins up there. Get them to help plan their new house. Show them Mount Glenmary from what will be their bedroom window."

"Rocky Ridge," I said, realising where on rangeland the section was. "Near Dobson River."

"Location's perfect," Luke offered.

"Perfectly inaccessible," I countered.

He shrugged. "That's why it's perfect."

Because it was somewhere Missy hadn't been.

I sat back in my chair and stared out the window. The sun had set, and inky fingers of darkness crept across the back garden. Petals curled in on themselves, waiting on the sun for reawakening. The scent of tulips and daffodils wafted in through the open window.

Even the guest house was more alive than our old home had been.

"Wouldn't take more than a few hours of hard labour to get a road in," Dad said into the ensuing silence.

"Still got a while before the snows hit," Luke added, tag-teaming him like a pro-fucking-wrestler team.

My eyes drifted towards Liv. She watched the exchange keenly.

An ache started up in my chest. Could I do this? I'd only thought far enough ahead to here. To this; squatting in Red Tussock's guest house. In all reality, we could use it indefinitely. If Finn and Momo visited from Auckland, they'd be welcomed at the homestead. It might be Luke's now, but it was still the heart of the station. If I insisted we stayed here, that we *needed* to stay here, no one would baulk.

I could wallow a little longer.

"Of course," Luke said in a drawl, "building a house is a big commitment. What with your job and the girls." He shrugged.

"Man's gotta pick his battles," Dad agreed.

"Land won't go anywhere," Luke added.

Both men looked at Liv. As if they'd fucking rehearsed this beforehand. Their heads ducked, their mouths tipped down in slight scowls and then they looked at me expectantly.

Yeah yeah, I got it. The land wasn't going anywhere, but Liv might.

My eyes met hers across the table. She arched her brow but didn't say anything.

She didn't need to. Those beautiful blues said it all.

Just don't expect me to leave.

I blew out a breath of air and tapped the table with my knuckles. Fuck this. Missy had her chance.

She'd bailed. I'd been holding on to a dream.

"Right then," Dad said as if it had all been settled.

"I'll get Charlie to do a quick survey tomorrow," Luke added, heading toward the door. "See what we need to do first."

"That a good idea?" I asked. Red Tussock's foreman would just as soon see me fail than lift a finger to help get me back on my feet.

Luke's face wasn't to me so I couldn't see the smirk. Somehow I just knew it was there, though.

"Might want to watch over his shoulder," he suggested, reaching for the door and heading through it.

Dad pushed himself to his feet.

"Right then," he repeated, trying not to crack a smile. "Mum will be wondering where I am."

"Good night, Dad," I said, feeling like I might have lost that round.

Thinking I might have to thank them for it.

Dad kissed Liv on the cheek and then went out into the night. Their ute engines slowly sounding less and less distinct as the clock on the kitchen wall ticked loudly. I stood in the middle of the room, increasingly aware that Liv was watching me. Unsure of what would happen next.

"Are you angry with them?" she asked, surprising me.

There were many times my brothers pissed me off, and Dad could be a hard-arse when he wanted to be. But now?

"No," I said. She nodded her head in agreement.

"What are you feeling, then?" she asked.

I let out a huff of air. "This how they trained you to get people to open up?"

She smiled, pink washing her cheeks. "I am a little off my game, I admit."

Something inside me loosened. I held her gaze for a few seconds longer and then decided enough was enough. Time to live.

I flicked the light off as I walked out of the kitchen.

"Is that a signal the conversation is over?" Liv asked, following me into the lounge.

I began switching the lights off in there too. The guest house was decked out in creams and beiges, neutral colours that complemented the cottage-like feel of the house. It was rented out on occasion, and used by Finn, of course. But aside from a bookshelf filled to the brim with books and games, there was no TV and no internet to keep you occupied. It was meant to be luxury accommodation without the clutter of technology to muck it up.

Mum's idea. I snorted as the last light went out.

Walking down the hallway, I was aware that I hadn't answered

Liv. She was following, though. Slower than I was. A little uncertainly, I think. I tried not to feel too anxious about that. Instead, I pushed open the girls' door and made sure they were both still asleep, then pulled it to and walked across the hall to the master bedroom.

Creams and beiges. I decided I liked them. Would Liv?

I started to peel off my t-shirt, chucking it into a hamper in the corner when I was done. Then sat down on the bed to remove my boots. Liv walked in and leant against the door frame. I didn't turn to look at her. Boots off, I kicked them into the corner too. Would Liv expect me to leave them at the back door?

I undid my belt and pushed the button through the top of my jeans. Then shoved them down my legs, stepping out. They went flying over the edge of the hamper, as well. Should I have folded them? Would she want me to? I shrugged.

Crossing to the dresser, I pulled open the top drawer, grabbing some deodorant. I never put deodorant on before bed. Feeling like a tool, I lathered up. Then shut the drawer and turned around to face her.

She was biting her bottom lip. Plump red flesh between white teeth. Her hair shone coppery and gold, the reds dimmed in the low light from the bedside table, but not entirely absent. She'd always have that alluring fiery shade of red.

I walked to the far side of the bed, my eyes on Liv. She didn't move. Slipping my hands into the top of my boxers, I watched as she sucked in a breath of air, then went completely still. I shucked them off, chucking them in the vague direction of the hamper, and then pulled back the coverings and slipped in.

Liv watched every inch of me every second I was uncovered. Even after I wasn't, she didn't stop.

"You coming to bed?" I asked, my voice a little rough around the edges.

Her eyes slowly came up to mine. That lip firmly caught between her teeth. She let out a breath of air on a rush.

"What do you want, Matt?" she asked. Such a simple question. So many complicated answers.

"I want you in this bed," I said. "Beside me. Under me. On top of me." I shrugged. "And I don't ever want you to get out."

"Never?" she asked, head tilted, eyes wary.

I understood her reticence. But I was done living my life for the dead.

"Well, I might let you go pee, but that's about it," I offered.

She didn't move.

I was going to have to work for it. Hadn't the striptease been enough?

Not for Liv. Not for my fiery school ma'am, who analysed and assessed and did shrink type things in her head. What was going through it now?

"I'm sloppy," I said out of fucking nowhere. "Can't be bothered picking shit up off the floor. I leave toothpaste all over the sink and mirror," I added. "Like to wear my boots in the house. I don't care if the carpet's been vacuumed. Or if there're flowers in the middle of the fucking kitchen table or not. But I'll never ask you to pick up after me. And I'll never ask you to have a meal on the table when I get home. And I'll never expect you to be anything other than who you are.

"Life can be shit, Liv. I've lived it. But here, in this house, or wherever the fuck we end up, with you and me and Rachel and Dani, it could be good. What did you tell me?"

She arched her brow. Silently. OK, I could do this.

"You could be good for me?" I said, repeating her words. "Well guess what, doll; I could be good for you, too."

I knew what was on her mind, on the tip of her tongue, on her kissable lips.

What about Missy?

What about her? I'd have to learn to forgive Missy, I knew that. Learn to forgive myself, as well. But I was not prepared to give my dead wife any more of me. Any more of my heart and soul and my life. My daughters needed their father. And I needed to be able to breathe.

Liv let me breathe. I don't know how she did it. She'd fucking lied to me. Granted, there'd been extenuating circumstances regarding her false identity. But somehow Liv's lies seemed different. Seemed acceptable. Fuck knows why.

Why was Liv different to Missy? Why was she so important to me?

More important than grieving my ex-wife.

I suddenly felt nervous. Liv hadn't said a further word or shifted a single muscle. Was she about to bolt? Head out to the sofa? Drive back into town to that shitty little flat? And the dead fucking cat?

"Give me something to go on here, Liv," I said softly. "Yes or no? It's that simple."

Was it, though? I looked at Liv and felt like I was at the edge of a precipice. One word and she'd push me off. Make me plummet.

I had the disquieting feeling that I'd never land. Not like with Missy, where the ground had come up and hit me. Hard. But in a way I knew I'd never quite come back from.

How could you fall for someone so very right while still tied to someone so very wrong?

Maybe you couldn't. Maybe I'd got it all wrong.

And then Liv moved...

And the ground fell out from beneath me.

CHAPTER 27

AND I DIDN'T CARE

LIV

I stood on the threshold of the master bedroom in Red Tussock's guest house thinking I might be about to cross over a different kind of threshold than the physical one before me. Matt seemed so sure. So certain.

I knew otherwise.

Every fibre of my body wanted to believe his mind was made up. And, I guessed, it was in a way. Except he didn't realise how emotionally unstable he was. How mentally incapable he was of making the right decisions for the long term.

And yet, despite my better judgement, I crossed the threshold and walked toward the bed.

I wanted to warn him. Prepare him for what might happen. I wanted to be the professional I was and treat this man with kid gloves. Give him space to come to terms with his epiphanies.

But I didn't say a thing.

My legs hit the edge of the bed, and Matt looked up at me; expectantly, hopefully, hungrily.

Sod it, he might hurt me in the long run, but right now Matt

Drake knew exactly what he wanted. He wanted my body, in his bed, beside him.

And I wanted that very much too, it seemed.

I slowly reached up and pulled my t-shirt off over my head. He let out a breath of air that filled the room with delicious anticipation. My bra came off next, and Matt finally smiled; white teeth glinting in the dim lighting. His hooded eyes devoured my breasts and then slowly coasted up my neck to my face.

"You're beautiful," he whispered. "So gorgeous."

I made quick work of my jeans then, slipping them off and letting them tumble to the floor. A soft huff of breath left him when I didn't make a move to pick them up. My panties met the same fate and then I was climbing under the covers and pressing up against the scorching heat of Matt's hard, muscular body.

He groaned, his hand shaking slightly as it came up and cupped my breast, his eyes glazing over as he stared at my distended nipple. He licked his lips, made a growling type sound and then lowered his head and sucked my areola into his mouth.

My body responded immediately as if he had the remote control to my libido. Warmth flushed through me, tingling against my skin, centring between my legs. My back arched as my legs pressed firmly together, Matt's soft chest hairs rubbing against my sensitive skin.

The fingers of his free hand pinched my other nipple, rolling it between them as he sucked and nibbled and licked. Wetness pooled between my thighs, a bubble of tension growing bigger and bigger down inside.

And then it burst in a rush of ecstasy, Matt groaning and sucking and rocking his hips up against me.

"Fuck," he murmured, laying kisses across my stomach, just under my breasts. "I love that you come so quickly."

His lips trailed lower, over my abdomen and across my mons. And then two big hands pressed my legs apart, and he stared at my vulva.

"I'm going to taste this pussy now," he said. "Been dying to. How long will it take, Liv? How long for my tongue to make you come?"

I made a sound, needy and embarrassing and like nothing I had ever uttered before.

His fingers spread my labia and then his tongue was lapping me up. I pressed up on my elbows so I could watch him. Dark blonde head of hair bobbing up and down as he growled and licked and fucked me with his tongue. His eyes came up and met mine. My eyes rolled back in my head. And then I was coming in a rush of champagne-like bubbles, my shoulders collapsing onto the bed, my eyes closed as I panted and moaned.

"Not long, huh?" he said, with a self-satisfied smirk. He laid a soft kiss on my inner thigh, and then another to my stomach. His body rested over my legs and pelvis, his elbows digging into the mattress either side of my hips, his fingers idly trailing a path across my torso.

"So white," he whispered, making me blink down at him. I took in his dark skin against the porcelain of mine. "You're like a china doll," he murmured. "With wicked curves and fucking amazing tits."

I giggled. It was entirely unexpected. His eyes shot up to mine, and he frowned.

"You think that's funny?" he mock-demanded. "Are you laughing at my infatuation with your body?"

The giggle became full on laughter. And then I was squealing as he tickled me and we were rolling all over the bed as I tried - unsuccessfully - to get away from his determined fingers. Several long stomach quivering seconds later, he positioned us so he was on top and I was trapped; breathless, lightheaded, tears streaming out from under my eyelids.

His hands softened, changing from tickling me to stroking me, warm palm running over scorching flesh. He cupped my hip, ran his fingers over the curve of my waist, brushed the underside of my breast, slid down my arm, palm circling my wrist. He never stopped touching me, stroking me, lighting my body on fire. It was heaven.

"I wonder if I could make you come by tickling you," he

murmured idly, his hand cupping my rear, smoothing down my thigh, lifting my leg up until I cradled him.

"More like pee myself," I said with a grimace, brushing back his hair so I could see his eyes.

He looked up at me, rubbed his cheek into my palm. Turned his face to lay a kiss against my fingers.

How could this tough policeman, who had suffered such heartache and loss, be so caring and loving in bed?

How could I fight this? How could I keep my own heart safe and protect his?

When Matt loved, I thought, he loved completely. With mind, body, heart and soul. Matt Drake did nothing in measures. He grieved with every ounce of his being. And he made love with every fibre of his soul.

"Do you need the bathroom?" he asked.

I rolled my eyes and shook my head. "Only if you tickle me."

"What if I do this?" he asked, face tipping down to my neck and his lips nibbling. A hot tongue came out and licked up to my ear. "And this?" he whispered, biting my earlobe carefully. "And this," he growled as his hands slipped between us and his very clever fingers found my clitoris.

"Matt," I moaned, my head falling back as his mouth sucked on the side of my neck.

I could feel him everywhere. I could feel him above me, around me, inside me as his finger dipped in and his thumb rubbed circles.

"Matt," I cried out as my body split apart from his simple attention.

His lips found mine, and he kissed me deeply. Slowly but no less hungry for it than I was. I pressed myself against him, spread myself wide for him, and kissed him back with my mind, my body, my heart and my soul.

He rocked his hips, the tip of his cock slipping into place between us. "Liv," he groaned, entering me an inch. "Baby," he said, hot breath mingling.

And when I rocked up to meet him, and he slid in so smoothly, so slowly, so deliciously big and wide, both of us gasped at the sensation. At the closeness. At the feeling of skin on skin, the hot, hard length of him squeezed inside me.

"I need to be inside you," he growled.

"You are," I moaned as he started to rock.

"More," he insisted, rolling his hips, thrusting forward, harder than he'd done before. "More," he pleaded, lifting my leg up and out, stretching me wide, rocking in deep.

Long thrusts, slow withdrawals, and then the inexorable roll forward as his cock filled me up and reached deep inside.

"Fuck, you're perfect," he moaned, his lips laying kisses against my neck, my jaw, my chin.

Deep and slow and lush and seductive.

He pulled back and looked down at me, one hand supporting my thigh as he held it up and out so he could press into me so very deeply on each thrust forward. The other wrapped up in my hair, cupping my head, holding me steady, as he stared down at me.

I gasped beneath him, feeling every inch of his hard body covering mine. My breasts brushed against the soft hair on his chest, my thighs trembled around narrow hips, my hands grasped firm butt cheeks, pulling him deeper into me.

I couldn't get close enough.

"That's it," he murmured. "Take me deep, baby. Take me long and slow, make me work for it."

"I...I can't..." I started.

"Yes, you can, Liv." He rocked himself deeper still, his movements measured, unhurried, so beautiful. Such a turn on.

"Faster," I pleaded.

"Not a chance," he said with a wicked smile. "Your tits look glorious wobbling beneath me like this. Your pussy's so wet, I don't think you need more."

"I do."

"Liv," he said. "Fuck," he moaned. "I'm going to come, babe. Just like this. Slow and deep and wet and fucking hot. Your pussy sucking me deep. Your body so soft beneath me. I can feel you," he rasped. "Everywhere. Fuck. Fuck. *Fuck!*" he growled as his movements stuttered and his eyes widened, and then he was burying himself deep, and his head hung down, and his breath rushed out on a long, torturous moan.

I felt him come. I felt the hot jets of his climax inside me. I realised what we'd done. What we'd forgotten to do in the heat of the moment.

And then I was coming because clearly I was insane, and Matt Drake was reckless, and I couldn't say no to this man. The orgasm stormed through me, on the heels of a tornado of emotions, and Matt groaned and pulled me closer and whispered how fucking hot it was that I came because he had.

How fucking much he loved that I came so easily.

How he was going to make me come again, right now.

He did. Still inside me. Still bare, skin on skin.

And I didn't care. Didn't stop to think of the consequences. Because Matt Drake made love with every particle in his being.

And the fool that I was longed for more.

CHAPTER 28

AT LEAST THIS I COULD HANDLE

MATT

THE SUN BEAT DOWN ON THE BACK OF MY NECK AS I PUSHED open the door to the shop, sucking in a deep breath and preparing myself. The fish was floating in the corner above a shelf full of pricey scarves. I wondered if I should pick one up for Liv. Merino wool from our farm.

Then I shook my head and reminded myself it was still warm out, and Liv wouldn't need a scarf for weeks. My eyes automatically went in search of what else I could get her instead. Kiwifruit lip balm?

The fish's tail swished and the fucking thing turned beady little eyes toward me. The camera lenses inside them no doubt zooming in on my blush.

I cleared my throat.

"I know you're there, Senior Sergeant," Alicia Parsons called out from behind the stack of postcards in the middle of the store.

"Your fish," I guessed, rounding the stand and catching my first look at the souvenir shop owner. She was dressed in a prim skirt suit; pink tweed was the only description that came to mind.

"I clocked you long before that," Ms Parsons said in her British accent.

I just raised my brow.

"New acquisition," she explained. "High-powered zoom lenses on all my hardware. I saw you park your car outside the Musterer's Hut."

It never failed to unnerve me that our resident peeping Tom kept tabs on everyone including the cops.

"Didn't double park today," I grumbled.

"No," she agreed, giving me a stern look in reprimand.

I resisted the urge to adjust my shirt collar.

"Need your assistance, Ms Parsons," I announced.

"I thought as much," she said dryly. "I was sure it wasn't a novelty sock that you were after."

Would Liv like a novelty sock? I shook my head. Thankfully, Alicia took the movement as an answer.

"The vandals," I started.

"I'd be more concerned with the boy racers."

I stared at her, not passing comment.

"But then you know who they already are," she remarked.

"The vandals," I started again.

"Yes."

"Have you caught them?"

"I'm not a police officer."

"On your video cameras," I stressed.

"Which don't cover the entirety of this street, let alone the whole town. At your insistence, I might add."

"If we could afford a CCTV system, the council would invest in one," I pointed out, yet again. "But allowing a member of the public such a liberty is not something the police service can condone."

Every time I came in here, we had the same bloody conversation.

"And yet, here you are, asking for my help. Does that not seem shortsighted to you, Senior Sergeant?"

"Ms Parsons, did you happen to catch the vandals or not?"

"I'm going with 'or not,'" she said, sweeping past me and rearranging a nearby shelf.

"Is that a literal 'or not' or an 'I want to piss the cop off because he's pissed me off or not'?"

Alicia turned around and stared up at me. "You're extremely frisky this morning."

I grimaced.

"Are the girls well?"

"Fine."

"Your brothers?"

"*Fine.*"

"Red Tussock?"

"Ms Parsons."

"Yes, yes, can't have the local senior sergeant opening up about personal things."

I really needed to get out of here. When Alicia decided to be contrary, there was no point in pursuing a lead through her surveillance system.

"If you do happen to spot the vandals on your cameras," I said, as I headed toward the front door. "Please consider letting the Twizel Police know. After all," I added, "their next target could be this shop."

She snorted delicately and then reached up and pulled something off a shelf.

And then promptly threw the fucking thing at me.

For a second, I thought she'd lost her ever loving mind and was attacking. And then I caught the object in my fist and realised it was just an 'I♥Twizel' fluffy sheep on a keyring.

"For your teacher," the blasted woman said. "So when you give her the key to your heart she doesn't lose it."

"I beg your pardon?" I snapped.

Alicia shrugged.

"This is Twizel, Senior Sergeant. Did you really think people wouldn't talk?"

Fuck. I scrunched the sheep up in my fist and stormed out of the door, practically running into Alan Bennet from next door.

"Whoa, Sergeant," he exclaimed, the 't' in sergeant silent. "Such an 'urry to escape our little voyeur."

"I wouldn't call her that," I immediately argued.

"Psychotic celebrity spotter?" he offered instead.

"Mr Bennet," I warned.

"'Tis nothing," he said, dismissing his words with a Gallic wave of his hand. His eyes darted down to the sheep I was still clutching. "For your daughters? Only one? Ah," he said with dawning understanding. "For your woman." He said 'woman' like the French always say woman, as if it was a sinful, naughty word.

"Um," I managed.

"Do not let the gossip mongers deter you, Sergeant," he said. "Love is to be cherished. Enjoyed. Revelled in, in fact."

"I really don't think..."

"Of course, *she*," he indicated the souvenir shop, "would not know the true meaning of love if her flying fish hit her on the side of the 'ead with it."

"Your French accent is very pronounced today," I offered.

He laughed. "Love does tend to bring out the Frenchman in me."

"And Ms Parsons?" I asked. "What does she bring out in you, Bennet?"

His sharp eyes met mine. "She is a menace," he said, dropping the accent altogether. Now he sounded more British. Not quite the same as Alicia Parsons' cultured tones. But somewhere between England and New Zealand in cadence. "I'd be very careful what information she gives you, Senior Sergeant. A woman like that has the capability to doctor her video footage. Not everything is as it seems."

With that carefully delivered warning, the pharmacist spun on his heel and entered his store. I stared at the front door of the souvenir shop and then up at the camera on the corner of the building. A red light blinked steadily as it filmed me.

Shaking my head, I went to cross the road. Cursing nosy townsfolk and imported residents and the crazy air in Twizel.

I'd made it halfway across the street before I heard them. The distinct sound of a souped-up high-performance Japanese car. I paused in the middle of the road and waited to see how many of them were coming.

Then promptly got horned by Helen Cameron in the mobile library.

"Daydreaming, Senior Sergeant?" the librarian called out of the rolled down diver's side window. "Can't blame you," she added with a salacious wink. "That woman's featuring in many a person's fantasies."

"Excuse me?" I replied. She only cackled as she drove away. And then I spotted Tanya Ruka watching on from beside my police ute.

Could this get any worse?

"What's the latest news, Matt?" she enquired cheerily. "Hear you've got a new roommate up at Red Tussock."

Fuck me. How the hell did everyone know everything about my life so damn quickly?

I shook my head, pushed past the busybody café owner, chucked the stuffed sheep onto the passenger seat, and slid inside. When the boy racers streamed through Main Street, I flicked on my beacons and tore out after them.

At least this I could handle.

CHAPTER 29

THE PROMISE IS BROKEN

LIV

MAGGIE AGREED TO ACCOMPANY ME TO CLEAR OUT THE LAST OF my belongings in the flat. The thought of going back there, where the stalker might know I had been staying, set my heart racing.

And not the good kind of racing Matt had managed to get it to do last night.

My mind wandered back to the way he had touched me, the way he had sought out every climax with dedicated care. The way his fingers had felt hot and sure and yet so soft and careful. How he'd made my body sing by going so slowly, so deliberately, with such care.

Matt had made love to me last night, his eyes on my face, his hands worshipping my body, his soft and steady movements a reflection of the man. I kept trying to make myself wake up to reality. Warn myself of what rushing into a relationship with him could mean.

I knew the answers. I'd seen them a thousand times before. I knew how the mind worked.

But the heart was foreign to me. And right now, my heart dictated my actions.

I wanted what Matt was feeling, what he was doing, choosing, to be true.

So I buried my head a little longer, and I promised myself that I'd take care. And I let him love me again in the early hours of the morning because I couldn't say no and he couldn't stop touching me and kissing me and loving me with such beautiful care.

I was falling for Matt Drake, a man who was only now coming out from under the fog of his wife's betrayal and murder.

I was an idiot.

"Penny for your thoughts, Doc?" Maggie asked. She'd taken to calling me that, now the cat was out of the bag.

And now I was thinking of the stalker again and dead cats at my back door.

Which made answering her that much easier.

"I'm hoping no more of the neighbour's cats have been hurt."

Maggie grimaced, her fingers tightening around the steering wheel. She shook her head. "Never a good sign when animals start being killed."

"No," I agreed. Maggie was an experienced detective. I'd found out she knew both Detective Sergeant Pierce and Detective Stone. She hadn't worked at CIB in the city, but out at Manukau, with Counties Police. The distance from the CBD, however, did not diminish her experience.

Maggie knew exactly what dead animals meant.

"I took a look at the photos," she said, conversationally. "The ones Matt had taken of the cat," she added. I nodded my head and waited for more. "If that cat was run over by a car, I'll eat my stab vest."

"Matt thought it had been," I argued.

"At first glance, yeah. But he agrees with me now. Four broken legs?" She shook her head, her blonde ponytail flying. "Nah, that's too perfect. Then the cave in of the skull. Without having seen the animal itself, I can only guess. But that looked too much like the work of a hammer."

A short, sharp breath left me. A hammer? How barbaric.

"I know it's not nice to hear that sort of thing," Maggie went on. "But you need to be aware of what we're dealing with."

"A hammer? That sounds so... opportunist."

"Really? I thought more adaptable. The type of thing someone would do thinking on their feet."

"So, we're dealing with a barbaric, highly changeable, psychopath with murderous tendencies."

"You're the shrink."

I stared out of the police ute's window at the fields rolling past. Tawny grass for miles and miles, rust-gold leaves adorning row upon row of heavy limbed trees, the odd white fluffy outline of a sheep nearby.

"When's lambing season?" I asked.

"July," Maggie said. "A few stragglers into September, but mostly they lamb early down here."

"Shame. They're so cute. I would have liked to see them."

Maggie snorted. "Don't let Luke hear you say that. They're stock. Not pets."

"I wondered why the Twins didn't have a pet sheep."

"They had a dog," Maggie said carefully. "It was in the car with Missy."

Oh my God. This just got worse and worse.

He took the twins out, but not the dog or Missy. There was just so much horror in that thought.

"You said this guy had ASPD," Maggie said, drawing me back to the present. "What does that mean exactly? Is he shy? Can't carry a conversation? That sort of thing?"

"It's not like that," I explained, noticing we were on the outskirts of town now. "They can carry a conversation, they just don't regard what the other person has to say. They're usually quite aggressive, often getting into fights; confrontation is not an issue. They also like to behave in ways that upset others. Push their buttons, so to speak. They've disassociated themselves from society as a whole, but that doesn't mean they can't slip through the system. Like every psychological disorder, there are varying degrees of affliction. A spectrum, if you will. My stalker has just moved further along the spectrum recently to become noticeable."

"Hence the rush to get you outta Dodge."

"Yes."

"So, what will he do next?"

I bit my lip as we turned onto Main Street, my eyes widening at the scene that greeted us, Maggie's question falling by the wayside immediately.

The pharmacist was arguing with the souvenir shop owner. Hands flailing around like the French so often do. For her part, the immaculately presented woman just stared at him, as if he wasn't worth the effort to respond. Mohawked Gribble, I noticed, was down the street, leaning against his car, as Matt wrote him out a ticket. The I ♥ NZ t-shirt wearing tourist watched on from outside of Smokey's, getting an eyeful of Twizel at its best.

Bizarrely a mobile library was parked across the road, blocking the boy racers' cars. A stout looking woman, with the shortest purple dyed haircut I'd ever seen, taunted Gribble and his peeps.

I snorted to myself. Peeps. Maybe I wasn't as old as I thought.

"Damn, those kids don't realise the shit they're stirring," Maggie said grimly. "Matt's ready to impound their cars."

"Can he do that?"

"Of course. Aside from the fact they disobey the road rules repeatedly, their vehicles are also over modified. It's illegal to have underbody lights."

"I didn't know that. So, why haven't they removed them?"

"This is Twizel," Maggie said in a decidedly angry growl.

"You don't agree with how Matt's handling it," I surmised.

"I'm not used to small town leniency."

I could understand that. Twizel was different. Beautiful but different. I wondered how I could ever go back to Grafton Road and think it was interesting.

I wondered if Matt would want me one day to leave.

"Come on," Maggie said, putting the car back into gear and

rolling off down a side street. "Matt's got it in hand, let's check out the flats and get ourselves back out to Red Tussock."

"Catherine's cooking a quiche for lunch, I've been told," I said.

"Have you tried her dark chocolate chiffon cake with fluffy rose-water frosting?"

"Ah, no," I said, trying not to laugh at Maggie's stomach grumbling.

"You have not lived until you try that," she said in all seriousness.

"I'll be sure to ask her to bake it for me."

Maggie smirked. "She'd bake you a dozen if she thought you'd stick around for Matt."

"What the hell does that mean?"

Maggie laughed. I didn't think there was a lot Maggie Blackmore didn't find funny.

"Fair warning," she said as she parked the car next to the mailbox. "That woman was born a matchmaker. But when she had sons, she got the degree."

"A degree in matchmaking?" I said on a chuckle.

"With honours."

I was laughing as I got out of the car, but the silence that seemed to envelop our flats had the smile slipping. I checked up and down the deserted street, but couldn't see anything untoward. The back step wasn't visible from where we were parked, but Maggie took off at a trot, and when she didn't call out a warning, I took it to mean there was no new dead cat waiting for me.

I shut the door of the police car behind me and walked over to the mailbox to clear it out. I'd have to get my mail redirected. Maybe get a post office box in town to avoid anyone knowing where I was. I hadn't even told David yet.

I lifted the lid on the mailbox and peered at the single letter inside. My insides immediately churning.

"It's all clear," Maggie said, walking up to my side.

I stared at the white envelope. At the handwritten name on the front, minus a stamp or address.

"What is it?" Maggie asked, leaning over the top of the box and then sucking in a breath of air. "Don't touch it," she ordered. "In fact, get back in the car."

"It's not a bomb," I said, feeling numb. It was too small, surely, to be a bomb. It was just paper.

"It doesn't need to explode to be a bomb," Maggie said.

I took a step backwards as Maggie slipped on surgical gloves. My heart racing, faster and more erratically than ever before. I thought back to last night, to the beautiful way Matt had made love to me. And then swallowed down bitter bile at the knowledge that the speed of my heartbeat now had outpaced even that.

Maggie opened the envelope up and peered inside and then seemed to relax. If you could call the minute downward shift of her shoulders relaxation. She reached in with finger and thumb and pulled out a photo. Nothing remarkable about it, save for the fact that it was a picture of Matt and me, sitting side by side at Smokey's bar.

Maggie turned the photo over and then swore under her breath.

I stared at the words, written in red, my heartbeat pounding inside my head.

The promise is broken. Your word is dead. Should he be?

I closed my eyes and let out a fractured breath. Then jumped out of my skin when a cat wrapped itself around my leg, purring loudly.

CHAPTER 30

I HAD MY WORK CUT OUT FOR ME

MATT

I WANTED TO HIT SOMETHING. I COULD FEEL MYSELF clenching and unclenching my fists. Sheila had taken one look at me and scurried from the room, back into reception. Annmarie had quietly retreated to behind her desk but hadn't relaxed enough to sit down. Mac, Maggie and Liv were the only ones who stood close enough to feel my wrath.

The fucking stalker was here. In Twizel.

"Well, at least we know the cat wasn't a coincidence," Maggie said steadily.

I turned around and kicked the desk, cracking the wood loudly.

"Of course," Maggie went on as if I wasn't about to rampage through the police station like a fucking lunatic, "he doesn't know Olivia has moved out."

I leant down, placing my palms flat on the desk, and stared at the photo of Liv and me sharing a drink at Smokey's.

"I didn't even pay attention to who was in the room," I said aloud.

"Maybe Mad Eye will remember," Mac offered.

"Go question him now," I ordered. Mac nodded his head, turned and snapped his fingers at Annmarie, and then walked out. Annmarie sighed but dutifully followed.

I should have been dealing with that situation, as well. But somehow Mac's constant disrespect toward his recruit seemed irrelevant right now. I looked across the room to Liv. She was studying me with an impassive but open face. Her psychiatrist face. I was acting crazy, so Liv was acting like a doctor. Alert. Approachable. Assessing.

I sighed. "Are you all alright?"

"Fine," she said. She wasn't. She might be able to deny her shock and fear by concentrating on my emotions, but sooner or later her feelings would come out and hit her upside the head. "Sit down," I said, pulling out a chair by my desk. "Sheila!" I called out.

"Yes, Matt," she replied, immediately appearing at the entrance to the bullpen, bejewelled fingers wringing.

I pulled a fifty from my wallet and handed it to her. Softening my voice, I said, "Can you get us a round of coffees and something to eat from the Musterer's?"

"Sure thing." She grabbed the note and practically ran from the station. Well, a close approximation considering her more than generous size.

"Coffee?" Liv asked.

"Would you rather tea?" I had no idea what Liv drank, I realised. How long had she been my kids' teacher? Long enough for me to have been aware of that.

"No," she said. "I like coffee. Just not when I'm riled up."

Good, she was admitting it. "It's OK to be riled up, Liv," I said, looking her in the eyes; offering what little support I could right then.

She smiled, arching her brow at me. "I was talking about you," she pointed out dryly.

Ah, that made sense. I scrubbed my face with both hands.

"I won't let anyone hurt you," I vowed. "There's only so many people in town. He'll stand out like a sore thumb."

"Considering he's a JAFA," Maggie said drily.

"Yeah, there's that," I offered, attempting to smile.

I looked back down at Liv. "Any ideas?"

She shook her head, lip firmly between her teeth.

"You said he was likely a patient," I pressed.

"Yes, David mentioned one of my former patients having gone AWOL."

"Got a name?"

"Callum Wilkes," she said, and Maggie promptly got on the computer.

"The Wanganui has him," she said after a few key taps. "Drunken and disorderly. Breaking and entering. Class A possession."

"That sound about right?" I asked Liv.

She nodded her head. "I wasn't aware of the Class A possession. That must have happened after I stopped treating him."

"Methamphetamine," Maggie supplied. "Eighteen months ago."

"The last time I saw him was three years ago," Liv said. "He'd managed to get his life in order, and the medication was working."

"What's he on?" Maggie asked. Liv just looked down at her fingernails. "Doc," Maggie said cajolingly, "you've already told us his name. There's an active warrant out for him and your files. CIB Auckland will be picking them up now if they haven't already."

Liv sighed. "It goes against everything we're trained to be."

"Patient confidentiality, I get it," Maggie agreed. "But this is your life we're talking about."

And just like that, my anger surged.

"Damn it, Liv! He's killing cats. Leaving messages in your letterbox. Took photos of you outside your home in Auckland. How much more do you need before you take care to protect yourself?"

"I'm here, aren't I?" Liv snapped back. "I uprooted my life and moved all the way down here, to the middle of nowhere. Dropped my current clients as if their needs weren't as important as mine. Left my friends and the life I knew to move to Twizel. Twizel!" she practically yelled. "How on earth would he have found me here?"

"Exactly," Maggie rushed to say, throwing me a scowl. Her attention was back on Liv in a heartbeat. "How does he know you're here? Who else knows you're here?"

"The detectives," Liv said, calming down at Maggie's steady and encouraging tone. "My clinic partners."

"Is that it?"

Liv nodded her head.

Maggie's eyes met mine. "That's not many. Unless he can hack the Police database." She looked back at Liv. "Was he a computer whizz?"

"Not that I know of."

"I don't get it," Maggie said, frustrated. "The net is too tight. How did it slip out?"

I had no idea either, but I wanted to find out. I stalked around my desk and lifted the handset on the telephone, then hit the speed dial for Auckland Central Police. In seconds I was put through to Detective Sergeant Ryan Pierce's cell phone.

"How did you know?" he said, the sound of cars rushing past beside him filling the line.

"Know what?"

"That Olivia Logan's clinic was broken into last night." Shit. "We're just arriving now. Her partners are beside themselves. Apparently, several patient files have been nicked."

My eyes darted to Liv. She was watching me carefully but clearly, couldn't hear Pierce's side of the conversation.

"Callum Wilkes one of 'em?" I asked.

Pierce sighed. "I've got the warrant in my hand. I haven't had the chance to serve it yet, but I'm guessing that'll be one of the files missing."

"Anything else?"

"Hold on," Pierce said. His voice when he spoke again was further away as if he'd pulled his cell phone down to speak to someone else. "David," I heard him say. "What else was taken? Just the patient files?"

"My laptop," I heard this 'David' guy say. "And my cell phone."

"What the hell was your cell phone doing here last night?" Pierce asked. Good question.

Unfortunately easily answered. "We had a few drinks after work last night and then headed to a bar on K' Road. I didn't notice it was missing until I went to call for a taxi to get home. I figured I'd just pick it up this morning, rather than pay for a cab back here and then home afterwards."

Pierce grunted and then spoke into the phone for me. "Hear all that?"

"Yeah, I heard it. Let me guess, he phoned Olivia at her address down here."

"I'll have to check, but they do seem pretty close." I didn't like that. "Why do you ask, Senior Sergeant? Has something happened?"

Liv had stood back up again, fear and worry etched across her already too pale cheeks. I looked toward Maggie, just as Sheila came into the station. Maggie nodded, holding my gaze, and then grabbed Liv's elbow, guiding her toward reception.

"Come on," she ordered, "let's get this set up so we can debrief."

I huffed out a breath of air. Maggie knew just how to make someone feel involved while keeping them at arm's length. Another reason to be thankful she stayed here.

"Well?" Pierce demanded in my ear.

"He's here," I said, my hand fisting. "He knows where Liv's been staying."

"*Liv?*" Pierce asked; too damn astute by far.

"Yeah," I said, not in the mood to go there. "Left a message in her mailbox."

"Fuck!" Pierce exclaimed.

Yeah, fuck. Twizel was now at the centre of this case. Auckland CIB would be answering to us from here on in. Somehow that didn't help the rage, though. Control was good, but having this dickhead dealt with would be infinitely better.

I settled down in my chair to talk things out with Pierce. One way or another, we'd get this guy. And then Liv would be free to go home to Auckland.

The desk groaned when I kicked it. Again. Thankfully, Pierce didn't hear. I was betting Liv did, though. I needed to control my emotions better. Knowing she was safe would be a start.

Knowing she'd stay in Twizel would be even better.

I had my work cut out for me.

CHAPTER 31

MAYBE SOME ANTACIDS FIRST

LIV

THE LIBRARY WALL HAD BEEN GRAFFITIED AGAIN. I STARED AT the pink glowing penis and thought the artist might have been improving. Maggie snorted as she held the front door open for me to proceed her in.

Without my usual resources on hand, I'd had to consider alternate avenues. I could have looked things up online at the Police Station, but Operation Shut Down Twizel had begun and getting out from under Matt's stomping size ten feet seemed like a good idea. I'd asked Maggie if the local library had a mental health section, under the guise of looking up some little-known facts about ASPD.

She'd fallen for it - I could be very convincing - and had jumped at the opportunity to give Matt some much-needed space to vent.

We'd left him yelling at someone down the phone line as Sheila, the Police Station's receptionist, cowered in her seat at the front desk. I'd almost asked her if she wanted to accompany us, but losing two people instead of just one very astute cop was too much even for me, right then.

The second we walked into the library my shoulders relaxed. The cool interior mixed with the scent of old glue and book dust, wrapped up in the soothing sensation of silence, allowed me to finally breathe. I exhaled long and loud and took in my bearings.

It was an unusually large room for such a small town. I'd seen the mobile library just this morning, of course, which had led me to believe Twizel's reading community was somewhat progressive. But seeing the row upon row of stacks, the twenty-foot high stud, ornate plaster ceiling rose and four grand matching library chandeliers, made me realise now that Twizel took reading to a *whole* other level.

"Kinda makes you think of the *Tardis*," Maggie whispered from beside me. "Of course, the pink penis on the outside wall does sort of ruin the effect."

"I had no idea," I murmured, unable to stop myself from gawking at all the intricate details.

"This is Twizel," Maggie said. "Expect the unexpected."

"Are you badmouthing our town again, Sergeant?" a stern voice demanded from behind a nearby stack.

Maggie grimaced. "Not at all, Helen. Just pointing out the juxta-position." To me, she whispered, "Use big words."

A woman walked out from behind the new releases. Late thirties, at a guess. I recognised her from Main Street earlier when the mobile library had been angled across the road as if cutting off escape routes for the boy racers. Her hair was a vivid purple, brutally cut into an unapologetically short style, which hid nothing of her stunning violet eyes. Had to be contacts.

Her face lit up, and a soft grin spread across her lips. I half expected to see a nose ring much like Gribble's. But although her hairstyle was on the punk side of rock, the woman wore zero adornments.

"Helen Cameron," Maggie said waving her hand between us, "Olivia Smith."

"The teacher," the woman said.

"The librarian?" I asked.

She nodded, her gaze running down my frame and then back up

again. I had the distinct impression I'd just been lasciviously checked out.

Heat stole up my cheeks.

"Oh, aren't you just the cutest," she exclaimed. "Look at that blush, Sergeant. So sweet."

Maggie cleared her throat and looked anywhere but at me.

I suppressed the nervous laugh that wanted out and returned the woman's smile.

"Thank you," I said, making her arch a brow.

"And what can I do for you, Ms Smith?"

I had to work at keeping the smile in place. Only a handful of people knew my real name, but that didn't mean it was any easier to hear my false one.

"Please, call me Olivia," I said.

"Of course," she replied with a knowing glint in her eyes. "And you most certainly can call me Helen."

"Lovely," Maggie said, evidently trying to move things along. "Olivia needs to look up a few things in your mental health aisle. Can you point us in the right direction?"

It was time to give Maggie the slip. I eyed Helen, trying to decide if being alone with the overly friendly librarian was a good idea. But I really didn't have much of a choice in the matter. Taking a step forward, I reached out and placed a hand on Maggie's arm.

"I might be a while," I said. "You don't have to stay. There must be more important things for a police sergeant to be doing."

Maggie ducked her head and lowered her voice, but what she thought she'd achieve by that was anyone's guess; Helen was watching the exchange avidly.

"Matt wouldn't like that," Maggie said.

"I think Matt has a lot on his mind," I offered. "And he doesn't even know about the new graffiti yet."

"New graffiti?" Helen asked.

"Outside," I said with affected innocence. "On your building's wall."

"What?" the woman all but yelled. "Tell me they haven't done it again, Sergeant," she demanded Maggie.

Maggie cringed. "You haven't seen it, then," she said, sounding resigned.

"Show me!" Helen ordered. Maggie shot me a glare but turned to lead Helen to the new wall art outside.

I allowed myself a small smile and then went in search of the library's computers.

A big sign in the entranceway had touted free internet access. I was counting on there not being any passwords required. My luck held. The computer wasn't state-of-the-art, but the wi-fi was fast enough to prevent me biting my nails in impatience. A few seconds later, I was inside our Grafton Road server, eyeing Callum Wilkes' file.

Detective Sergeant Pierce had sent through a hastily collated list of all those physical files thought missing from our Grafton Road offices. Callum Wilkes' file was one of them. Matt and Maggie had suggested my former patient might have wanted to cover his tracks by removing all reference to himself in our office. But the Callum I remembered, while not a computer genius, had been a big *Halo* fan.

How many video game players out there couldn't open a laptop and find their way into a business's digital files? David did have password protection on his computer, but he'd never been very creative with the passwords themselves; he always forgot them. Writing them down on his calendar on the first of every month when the system requested he change it.

My stalker had already proven he wasn't in a rush to leave the office, taking his time with the picture he'd hung that had led me to move to Twizel. I couldn't see him not taking his time with the theft of the files, either.

So, why was Callum's digital file still in the system?

I skim read it, then emailed it to myself. Then checked the list Matt had given me from Detective Pierce. None of the names had been removed from the digital archive. I emailed myself a copy of each one and then hacked into David's login.

It didn't work. The last password he'd used failed. I checked my watch. I'd been in Twizel a month already. At some point, David had changed his password like a good little network soldier. Without being able to see his calendar on his desk, I couldn't begin to guess what he'd used on this latest occasion.

I tried a few different words just to be sure, but nothing worked. And on the tenth attempt, I was locked out.

I leant back in my chair and stared at the screen. Callum Wilkes was missing from his home in Auckland. A hand-delivered envelope had been left in my mailbox down here in Twizel. Someone had been in Smokey's that night to have taken a photo of Matt and me sitting at the bar.

Everything pointed towards Callum.

I signed into my email account and clicked on the first attachment. One last look around the library to determine I was still alone, I opened up Callum Wilkes' file.

Callum didn't have a personality disorder such as ASPD. He didn't even have psychosis. Both of which my stalker had to have to a certain degree.

No, Callum Wilkes had stock standard depression. Dysthymia, in fact, a *mild* form of chronic depression. Low self-esteem. Sadness. Fatigue. Poor appetite. But no sign of aggression, psychosis, or something like ASPD. And the last time I saw him, his medication had been working. Even if he'd stopped taking it, which wasn't a given, the return of his symptoms would not have led him to this.

Stalking me.

It wasn't Callum Wilkes, I was sure of it. But when I looked back over all the missing files I'd sent myself, none of them met the criteria either. None of them fitted the profile I'd created.

Had I got it wrong? I couldn't have. Everything had pointed to ASPD with a side order of psychosis. The perpetrator might be suffering from depression as well, but he had to have at least a personality disorder. And to kill the cat, psychosis was now a given as well.

But just depression based illnesses? Which all of the names Matt had given me had.

No.

None of this made any sense. None of these patients had it in them to kill a cat, paint a message in blood, and talk about cold knives and murder.

This was all a red herring.

I was missing something. Which meant the police were, too.

Which meant it was time to face Matt and tell him what I'd uncovered.

Which meant I'd have to explain why I didn't do this at the police station.

I swallowed thickly.

Which also meant I needed to decide if my suspicions were correct.

Was it David screwing with me?

My stomach somersaulted, an uneasy feeling settling in my gut.

Maybe some antacids first.

CHAPTER 32

EVERYONE WAS SO DAMN SENSITIVE ABOUT MY DRINKING HABITS

MATT

I pushed open the door to the pharmacy and heard Liv's voice as she asked for something at the counter. Maggie was picking through a sparkling stand full of garish hair ties or something similar. I didn't look too closely. Her eyes met mine as soon as the door jangled closed at my back.

"Did Sheila tell you we'd be here?" she asked.

"No, Helen Cameron did. What did you do to our town librarian, Maggie?" I'd been read the riot act from the short and extremely irascible woman. Helen might have been an import to Twizel, but she'd claimed the town as her own to defend.

And defend it she did; with sharp words and hard stares and an attitude a t-Rex would be proud of.

"Pfft," Maggie huffed. "She took one look at the latest penis presentation on the library wall and started whacking me over the head with a library card."

"She did not," I said, trying not to laugh out loud.

"Well," Maggie said, smiling slightly. "Maybe she just threatened me with one."

"I can see why you're hiding in here, then," I quipped.

Maggie rolled her eyes. "It's not me you should be worried about."

"I'm not worried. You can handle yourself."

"It's Liv," she said, ignoring the compliment. "Helen took a shine to your teacher."

I scowled. "Helen takes a shine to anybody new in town."

"Anybody?" Maggie asked with a knowing smile.

I scratched my head and made a sound which could have been agreement or denial, and left Maggie to her shit-stirring and fancy-hairband-shopping. Now there's a combination you don't hear every day.

I walked up to the counter, my eyes taking in Liv's perfect behind encased in tight fitting jeans, and then flicked my gaze to Alan behind the counter. He smirked when my eyes met his, letting me know in that Gallic way of his that he'd seen me checking out my woman's assets.

"Mr Bennet," I said, startling Liv. Clearly, Helen had got her rattled. Or maybe that was the renewed threat of the stalker. My scowl deepened.

"Senior Sergeant," Alan greeted. He was going with 'French' today. "You 'ave come at an opportune moment."

"How's that?" I asked, coming to stand beside Liv. I wanted to reach out and touch her. I wanted to pull her close and let her lean against my larger frame. I wanted it so much my hands shook.

But I did not want to spook Liv.

I shoved my hands deep inside my pockets. Patience, I told myself. Not my strong suit.

Alan Bennet didn't miss a thing, though. His eyes came back up to my face, and he asked, "'Ave you seen how busy the town is?"

"Fine weather brings out the tourist," I countered. Where was he going with this? Alan didn't usually talk unless there was something important to stay. Or if he wanted to wind up his neighbour.

"So many new faces in Twizel," the pharmacist said.

"I'm a new face," Liv offered.

"Oh no, *ma chérie*, you are a local now. Yes?"

My hands fisted in my pockets

"Well, maybe not quite yet," Liv demurred.

"You are living with the senior sergeant," Alan replied immediately. "Does that not make you more than just a tourist?"

My hackles rose. Just how the hell did he hear about our new living arrangements?

"News travels fast," I grumbled. My eyes watching the pharmacist's face for any clues.

Unfortunately, Alan Bennet was a dab hand at hiding his reactions.

"You are the talk of the town, Senior Sergeant," he said with a casual shrug of his shoulders. "Even Mad Eye has placed a bet."

"A bet?" Liv asked as I pondered that tidbit of information. Tom Moody had a lot of vices, but gambling was not one of them. And gossip sure as hell didn't feature on his radar.

Just what the hell was Bennet insinuating?

"Yes, *Mademoiselle* Smith." It was hard to tell which word he put the emphasis on. The French title or Liv's fake surname.

There was more to Alan Bennet than met the eye.

"The whole town is eager to know the outcome."

"The outcome?" Liv asked. "Of what exactly?"

"Why, how long you will take to reform our senior sergeant, of course," Alan replied pleasantly.

Liv blushed a beguiling shade of pink. I couldn't stop myself from reaching for her if I had tried. My hand landed on the small of her back and my thumb stroked across the hollow at the base of her spine reassuringly.

"I'm sure no one is interested in any such thing," I said.

"Oh, for a certainty," Alan remarked, "there is much interest in Ms Smith."

The abrupt drop of his French accent had my hand stilling. I could feel the return of tension to Liv's back. We both stared at the

Frenchman. God knows what Liv was thinking, but the fine hairs rising on my arms left me very wary of Alan Bennet.

"You don't say," I stated in a low tone of voice.

Alan met my challenging gaze with a neutral expression.

"Some tourists," he said, "stand out more than others."

"Which tourists would they be?" I asked, my body tight.

Alan shrugged his shoulders again in that damn Gallic movement of his that could mean nothing at all or everything at once. On this occasion, I was betting it meant he was stalling for time or trying to downplay his message.

Because sure as the dags hanging off the arse of a merino, Alan Bennet had shit to say.

"Perhaps," he said, "one should look for the unusual in what appears to be usual."

"Riddles," I said in disgust.

"It is the French way."

"Sometimes I wonder," I said gruffly, "whether you actually are French at all, Mr Bennet."

"Oh, I assure you, Senior Sergeant, I am *le français*. I am just a little of something else, too."

It was the most the man had ever talked about himself. Alan Bennet kept things close to his chest. His antagonism toward Alicia Parsons, who happened to be very British, was the only time he ever displayed anything other than rigid control. He might shrug like a Gaul, and speak like a Parisian on occasion, but the man was a block of ice inside.

A chill raced down my spine and I turned to Liv.

"You done here?"

"Yes," she said, biting her lower lip. She knew something wasn't right in Twizel's drug dispensary, too. I wondered what the psychiatrist in her made of *Monsieur* Bennet.

I looked back at Alan and nodded my head. "Thanks for the warning," I said. He smiled.

I kept my hand on Liv's back as I guided her out of the store.

Maggie caught my eye, her eyebrows raised slightly, but no one said another word until we were out on the sidewalk. I glanced up and down Main Street, my eyes landing on Smokey's Tavern. For a moment, I was struck immobile, unsure how to proceed.

"That was interesting," Maggie remarked quietly at our sides.

"Very," Liv agreed.

"Do you think he knows something?" Maggie asked.

"It would seem so," Liv replied just as quietly.

"Matt?" Maggie pressed.

"Fancy a drink?" I asked, slipping my hand into Liv's and starting across the road to the tavern.

"Um," Maggie said, almost running to keep up with us. "It's four o'clock in the afternoon."

"Live a little, Sergeant," I said, stepping under the tavern's awning. The happy hour sign had already been lit up. Outstanding.

"Ah," Maggie said, right before I pushed open the door. "I'm bowing out of this one."

I turned to look down at her.

"Just one drink."

"No thanks. And I don't think you should, either," she replied.

My brow arched. "Giving me drinking advice, Maggie?"

"Just *friendly* advice, Matt."

I sighed. Everyone was so damn sensitive about my drinking habits.

"You know," I growled, pushing open the door, "they do sell non-alcoholic beverages in here, as well."

Maggie winced, but I didn't wait to see if she had a reply. I stepped into the familiar. Too familiar. And searched for the unfamiliar.

Or more precisely, the unusual in what appeared to be usual, as Alan Bennet had said.

CHAPTER 33

HOW MUCH CONTROL WOULD HE NEED TO SURVIVE THIS?

LIV

The antacids weren't going to help. That exchange with the pharmacist had left me feeling even more queasy. There was something distinctly secretive about that man. A hint of danger hidden beneath a thin veneer of civility. The Frenchman he portrayed was real, I was sure of it. But whether or not Alan Bennet used that as a distraction, I wasn't so certain.

The man had a social conscience, that was obvious. His "message" or warning indicated as much. But underlying that concern for my wellbeing was an even greater narcissism; the French distraction.

He was hiding something and very sure of his ability to continue to do so.

Intriguing, but not an immediate threat.

I looked up at Matt as he led me toward the bar at Smokey's. His brow was furrowed, his eyes dark with emotion, and his mouth set in a thin line. The hard angle of his jaw drew my attention. Even in anger, he was stunning.

But I still didn't understand why we were here.

Maggie hadn't followed us inside. I'd seen the regret on her face before the door had shut at our backs. Everyone was worried about

Matt's drinking. I had no such qualms. He might be full of fury and angst right now, but Matt Drake was a man who could control his demons.

Even if it killed him to do so.

"Tom," he said, helping me onto a stool in front of the barman.

"Matt," the man answered, continuing to clean a glass with a fluffy white towel in hand. His eyes, the good one and the bad one, never left Matt's face, but he added, "Ms Smith," in greeting to me, as well.

Matt took a seat and tapped his knuckles on the worn wooden counter.

"Diet Coke for me," he said. "Liv?"

"Lemonade," I offered with a smile. If I couldn't slip an antacid, I'd at least settle my churning stomach with something mild.

Tom grunted in obvious bemusement and began filling a glass with ice. His hook clunked against the metal siding of the ice bin periodically, as if to draw the eye. I wondered if the movement was purposeful.

I had the feeling not many people did anything accidentally in Twizel.

Tom slipped the drinks across the bar top one after the other and then "hooked" a glass and began to clean it.

"Tell me," Matt said, taking a sip of his Coke. "Many tourists in lately?"

Tom stared at Matt as if he'd gone mad.

"Always tourists in Twizel," he muttered.

"Any standout?" Matt pressed.

"No more than usual."

"And how do they stand out usually?" I asked.

Tom spared me a flick of his unsettling and uneven eyes. "Take photos."

I screwed up my nose trying to decipher that.

"Of their food," Tom added. "Their beers. Their fluffy coffees."

"It's called Instagram," I offered.

"It should be called Instasanity," Tom replied.

"Did you just crack a joke?" Matt asked, the harsh lines of his face relaxing.

Tom merely grunted.

I smiled into my lemonade. I kinda liked the gruff, taciturn barman.

"What about tourists talking to Alan Bennet?" Matt suddenly asked.

My glass hit the bar top too loudly. Just where was Matt going with this?

Tom arched his brow. "There was one."

I turned in my seat and stared across the bar. I remembered now seeing one talking to Mr Bennet the night I came in here to rescue Matt from himself. Matt had managed to drink at least one glass of whisky that night and then sat before another without breaking.

The temptation at the time must have been enormous. But Matt had managed to control himself.

"Your teacher saw them together," Tom said bringing me back to the moment.

"You did?" Matt asked. I nodded. "What did he look like?"

"He wore an I♥NZ t-shirt," I said, recollecting.

"Didn't even try to blend in," Tom said with disgust.

"Did he take any pictures?" Matt asked tensing.

"They all take bloody pictures," Tom grumbled.

"And he was talking to Alan Bennet?" Matt pressed. First looking at Tom and then at me. I nodded. "Fuck," Matt said under his breath.

"What does it mean?" I asked. I couldn't begin to connect the kitschy t-shirt wearing tourist and the secretive French speaking pharmacist with my stalker.

"I don't know," Matt admitted quietly. He pulled a ten dollar note from his pocket and laid it down on the bar surface. Tom nodded his head and slipped it into the till. Matt eased off his stool.

"Where to now?" I asked.

"Home." That one word seemed to fill me up inside. Almost overfill me. To bursting. Excitement. Anticipation. Nervousness. It was all there. With a healthy dose of anxiety.

Home. Was home with Matt and the twins? I wanted it to be, dear God I did, but Matt had so much more healing to do. So much more progress to make before he could truly let go of Missy.

And the girls? They'd come so far, bless them, but they weren't out of the woods yet.

"You're quiet," Matt said as he held the door open to Smokey's. I proceeded him into the late afternoon sunlight. Twizel was winding down for the day. A ute was parked across the street, mud splattering its tyres. A mother and two children were exiting the Musterer's Hut. A dog barked from a rear mounted kennel on a truck.

It all looked so ordinary. So simple. A farming community. A family community. Small town New Zealand with a majestic back-drop. The sunset on Mount Glenmary. Golden. Sparkling. A jewel on the horizon.

And yet everywhere I looked I felt eyes on me. Threatening.

I had to tell him about David. I had to admit I was doubting my closest friend. I had to say something before it became a secret and speaking about it became harder than it should.

"Liv?" Matt pressed, aware I hadn't answered his question. His hand rested in the hollow of my back as he led me towards his police ute. The heat of his palm sent tiny tingles sparking out from where he touched. My legs felt wobbly. My balance off.

Matt Drake had tipped my world on its side.

"I've been thinking," I said.

"Yeah?" he offered when I stopped talking.

"About who it could be. Or more precisely, who it can't be."

"Can't be?" He knew exactly what I was talking about. My stalker.

"Callum Wilkes doesn't have the correct personality," I explained. "He suffered from a mild form of depression. Doesn't have, to my knowledge, a personality disorder. And from what my notes told me, he lacked any form of psychosis. Simply put, he doesn't fit the profile."

Matt stopped next to his car. His gaze was off over the street towards the hairdresser's, but I was sure he didn't see the Shearing Shed at all.

"How did you get your notes, Liv?" he asked.

If I needed proof that Senior Sergeant Matt Drake was an observant police officer, I just had it. He'd seen through my entire speech to the crux of the matter.

"I signed into our online server." I bit my lip and waited.

"All your files are backed up?" he queried, still staring off into the distance. As if he couldn't, *wouldn't*, look at me.

"Yes."

"And none of them were missing?"

"No."

"Wilkes might not have known you had digital back-ups."

"The photo of me outside my house was painted whilst in my office. Drops of cat blood were found on the carpet beneath it. He took his time."

"Your point?"

"He would have taken his time with the files, as well."

"Meaning?"

I closed my eyes. Matt sounded relaxed. He even looked relaxed. He was so far from relaxed it wasn't funny.

"He would have looked in our desks. On our desks. David's laptop was right there. The thief would have seen it. Seen his desk calendar." I took a breath. "Seen his password for his laptop written in red on the first of the month."

Matt let out a huff of breath. Then reached forward to the ute and opened the passenger side door. "Get in," he said.

"That's it?" I asked.

"Get in the car, Liv," he repeated. He was fuming.

I slid into the seat and buckled up, letting him close the door with forced casualness. He rounded the bonnet and opened his own door, bringing the scent of country and man with him.

He didn't start the car.

"When did you find this out?" he asked. And there you had it. Perhaps not the only reason for his anger, but a damn good chunk of it.

"At the library," I said quietly.

He started the car and pulled out onto the main road in Twizel.

"It's a ruse," he said. "An act," he added.

I nodded.

"It's OK," he murmured. For himself or me, I couldn't tell. "It's also his first mistake."

I stared out of the windscreen at the fields that rolled out around us and wondered how such simple words could have my heart palpitating.

David had made a mistake.

But had I just made a bigger one?

Matt had control. Unprecedented control. I admired that in him.

But he was also damaged. Emotionally, psychologically. He'd lost his wife to a psychotic, sadistic murderer. The woman he was sleeping with, *living with*, now was being threatened by her business partner. Bringing the danger right back to his doorstep.

How much control would he need to survive this?

CHAPTER 34

JUST SAY IT

MATT

OLIVIA THOUGHT HER BUSINESS PARTNER WAS THE STALKER. I couldn't begin to imagine what strength of character it took to face up to that horror. Someone she'd trusted, not just for a few months, but years. She'd told me they'd been at university together. That they'd flatted together for a while. That they'd had a sexual relationship for long enough for it to count.

Fuck. I rubbed a hand over my face, feeling thirsty. Thirsty for more than just water.

"You look like shit," Zach said from across the table. Justin grunted in agreement.

"You don't look much better," Luke shot back at him. "Where the hell have you been?"

"Checking the back pastures."

"Did I tell you to check the back pastures?" Luke demanded.

"Chill. I was reacquainting myself with the station."

"Charlie said he saw you talking to someone out in sector three." Justin and I stilled.

"He was mistaken."

"Charlie's got good eyesight," Luke countered.

"It was nothing," Zach growled back. "Leave it."

"Saw you exchange some cash for something in a paper bag," Luke said softly. I sat forward. Justin flicked a startled gaze toward me. I shook my head slightly, keeping my eyes on Zach.

"We gonna talk about this now?" Zach snapped back. "Or we gonna discuss the immediate threat?"

"So, you admit what you're doing, whatever the fuck it is, is a threat?" Luke asked.

"It was nothing," Zach repeated, practically rolling his eyes in frustration.

"Then what was in the bag?" I asked.

"Not you, too," he groused.

"Just tell us," Luke pressed. "Better out than in."

"That's for a hangover, dickhead," Zach said.

"We're family," Luke began.

"Fuck this," Zach said and pushed back from the kitchen table. "If you want my help with this stalker business," he said to me, "just buzz my phone." He slammed out of the back door without a backwards glance.

"Paper bag?" Justin asked.

"Brown paper bag," Luke growled.

"Doesn't necessarily mean anything," I offered.

"Then why didn't he tell us what was inside it?"

"Ever heard of privacy?" I asked, my gut churning. Zach liked his privacy. But that was the problem. Sometimes it was as if Zach led an entirely alternate life. One that didn't involve four brothers, a 50,000-hectare merino station, and Twizel. I was damn sure he'd joined the army to give himself even more privacy. Which, in and of itself, boggled the mind.

Where in the army does one find privacy?

But if anyone could, it'd be Zach.

"He likes his privacy," I said, wanting to give my brother the benefit of the doubt.

"We need to watch him," Luke advised. "He's not sleeping. Barely eats. Has to keep busy."

"You're thinking drugs," Justin said, sounding shocked.

Luke ran a hand through his hair, making it stand up on end. "Fucked if I know. But he's changed."

Yeah, he had. The Zach I knew would have been blustering about an invasion of privacy. Or misdirecting with a heated word or two about the danger Liv had brought to Red Tussock. Or simply organising a posse to go after David Jenkins. It would have been a toss up between which avenue of attack he would have taken. But it *would* have been an attack.

Not a retreat, like he had just done.

"Agreed," I said into the strained silence. "We keep an eye on him."

"Agreed," Justin said as Luke nodded.

The sound of Maggie and Liv talking reached us and before long they opened the back door and stepped into the kitchen. Rachel and Dani in tow.

"We found flowers to press," Maggie announced. "A bright yellow one and a purple and blue one."

"Gerbera and delphinium," Liv explained.

I suppressed a smirk. "Yellow and blue one, eh? Good call, Sergeant."

"Oh, shut up," she muttered, taking a seat beside Luke. His arm came out around the back of her chair, and he immediately started playing with her ponytail.

I glanced over at Liv wanting her to sit beside me as well so I could touch her like that. But she kept her distance. Fussing over the twins. Making sure they knew what to do to press their flowers.

"Now, go and write down what we discussed about the seasons and why there are fewer flowers at this time of year," Liv instructed.

The girls nodded their heads and scurried off into the lounge to do their homework.

"Just as well you shifted here," Justin said. "No flowers at the old place."

Liv's eyes cut to mine and then darted away. I leant back in my chair and cocked my head as I studied her. I knew she'd been nervous about admitting her suspicions regarding her clinic partner. But I didn't realise it went deeper than that.

Liv was nervous about me.

Oh, not in the don't-come-near-me way. But in the is-he-going-crack way.

Didn't she realise with her at my side I was stronger, mentally, emotionally, hell in every possible way, than I'd ever been in my life?

"Come sit down, babe," I said, patting the seat beside me. Her bottom lip rolled between her teeth. I arched my brow. I could reassure Liv later, but right now, with Justin and Luke still here, we needed to strategise.

"This guy, David," Justin said, picking up on my need for focus elsewhere. "He's still in Auckland?"

Liv let out a breath of air and moved to take the seat beside me. I immediately pulled her chair closer and slipped my hand into hers on her thigh. I squeezed it gently. It took a moment, but she finally squeezed it back in reply.

"Last time I spoke to him, yes," Liv said.

"And that last time," Maggie pressed, "what stood out?" What set the alarm bells off inside Liv's head?

"He was more aggressive than I'd heard him before. Not less supportive, but more judgemental." Her gaze slid to me and then away.

Ah, he'd called her out on us. Jealousy wasn't unique to psychotic stalkers.

"Understandable," I said. Luke snorted.

"What else?" Maggie asked in her caring cop voice, offering up a glare to both Luke and me.

"He swore a lot. That's unlike him. Usually, he's very circumspect. Even with me."

"And?" Maggie pushed, aware Liv was holding back.

"Melodramatic," she said. Then remained silent.

"How so?" Luke asked, stepping in to tag team with Maggie. I couldn't speak. I couldn't press Liv on this.

Right now I was as much a problem as David.

"He said." She had to clear her throat. "He said 'pillow talk can be deadly.'"

Justin whistled and received a kick under the table from Maggie. "Sorry," he mumbled, ducking his head. "But that's a bit telling, isn't it? And then he leaves a picture of you and Matt in your mailbox?" I had to force my hands not to fist.

It didn't help that I was still clutching one of Liv's and hers was damp with obvious distress.

"But how did he get it down here if he was still up there?" Maggie asked.

"Was he still up there?" Luke asked.

"Yes," I said, my voice hard. "Detective Sergeant Pierce interviewed him at Liv's Grafton Road offices when the files were stolen."

"Not to mention his laptop and cell phone being stolen," Maggie added.

"Then who left the photo in the mailbox?" Luke asked.

"Good question," Maggie agreed, offering her man a nod of approval. Luke simply reached up and tucked a strand of her hair behind her ear, his calloused fingers gently stroking the soft skin down her neck, above her pulse.

I blinked away, noting Justin was looking at anything but them as well. How had Luke found someone so perfect for him? How did I look Maggie in the eyes at work knowing exactly the sort of woman Luke needed?

Liv started to smile. Just a small one, but it was there.

And I forgot all about Luke and Maggie.

"Haven't seen that for a while," I whispered to her.

Her eyes met mine.

"Seems wrong to smile when so much is up in the air," she whispered back.

"You really think it's him?" I asked. I wasn't sure yet. But I sure as hell wouldn't let him near her until I was certain he wasn't the man we were after.

"I don't know," she admitted. "He was different on the phone the last time we talked." I wrapped my arm around her shoulders and pulled her close.

Fuck it! She was mine, and I was sure enough of that fact for the both of us.

"But there's more," she said, drawing everyone's attention.

I stilled, breathing in her scent and using her heat to calm me.

"What more?" I asked quietly.

"I profiled him," Liv said. "When we first met."

Ah, shit. I wasn't going to like this.

"And what did you determine?" Maggie asked.

"Bear in mind, he'd just lost his sister to suicide," Liv rushed to say. "At the time, I didn't know. I was new to profiling. When I did realise what was happening in his personal life, I redid the profile, and it came out completely different. Sometimes that happens, you know. External influences affect the assessment. Experience, too, I suppose."

"Liv," I said softly, drawing her face to mine with a finger and thumb gently placed under her chin. "You're rambling, doll. Just say it."

She nodded her head, not moving away from my touch.

Then licked her lips and said, "He was on the high end of the spectrum for classic ASPD."

Antisocial Personality Disorder. The serial killer mental illness of choice.

Fuck!

It's not as if David had harmed me. Sure, he'd scared me. Taken photos of me. Killed cats and left messages for me in their blood. Even threatened to kill Matt.

Ah, hell, who was I kidding? That alone was enough to have the entire Twizel police force on high alert. Not to mention CIB Auckland moving to bring my best friend in for questioning.

But David hadn't hurt me, and I wasn't certain he would. Part of me knew that was transference; my attempt to explain his behaviour away with what I thought our relationship to be. Built on trust.

But I never told David I'd profiled him in college. I never admitted I'd suspected him of having ASPD. The second profile had found him to be completely stable, so I'd refrained from admitting my findings. He'd been depressed over his sister's sudden death, angered over his perceived failure to help her, and struggling to keep up with his studies. But stable despite the emotional turmoil he'd been suffering.

So, I'd left well enough alone.

But had I got it wrong? That second time and not the first. Had David regressed and somehow used me as a springboard to his past tendencies? Had our breakup, romantically, meant more to him than he'd let on?

And if so, what did he want now? To reunite? No, to make me pay. To hurt me as I had hurt him.

I felt sick with the knowledge that I'd hurt him at all. Sick that he hadn't been healthy enough to express that pain at the time. But had instead waited ten years.

I shook my head and stared out at the fields as the morning sun rose above Red Tussock. We'd talked most of the night away, and even after the twins were put to bed and Luke, Maggie and Justin had left, Matt and I had kept talking. About nothing and everything and not nearly enough.

Matt had held me as I'd tried to fall asleep. He'd soothed me with soft words and softer touches. I'd allowed myself to fall into the perfect world he'd created. In our borrowed bed in a borrowed room in a guest house.

I'd been too weak to say no. And he'd been too much the gentleman to deny me.

Guilt washed over me. We hadn't discussed "us" last night. We'd talked about so much, he'd asked me question after question about David, but not once had I asked him about us. About him and Missy and what that meant for our future.

Missy was dead. But was she dead enough for Matt?

"We should hear from them soon," the man in question said as he entered the room. He was talking about Detectives Pierce and Stone.

"I've been thinking," I said, pushing all other doubts and fears aside for the time being. "The tourist."

"Yes," Matt said simply, lowering himself to sit beside me on the couch. His hand found mine unerringly. "It's the only explanation. He sent someone down here to mess with you. The cat on your doorstep. The picture from Smokey's delivered to your mailbox. What I can't understand is how Alan Bennet figured it out."

He scratched at his jaw. It was smoothly shaven. For a moment the need to touch it overrode all else.

Matt smirked down at me, too aware of my improper thoughts.

"You've got stubble burn," he said, voice lowering. "Here," he added, running a finger along the side of my jaw. "And here," he added, trailing his finger down over the side of my neck. "I'd forgotten how soft a woman's skin can be. How easy it is to leave marks."

There was so much to take away from that, that I decided to leave it for now.

Cowardly? Perhaps.

Or maybe just practical. I couldn't stop Matt remembering his wife. I couldn't even stop him from loving her still. But I could be the one beside him, here and now, supporting him, loving him.

Being good for him, somehow.

"Got something for you," he said, reaching into his back pocket. He placed a small stuffed sheep on the couch beside me.

"Ah, what...?" I started.

"Merino," he said, gruffly. "For your keys." He even blushed. Then shrugged. "You know, so you don't lose 'em."

I reached forward and picked the fluffy keyring up, staring at the I ♥ Twizel "t-shirt" adorning the woolly sheep. Then fingered the key attached to the ring.

"What's this for?"

"The house," he said indicating the building around us. "I took it off your keyring and put it on this one."

"Why?" I studied him, unsure why he'd go to the trouble of grabbing that key and not the rest.

"Liv," he said with a put-upon sigh, "for a super intelligent doctor of psychiatry you can miss the bleeding obvious sometimes."

"Huh?"

He scrubbed the back of his neck.

"Couldn't give you a key to my heart so I'm giving you a key to my house instead."

"A key to your..." Oh, hell. He felt the need to remind me he couldn't fall in love with me. I couldn't ever have his heart. "Oh, OK,"

I said, shoving the sheep, the key and the I ♥ Twizel message into my handbag.

"Liv?" he said, his head cocked to the side, and eyes narrowed. "You do realise if I could have made a key and it could have fitted my heart, you'd have it, right?"

I blinked.

"Damn it," he said. "I'm not good at this. What I'm trying to say…"

The front door opened, and Joshua and Catherine Drake walked in with the twins scurrying behind.

"This conversation is not over," Matt growled, pushing up from the couch and opening his arms for Dani to climb into. Rachel watched from the other side of the room, big eyes devouring her father.

So fragile, these girls. And yet they had their father's strength of character. They were survivors.

Rachel walked over to the couch and sat down beside me. I wrapped my arm around her shoulders and let her lean against me. It wasn't a cuddle, as such. She wasn't reciprocating. But it was her way of seeking comfort without having to ask.

"How about I make some lunch?" Catherine said, then hesitated. "You don't mind, do you, Liv?"

I smiled up at Matt's mother and shook my head. "Not at all. Go right ahead." She nodded her head and sashayed into the kitchen.

"Any word?" Joshua asked, taking one of the armchairs.

"Not yet," Matt said, tickling Dani. "How about you girls go help Grandma in the kitchen."

"Aw, do we have to?" Dani whined. It was the sweetest sound I'd ever heard. I was thinking Matt thought the same, too.

"Do as you're told, baby-girl," he said, swatting her playfully on the rump.

Rachel didn't move.

"How about you?" I asked, nudging her.

She shook her head and snuggled in further. It was manipulation, pure and simple. Rachel didn't ask for hugs. She was using this quasi-request for comfort as a foil against having to help out in the kitchen.

Rachel had a lazy bone. I smiled.

"Tell you what," I said. "Have you checked the flowers?"

She shook her head. "Which one was yours again?" I knew which one, but Rachel would regress if not pushed hard enough. Open-ended questions as prescribed.

"Yellow," she whispered.

"What was that one called?" Matt asked, falling into the routine with such practised ease it warmed my heart.

"Gerbera," Rachel said, louder this time. Getting into the swing of things.

"You picked a Gerbera?" Joshua asked. She nodded. He stifled a cringe, aware of his faux pas immediately. Scratching his jaw, he asked, "What kind of flower did Dani pick?"

I was so proud of them all. So proud of their combined efforts. Their support of each other. Of the progress they were making with these precious children.

"Delphinum," she said, slightly mispronouncing it. My heart just about burst from my chest.

"Well now," Joshua said. "That's Grandma's favourite. Bet she'd love to see what it looks like pressed."

And just like that Rachel was off the couch and running down the hallway to her bedroom, in search of their pressed flowers.

Joshua blinked a few times, and Matt cleared his throat. In a world which had been so dark for so long for this family, a little bright light had begun to shine through the clouds.

"You've done wonders, Liv," Joshua said, once Rachel had traipsed through the lounge to the kitchen with the girls' flower pressing book hugged to her chest.

"She has that," Matt said with no small measure of pride.

I smiled, but words failed me. Such gratitude was uncalled for. They'd been the ones to rally, to change their perceptions, to trust.

Matt opened his mouth to say something when his cell phone

sounded out. His eyes cut to me. Joshua stilled. I could hear Catherine pause in her talking to the girls.

"Drake," he said into the mouthpiece. A short pause. "I see. OK, thanks, Pierce. I'll be in touch."

Detective Sergeant Pierce. My heartbeat faltered. My breaths stalled. I swear sweat beaded my brow.

"David?" I whispered, my fingers trembling.

"Liv," he said carefully, just as Dani screamed from the kitchen, "Fire!"

CHAPTER 36
BLUE LIGHTS

MATT

I could smell the smoke as soon as I stepped out of the front door. A swathe of black reached up into the bright blue sky like a crooked and necrotic finger. The letterbox let out a loud crack and then fell to the side, flaming bits of wood falling into a nearby garden.

Dad raced out of the house with the fire extinguisher from the kitchen and proceeded to douse the entire thing while my heart beat too fast and my fucking feet refused to work.

This was no spontaneous combustion.

This was sabotage. Arson.

He'd found Liv.

Panic unlike anything I had every felt before consumed me. Making my vision blur and the world around me warp in and out like a demented fairground ride short circuiting. Nausea welled up in my gut, sweat broke out down my spine. My hands fisted.

Then sound and sensation came crashing back in, and everything returned to sharp focus.

"Stay inside the house," I said to Liv and Mum and the girls behind me. I stepped off the porch and approached Dad, as he kicked at the smouldering ruins of the guest house letterbox.

"Nothing inside," he said. "Smells like straight petrol."

I inhaled, my eyes scanning the road in every direction. Unlike the homestead, the guest house was close to the road; a smaller tributary to state highway one, so not a lot of traffic. But you could see in all directions for hundreds of metres, and not a thing stood out.

"No traffic," Dad mused. I stepped out onto the road itself and stared at the ground.

"Tyre marks. Not big enough for a four-wheel drive."

"Unusual for around here," Dad offered.

I crouched down, taking in the tread and size of the tyre, where it had pressed an imprint into the dirt at the side of the road.

"Left in a hurry," I observed, noting the dirt and mud splattered across the picket fence along the side of the property. I stood up and looked back at the house.

Liv was standing on the porch, but Mum had obeyed my direction and taken the girls inside. Liv's face was white, her hands were wringing, eyes too intelligent by far met mine.

"It's him," she said. I nodded. "He's here," she whispered and then turned to go inside.

I frowned, unsure what to make of that. She'd looked determined. Determined about what?

"What are you going to do, son?" Dad asked beside me.

"Find him," I said, heading back to the house.

Dad muttered to himself about cleaning up the mess, but I had bigger things on my mind. I pushed through the front door, but Liv wasn't in the lounge. I started toward the bedrooms at the back of the house, then heard Rachel crying in the kitchen and changed course.

Dani was standing at the kitchen sink, looking out the front window towards Dad. Rachel was shaking like a leaf in Mum's arms, tears running down her pink cheeks, snot dripping off the end of her little nose. Mum wiped a tissue across her face and lifted worried eyes to mine.

"Hey," I murmured, walking closer. Dani looked over her shoulder at me; dead eyes. That's what I'd call them on anyone else other than my daughter. Eyes that showed nothing of the turmoil inside.

There're not too many things in this world that bring me to my knees, but my kids' pain is definitely one of them. The fact that they can't process it, emote it, leaves a hole in my chest the size of Canterbury. When would this agony end? When would our lives be ours to enjoy again?

I'm not much for prayer, but I said a quick and fervent one then, hoping God was still listening. *Please, just, please. Make it end.*

I walked over to Rachel and laid a hand on top of her head. "It's gonna be all right, baby-girl," I said. "Everything's gonna be all right. I swear."

She hiccupped, but the tears slowed down, her still snotty nose delving into the crook of Mum's neck. For her part, Mum just cuddled her closer, running weather-beaten hands down Rachel's long hair. Again and again and again.

I crossed the small kitchen to Dani.

"Come here, bub," I said, opening my arms to her. Dani was the one who usually sought comfort in cuddles, not Rachel. The switcheroo had me holding my breath.

But in the end, Dani couldn't refuse. It could have been that I stood there for a good long two minutes of silence, my arms open, my shoulders beginning to ache as much as my chest. But finally, she walked into my embrace and let out a slow breath.

"You're safe, OK?" I whispered, running a hand through her hair just like Mum was to Rachel. "Nothing's gonna harm you. Ever."

Stupid to make promises you can't keep. But I'd be damned if I didn't keep this one. To both of them. My girls had seen more than any grown person should have to see, let alone mere six-year-olds. I was going to do everything I could to make sure they were spared that terror again.

I held Dani close and sent up another prayer. Hell, at this rate, I may even go back to attending church on Sundays. Especially if my girls were safe.

Please let them be safe.

I pulled back and crouched down until I was at eye level with Dani. "You OK?" I asked. She nodded. "Wanna talk about it?" She shook her head. "You know, Liv says talking sometimes helps. Let's you get it out so someone else can hold half the weight of it for you. Does that make sense?"

She nodded her head, empty eyes brightening.

"You like Liv, huh?" I asked.

Another nod of her head.

"What do you like about her?"

Dani held my steady gaze with one of her own. She wasn't stupid. She knew what I was doing. These girls had cottoned on to the whole "open-ended questions" thing right from the beginning. But it'd been Rachel who had fought it the most. Despite ending up being the first one to crack under pressure and speak.

Dani was more expressive than Rachel. Well, she used to be. More demonstrative, Liv had called it. I prayed with all my might that she wouldn't regress. Wouldn't go where Rachel had so recently been; so full of anger; so tightly held together; unable to show a thing.

Please let my daughters be all right. Please.

"She's clever," Dani finally said, allowing me to breathe again. I felt a little dizzy, truth be told.

I offered my girl a beaming grin. "She is, isn't she? She says you're clever, too."

"I am," Dani murmured.

"Then," I said, sucking in a breath and holding it. *Fuck, please let me be doing the right thing.* "Wanna talk about it?"

She stared at me; her eyes no longer dead, but not normal either. Not healthy. There was no fear. No anger. Nothing of what she must be feeling. Just a keen look relaying attention. Focus. As if she could stare at me and get me to see everything.

"I can't know what you saw unless you tell me, baby-girl," I whispered. "I can't read minds. I don't know what you want me to see."

Frustration entered two big pools of brown and blinked at me.

When her eyelids lifted, the frustration had retreated. Replaced with... nothing.

If raging could have made a difference, I would have done it. If cursing God had made a difference, I would have repeated it. I'd drunk my way through the pain. I'd beaten myself up with the guilt. I'd closed myself off from all hope.

I knew it all. Every trick in the book to make life liveable. Bearable. To fool yourself into thinking everything was fine. OK. Breathable.

But Liv had taught me something. Something I hadn't ever thought I'd need to learn. Me. Matt Drake. Forty-four years old. Senior Sergeant of Twizel Police. Father. Brother. Son.

Liv had taught me that there *was* life after death. That there was love after heartache. That there *could be* hope after defeat, after all.

I was not going to give up on Rachel and Dani. I wanted them to see the light. To see the light like I did. To wake up after that long night of darkness, like I had woken up with Liv.

"Baby-girl," I said. "You are the most caring person I know. So like your Mummy. Caring for things is a good character trait to have. They call it empathy, Dani. And I know you feel it the most. You worry about your sister. And you worry about me. I think you worry about so much that sometimes you just don't want to feel anything. I understand, bub. I do. Sometimes I want to do the same; switch it off; turn away; pretend it doesn't matter to me. I did it for a long time, Dani. But I'm not going to do it anymore. You know why?"

She shook her head, her eyes locked on mine, her little body thrumming.

"Because I love you too much. Because I don't want to miss a moment with you. Because you and Rachel, and Gramps and Grandma, and Uncle Justin, and Uncle Luke and Maggie, and Uncle Finn and Momo, and Uncle Zach are all so important to me. You're everything."

"And Liv?" she asked, voice scratchy. My heart ached. My chest hurt. My head pounded with the rush of blood through my veins.

"And Liv," I said. "Very much Liv. Liv is part of our family now. OK?"

She nodded her head and then looked across the kitchen to Rachel. Her twin's eyes met her gaze. Rachel nodded; giving permission, agreeing with her sister.

Dani looked back at me.

"Blue lights," she said, not making any sense at all.

"Blue lights?" I asked.

"Under the car, Daddy. I saw blue lights flashing under the car as it left."

CHAPTER 37

ARE WE YOURS, TOO?

I was closing my suitcase when Matt walked into the room. The zip wouldn't quite mesh together, and I was holding my breath, while I pressed all my weight onto the overstuffed bag, and struggled with the recalcitrant zipper.

One look at Matt's face and all air left the room.

I couldn't have sucked in a breath to save myself.

He looked devastated.

Trashed.

Burned as surely as the letterbox had been.

I swallowed, eased up off the suitcase, and prepared for the fight to come.

"So, that's it," he said quietly. "You're leaving."

"I'm endangering you all. Endangering the girls," I added. My argument was a good one, and he knew it.

"And where will you go?"

"I was thinking Wellington." I laughed. It wasn't humorous. "Olivia Smith is from Wellington. I might as well go and see it."

"He'll find you."

"But he won't find you," I whispered.

Matt didn't even blink.

"You're running away," he murmured.

"I'm protecting you."

"Bullshit," he snapped. "You're running away. Hiding. Giving up. Chucking it in. Call it what you will, but you lied. To me. To the girls. You're lying now to yourself, but you can't see it."

I stepped toward him. His body seemed to grow larger. Shoulders wider. Face harder. An imposing giant swelling up before my eyes.

"You can't want me here, Matt," I said carefully. "Think about it. I represent everything you've tried to leave behind and nothing of what you want to keep."

"What the hell does that mean?" he demanded.

I shrugged, feeling nothing like the nonchalance I was trying to effect. This hurt. He'd said he'd hurt me, but it was me hurting myself.

Not that things would have ever ended differently.

"I've done what I came here to do. The girls are healing."

"They need you still."

"They've got a family who is united in their efforts to help them. You don't need me anymore. *They* don't need me anymore."

"You're blind if you believe that."

"Oh, I see everything clearly. It's you who's blind to the truth."

"And what truth is that, Liv?" he asked silkily.

I searched his eyes, trying to understand the tension emanating from his frame. Trying to calculate from where the next hit would come. His soft tone belied the uncertain atmosphere. His words, said so certainly, contradicted reality.

"You're still in love with her," I said, steeling myself for the imminent pain.

I huffed out an unamused breath at myself. I was already hurting. Confirmation of what I knew to be true couldn't hurt me any more than I already was.

"Who?" he said, almost sounding confused. I stared at him,

thinking he really had created a false reality for himself when thunder clouds darkened his eyes. "Missy?" he said incredulously.

Then he took a step into the room, turned around and shut the door, and flipped the lock.

His shoulders were rising and falling too swiftly. His back looked carved from stone. He hadn't clenched his fists, but one curved around the door handle and looked like it would snap it off if I so much as moved.

I held my breath. Pressure pushing in from all sides. My chest throbbed, but I was unsure if that was the heartache of our impending separation or the strain in the room.

Matt Drake could be damn scary when he wasn't saying or doing a bloody thing.

"I did love Missy," he said to the door, his voice low and hard sounding. "At least, I thought it was love. And in some ways it was. Very much so. She was my childhood sweetheart. My best friend while I transitioned to adulthood. She knew me when I was young and impetuous, and when I became something of the man I am today. She loved Red Tussock as much as I did. Cursed the busybodies in town along with me.

"Fuck," he said. "She was the mother of my girls. How could I not love Missy?"

He turned around and took a step toward me.

"And then she tore out my heart and stomped on it," he said, stopping a few feet away from the bed and me. "I thought she'd crushed it beyond repair. I thought it had been hers and hers alone, and when she'd thrown it away for a better one, a newer one, a more dangerous one, mine was destined for oblivion. Because who else could know me the way she did? Love me the way she did? Love my girls as much as me?"

He took another step. So close now, I could feel his warmth. Hear his ragged breaths. Reach out and touch that vibrating mass of muscle if I was crazy enough. I kept hold of my breath.

"And then I met you," he said. "Everything Missy is not. Strong and capable. Worldly and sophisticated. Dedicated and loyal. To me. To my girls. My fiery school ma'am, who analyses and assesses and does shrink type things in her head. Who loves my girls and me as much as I love her back."

Oh, dear God.

"There is nothing of Missy in you. And I thank God every day for that fact. Because you're all I can think about. You consume my every thought. Your happiness is my happiness. Your pain my agony. Your fear my kryptonite. My first thought when I walked in here and realised you were running was to run with you."

Oh, good Lord.

"But that's not why you love me." He knew. He could see right through me. I hadn't stood a chance. "Not because I gave up on my life, walked out of my girls' world. But because I stayed and I found a way back."

He drew in a deep breath, then took one last step to reach me. He didn't touch me. He just stood there, looking down at me with such longing in his eyes I almost crumbled, so stripped bare.

"Listen up, doll. And listen well. Because I'm going to tell you something about Missy and me. Something I never want you to forget. I might have loved Missy in some way, but I am *in love* with you. Not just a fleeting thing. Not just a lust based longing. This, what you and I have, it's different." He shook his head, his face softening. "I didn't know you could love someone like this. I didn't know it was possible. You stormed into my world, turned it on its head. Made me feel things I have never felt before in my life. Not with Missy. Not with my girls.

"This," he reached out and placed his flat palm on my chest, over my heart, "is mine. Mine to treasure. Mine to protect. Mine to worship. And this," his hand slapped his own chest, above his heart, "is yours. It's *never* been anyone else's. Not even Missy's. Do you understand?"

"The sheep," I said. He laughed.

"That fucking sheep. Alicia Parsons gave it to me to give to you," he admitted. "Fucking saw the writing on the wall before I did."

"She's very astute," I acquiesced.

"But is she as clever as you?"

I looked up at him, really looked up at him. Took in the hard jaw, the firm lips, the honesty in his eyes. So clear. So deep. So dark, but comforting.

"Life has a way of throwing curve balls at you," I said.

"You just gotta be prepared to catch them," Matt finished for me.

Could I catch him? Could I catch this? Was it real?

I was a highly educated and successful psychiatrist, but when it came to my own love life, I was a mess.

"No one said love would be easy," Matt murmured. "But they sure as hell didn't say you had to do it alone. Love me, Liv. And let me love you. Let the girls love you. We can do this."

"Are you sure?" I asked; the only question I *could* ask.

"Never been more sure about anything in my entire life."

"The danger..."

"Does not compare to the loss of you."

"The girls..."

"Are nowhere near ready to let you go. Like me. Face it, doll. You're ours. Completely. Are we yours, too?"

I was theirs from the moment I walked into their lives.

And they were mine, whether they knew it or not, from that day onwards, too.

I nodded my head.

Matt let out a relieved sigh... and then he moved.

CHAPTER 38
AND I LOVED IT

MATT

She didn't see me coming. But then, I hadn't seen her coming, either. This redheaded vixen with a heart so big and a conscience so heavy, it shadowed her every move.

When I'd walked in here and seen the suitcase, I'd almost exploded. But something rational inside me told me to wait. To hold back. That this here was important. Perhaps the most important moment of my life.

She'd almost left me. Left us. I shuddered at the thought.

Then I reached her. Touched her. And all thought vanished, but this. Liv. Smooth skin. Hot flesh, Supple body. Mine.

It had been an epiphany, really. Not that I loved Liv. I'd already accepted that fact. But that I loved her differently than I had loved Missy. Missy had been warmth and comfort and a place to rest. Liv was like waking up after a long night of darkness. Waking up to red hair and bright blue eyes and a world full of her, full of colours. Full of life and promise and hope and wonder.

When I looked at her, I saw the future, not the past.

When I was with her, I was *home*. No doubt. No argument. It just was. Olivia Logan had become my home.

If she'd run, I would have followed her.

If she'd baulked, I would have stayed the course.

If she'd fought me, I would have relished every entanglement, every delicious friction-filled moment, every fiery outburst.

My hand wrapped up in her hair as my lips laid a trail over her jaw. My hot breath fanned her earlobe as I whispered in her ear.

"I need you," I said. Nothing fancy. Nothing poetic. Just fact. I needed Liv. God damn, I needed her so much.

It should have scared me. Maybe it did scare Liv. But she arched her back, pressed her beautiful breasts into my chest, and welcomed me home.

"Oh, baby," I whispered, lifting her t-shirt up over her arms, my hands immediately finding her round tits, my fingers and thumbs rubbing her nipples.

"Matt," she moaned softly. Not loud enough to startle the girls or disturb Mum and Dad. But I knew how small the house was, and it made me realise the next one, the one we'd build together up on Rocky Ridge, would be big. Huge. A room each for the girls downstairs, and a whole master suite upstairs for Liv and me.

"You gotta be quiet, doll," I said. I stripped her jeans down her legs, nuzzling my face into the V between her thighs. "Can you do that?" I asked on a rasped breath of air. Air filled with her sweet scent, making me wild.

"Oh, God," she breathed. "We can't do this now. Not with your parents and the girls out there."

Fucking hell, what was wrong with me? I should have said nothing.

So, I pulled the material of her knickers to the side and licked up her pussy.

"Matt!' she whisper-shouted. I growled, tightened my hold on her hips and buried my face in heaven.

"Oh, Matt," she whisper-purred.

"That's it, baby," I said, tearing her underwear away completely and feasting on my woman.

She tasted like spring to me. Bursting with flavours. Making my senses come to life. I felt every inch of her heated flesh beneath my fingertips. I felt every shudder and spasm of her body beneath my touch. I felt every indrawn breath and sharp exhale. I felt it all as if I was feeling it all for the very first time.

I licked and sucked, occasionally nibbling on her clit. She writhed and whisper-moaned, and did everything in her power to remain quiet. I chuckled at the whimper that came out, low and desperate and needy. And then I sank two fingers inside her channel and flicked her G-spot.

She came apart beneath me in a fiery wave of blissful release. My firecracker. My little sensual shrink. I'd barely gotten started. But that was Liv. Bursting with energy, begging to come. So quickly tipped over the edge.

"Fuck, you're addictive," I murmured, kissing up her thigh, then licking along the crease between pelvis and leg. "So fucking amazing," I added, unbuckling my belt and pushing my uniform trousers down off my legs. My boots hit the floor. My cock sprang free. I gripped it, my breath panting out over moist folds, Liv still moaning and writhing beneath me.

I fished out a condom, well aware we'd forgotten that little gem last time and not wanting to complicate matters any more than they needed to be. There'd be time. Hell, I might be forty-four, but I was still firing. And Liv. Liv was beautiful. Thirty-five and full of enough love and energy to give a horde of kids.

But if that wasn't what she wanted, then I was not going to trap her into it. I wanted Liv. Pure and simple. I wanted Liv, Rachel and Dani. And anything after that would be added bliss.

I rolled on the condom, moved up over her body, and stared down into the eyes of the woman I loved.

Loved.

No. LOVED.

I loved this woman. I fucking loved her.

"Liv," I said, my hands shaking as they rested on either side of her head, cupping her gently. "Got no fancy words for you, babe. Just my body. My heart to give." I laughed. She smiled. "But you've already got one, so I'll go with the other." I shifted my hips, letting my bouncing cock fall into position at her entrance. "This is me. Loving you. So damn much."

I thrust forward slowly, carefully, excruciatingly gently. My cock straining, so hard I was sure it would break off. Then her warmth surrounded me. Her walls gripped me. Wetness met my balls, ran over my thighs.

My fiery, erotic, combustible redhead.

"You feel so good, babe," I groaned, lowering my head to her forehead.

"Move," she pleaded.

"Like this?" I whispered, pulling out slowly and pushing back in.

"Oh, God, yes," she moaned, arching up to meet me. Her hands gripped my shoulders, then ran down my arms, over my torso, towards my butt. Then she pulled on my cheeks, hard, bringing me in. Bringing me home. Holding me tight.

"That's it," I said. "Hold on, baby." And then I started to rock.

I watched her the entire time my dick stroked in and slowly pulled out. I watched her move and breathe and come apart. I watched her do it all twice over and then I couldn't hold back. And I lost myself to the rhythm, to the sensations, to the taste of her lips and the sound of her sighs.

I lost myself, but I knew that wasn't quite right.

Because I might have lost myself in Liv's body, but I had, in fact, been found.

By this woman. By this connection we'd had from the start. By her smiles and laughter. Her serious frowns and intelligent eyes. By her care and attention. Her unfailing loyalty and commitment. By her words and her actions.

And by her heart.

I'd been wandering around my world in a dark haze, never quite emerging, never quite seeing what was right in front of my eyes. Never quite believing I deserved anything else.

But as I came apart, Liv holding me so close, so tightly, as if she couldn't let go, would never let go, needed me as much as I needed her, I realised this was right. This was good. This was all mine.

And if I ever thought I didn't deserve Liv Logan, then I'd do everything in my power to make sure I did.

I would be a better man because of her.

I would be a better cop because of her.

I would be a better father because of her.

And I would be everything she needed me to be and then more. Because Olivia Logan deserved the best life could give her.

How could she not? She'd given me the best of herself.

And I was keeping her.

I was never letting her go.

She was mine.

As our breaths slowed and our bodies released the last of their climaxes, I buried my face into the side of her neck and hugged her tight.

Liv was mine. We were hers. I would kill anyone who thought differently.

I'd kill David Jenkins, if I had to.

I just had to kill him without losing my own life.

Because life was good. It was fantastic. Right now, right here, with Liv's satiated body beneath me, life was fucking wild.

And I loved it.

CHAPTER 39

I SHOULDN'T HAVE FELT SO HAPPY ABOUT THAT

LIV

I walked into chaos. The kitchen full of people. Phones ringing. Laptops open. Keys tapping. Voices humming. The guest house had been turned into mission control. I took one look at the organised chaos caused by the Twizel Police Force and turned back around in search of the twins.

Joshua and Catherine were in the lounge, talking quietly. I heard my name mentioned as I walked past. They didn't see me, thankfully, but they were talking about me. The topic of conversation was a toss up between Matt's and my private moment of minutes ago and the mailbox message from my stalker.

My stalker. It had seemed such an impersonal title to give him. Even though it was me, he was stalking. Me he was photographing. Me he was reaching out to through messages written in blood. "My Stalker" had allowed a level of detachment that had helped me to keep going, to disassociate, to compartmentalise.

He was no longer "my stalker" anymore.

How could David have done this? Academically, I understood the motives, the twists his mind had taken. I wanted to help him. But choosing to stay here had forced me to change my plans. I hadn't told

Matt that I'd intended to go back to Auckland and confront David. I still thought a direct approach was best; this hiding out and waiting for his next move seemed ineffective. In a way, we were encouraging him. The further along the spectrum he moved, the harder it would be to treat him in the end.

But Matt had ruined everything and conversely changed my life in a miraculous way. His confession had been entirely unexpected, but so very much wanted.

I was in love with a man who loved me back.

I was staying in Twizel.

I smiled to myself as I came to rest outside the twins' borrowed bedroom. They were playing with their Monster High dolls on their beds. Tiny dresses lay scattered over the duvets, delicately decorated hair accessories dotted the landscape. Glitter hair lotion was smeared over their fingers and sparkling through their dolls' poofed up hair.

Children were so adaptable. So capable of mending what was broken inside. With the correct guidance and care, a nurturing environment and time, they could become whole again. It wouldn't be the same for David.

Dani looked up and spotted me, a crooked smile gracing her lips. She cocked her head to the side, studying me. Then she reached out, picking up one of her dolls, and held it out to me.

I crossed the room, garnering Rachel's attention also, and sat down on the side of the bed.

"Would you like me to brush her hair?" I asked and received the go-to nod of the head. "What should I put in it?"

"Glitter," came Dani's quiet reply.

"OK. Glitter it is." I sat silently beside my peaceful little princesses and stroked a teeny hairbrush through the doll's hair.

In some ways, I understood why they did this. It was therapeutic. Repetitive but soothing. It allowed the mind to wander but kept the hands still.

I wasn't sure my mind wandering was a good idea, though. All I could think about was David. The years we'd known each other. The short time we'd dated each other. The last time I'd seen him and his apparent concern for my fate.

I couldn't reconcile the man I knew with the man who was burning down mailboxes. Perhaps, back in college when I first met him, he could have fit that profile. He *did* fit that profile. But had I been working since with a stranger?

I finished the doll's hairstyling, glitter coating my fingernails, too. The sparkles caught the light streaming in through a nearby window. I turned the doll one way and then the other, and then looked at Dani's efforts.

"I think you're better at this than me," I said with a grimace. My doll looked like she'd fit in well on K' Road late at night with the strip clubs and prostitutes and druggies.

"Mummy wasn't very good at it, either," Dani said.

I slowly lowered the doll to the duvet and settled my hands on my lap.

"Did she play with you often?" I asked.

Both girls nodded their heads in unison.

"You must miss her very much," I offered.

Their heads paused as if controlled by the same remote. Their actions in sync in a way that made you believe those studies on twin behaviour. Sometimes they were so different from each other, and then they'd synchronise their movements like this.

"You don't miss her?" I asked casually. My heart beat a little too fast.

"She stopped playing with us," Rachel said.

"When did that happen, darling?"

Rachel looked away, and Dani bit her lip.

"It's all right to say it," I promised. "You won't get in trouble. Sometimes it's better to get it off your chest."

"Hold half the weight," Dani said, quoting her father at a guess.

"That's right," I said. "Well done. Sharing something halves the weight of the thing you're sharing."

Dani just blinked at me. Rachel held her doll close to her chest but stared out of the window at nothing.

Whatever Ivan Marinkovich had done to these girls, he'd done it too bloody well. They were still in his grip, and if I could have faced the man who had tormented them to such a degree, I'm not sure my professionalism would have won out. Not now. Not now that I'd fallen for them. Knew them. Felt their pain along with them.

I'm not a violent person, but I knew if anyone tried to harm these girls again, I would attack first and ask questions later. The desire to physically stand between them and any danger was shocking. I'd never felt such guardianship over anyone before.

It made me wonder what I'd have been like as a parent. A child of my own to protect. It might be too late to have a daughter or son of my own, but I did have Rachel and Dani. Two little girls who had stolen my heart completely.

I would guard them with my life if I had to.

I cleared my throat. "Was it when Mr Marinkovich became your Mummy's friend?"

Rachel turned back to me, a hardness in her eyes that would have caused a lesser psychiatrist to backpedal. I held her stare with an open one of my own and waited.

"He was a very bad man," Dani whispered. "Like the man I saw today."

My head spun as I turned to look at Dani. "You saw him, sweetheart?" I thought she'd just seen the car and the blue lights underneath.

She nodded.

I licked my lips. My pulse racing. If she described David, my heart would break.

"What did he look like, Dani?" I asked.

"Purple," she said, not making any sense at all.

"I thought the car had blue lights underneath?" I queried.

She nodded. "But he had purple hair."

I stared at her, wondering if she had seen things. Then noted the absence of the purple glitter from the stock of hair colouring lined up on the bedside table. I stood up on shaking legs and walked to the corner of the room, peering down into the wastepaper basket.

A lone purple glitter container sat at the bottom of the bin. Discarded.

"Purple," I said.

"I don't like purple anymore," Dani announced. "Just like I don't like pictures on people's skin anymore, either."

Tattoos. She meant tattoos. Like the tattoos on Ivan Marinkovich's arms.

I reached down and picked up the purple hair glitter. "Can I keep this, please?" I asked.

Dani shrugged. Rachel ignored me.

I wanted to tell them it would be all right. I wanted to reassure them as a parent would.

But all I could think was David didn't have purple hair. All I could feel was an astounding sense of relief.

I offered both girls a kiss on the head and walked out.

It wasn't David. It wasn't the man I had shared a business with for almost a decade. It wasn't my friend.

My stalker was back to being nameless. I shouldn't have felt so happy about that.

But I did.

CHAPTER 40

FUCK, IT DIDN'T GET MORE ECLECTIC THAN THAT

MATT

THE BELL JINGLED OVERHEAD AS I ENTERED ALICIA PARSONS' store. I walked past the stuffed sheep, reaching out and stroking one, and found Alicia waiting by her bank of computer screens.

"Boy racers," I said in way of greeting.

"Boy racer cars, to be precise," she offered in return.

How this woman knew so much about Twizel was a mystery I would one day solve. For now, I had to keep her on side. Tread carefully.

Alicia Parsons was very proprietary about her video surveillance efforts. She referred to her videos often as her art. The top quality equipment she possessed was a testament to her dedication. In a small town like Twizel, the souvenir shop boasted at least twenty thousand dollars worth of high-end tech.

One day I'd get a warrant for her bank account records and see just how much the woman was worth.

"What can you tell me about them, Ms Parsons?" I queried.

"They have multiplied," she said without missing a beat.

"Have they now?" I murmured. "How many are we talking about?"

"Four."

The last time I'd pulled over Gribble and his gang, there'd been only three souped-up Subarus. All with underbody blue LED lights.

"And who owns the fourth car?" I mused.

Alicia smiled. "Now that would be telling."

And here we meet the Alicia Parsons' brick wall.

"But you like telling, Ms Parsons," I said.

"No, Senior Sergeant. I like knowing." She waved a hand toward the video screens.

"And what do you *know* about the fourth boy racer car?"

She pursed her lips together. She looked immaculate again today. Soft blonde hair pulled back in a tight twist at the nape. No loose tendrils about a perfectly made up face. Small pearl earrings adorned her ears, a matching choker necklace around her neck. A silk skirt-suit hugged a very well toned body. In red that matched her lipstick and nails.

She was as cold on the outside as Alan Bennet was on the inside. I wondered if that was why they rubbed against each other so much.

"I have one image of the new vehicle," she finally acquiesced. In graceful movements, she had the video up on the centre screen and had it playing. A white WRX streaked past the camera, familiar storefronts across Main Street behind it. The Happy Hour sign at Smokey's was lit up. Blue flashed intermittently beneath the car's body.

For all intents and purposes, it was a replica of Gribble and his mate's cars. No driver could be seen behind the wheel, though. The windows were illegally tinted. Of course.

"That's it," Alicia said, leaving a still image of the new vehicle on the screen for me to stare at. "A new boy racer car."

"When was this taken?"

"Last night."

"And you've not seen it before?"

"I've not filmed it before."

My eyes lifted to her flawless face.

"Why the distinction, Ms Parsons? 'Not filmed it' instead of 'not seen it.' When did you see it?"

"Last night."

"Where did you see it?"

"On the video."

I forced myself not to react. But if wishes were horses, she'd have my hands around her neck, and I'd have a new horse to stall next to Zoro at Red Tussock.

"And where else?"

"Oh," she huffed. "You're no fun anymore, Senior Sergeant. You've figured out all my foibles. I really must mix things up a bit. Perhaps change my name? I hear 'Smith' is a very popular choice these days."

I blinked. "You hear a lot of things."

"Yes. Twizel is a hotbed for gossip."

"But that's just it," I pointed out. "It's gossip."

"Is it? Your teacher is a Smith, correct?"

"Yes." My jaw was aching from how hard I was clenching it.

"Just a curious choice for a surname."

"You don't get to pick your surname, Ms Parsons."

"Don't you? How odd." Was Parsons even hers?

"The boy racers," I repeated, bringing her back on track. "Where else did you see the new car?"

"Outside the library," she said with a small knowing smile. "Next to the new graphic art."

Don't tell me it had been graffitied again.

"Penis?" I guessed.

"The one and only. Well, that's not strictly true. There's been so many."

"And the new car? Wouldn't have got a license plate at all, would you?"

She leant forward, resting her elbows on the shop counter, her suit jacket gaping attractively to show me her assets should I look. I kept my eyes firmly on hers the entire time.

"No licence plate, sorry."

"That seems a gross miscalculation," I commented mildly, enjoying the tightening of skin around her mouth.

"Not everything is as it seems, Senior Sergeant."

Strange, Alan Bennet had said the same thing to me about her.

"Then what is it, Ms Parsons?" I asked.

"The car is new," she said.

I frowned. How is that not as it seems?

"And?" I pressed.

"And what?" she said. Then promptly placed an angry redheaded bobblehead-doll keyring on the counter between us.

On it were the words, *You don't scare me, I'm dating a redhead!*

"For you this time, Senior Sergeant. To keep your morale up."

I let out a little growl.

Alicia Parsons just smiled. "There's plenty more where that came from." I just bet there was.

"If I take it, will you leave me alone?"

"Now, where would the fun be in that?" She laughed throatily and turned her back on me, picking up the remote control for her flying fish camera. "I'll know if you don't use it, Senior Sergeant."

The fish floated over and turned beady eyes on me.

I muttered something unsavoury under my breath, then swiped up the keyring. By the time I reached the door, flying fish in tow, the first few lines of my song were floating through my head. As I stepped out onto the sidewalk, I felt a lot calmer. I stared down at the keyring in my hand and then glared at the fish. I wasn't going to be browbeaten into using a kitschy keyring just because the resident kooky surveillance expert ordered me to do so. I shoved it in my pocket and smiled for the camera. Then headed to my ute.

My cell phone rang as I shut the door on the snooping salmon. I fished it out of my pocket, chuckling at the thought, and answered on the third ring.

"Drake."

"It's not Jenkins," Maggie said down the line. "Dani's just told Liv the arsonist had purple hair."

I slowly reached into my pocket and pulled the keyring out. Maybe Alicia Parsons was right. Liv sure knew how to advance a case.

"Purple, eh?" I said, attaching the keyring to the air vent on the dash.

"You're thinking the Gribble boy?" Maggie guessed.

"Who else could it be?"

"I'm not liking him for this," she admitted. "Well, for *all* of this. Some of it maybe. But we can't forget what's happened in Auckland, and Derek Gribble has been down here the entire time."

I let out a long sigh and started the car. Maggie was right. We couldn't approach this from only one direction. Too many variables already existed. The original photo and message on Liv's office wall. The dead cat on her doorstep in Twizel. The photo from Smokey's in the mailbox, also in Twizel. The Grafton Road offices break-in up north. And the burned out mailbox at Red Tussock.

And now this. Boy racer cars, blue underbody lights, and purple hair.

Fuck, it didn't get more eclectic than that.

CHAPTER 41

THIS IS WHAT MY LIFE HAD COME TO

LIV

My cell phone rang while I was peeling potatoes. I dried my hands off and moved toward where it sat next to the plethora of papers and files and photos on the kitchen table.

Maggie reached it first.

"You might want to let it go to voicemail," she said, noting the name that flashed up on the screen.

David.

"The stalker is not David," I said, stretching out for the phone. Maggie held it just out of reach of my hand.

"We don't know who it is yet."

"David doesn't have purple hair."

"Someone had to be in Auckland to carry out the offences up there."

I hesitated, my hand hanging in the air between us. My stomach somersaulting all over again.

"What are you saying?" I asked.

Maggie sighed and placed the phone down on the table. It rang off. No doubt directing David to voicemail.

"Listen," she said. "I know it's hard to accept it might be him, but he's the best bet we've got. It's personal. He has motive. You've profiled him in the past, and he fits. And he's been in Auckland the entire time."

"But who would he know down here?"

"The tourist."

I'd forgotten about the tourist. "He didn't have purple hair," I pointed out.

"No, but there is someone here who has shown an interest in you who does."

"Gribble."

"Exactly."

"But..."

"Look, Liv. We just don't know right now how this all connects. But we're getting warmer. Trust us to work this out for you. Just..." She grimaced. "Just hold off on returning Jenkins' phone call until we've got a bit more info. All right?"

She couldn't even call him David anymore.

I nodded my head.

Maggie continued to watch me and then started tidying up the table. I returned to the potatoes, my mind whirring.

"Where is David?" I asked, watching her reflection in the glass above the sink.

She paused, her hands stilling over a pile of scattered photos. "Not in Auckland," she finally said.

I spun back around and leant against the bench.

"When did you find that out?"

"Earlier today."

"Why wasn't I told?"

"Matt didn't want you to worry."

I sucked in a breath of air and tried to calm myself. Usually, I could meditate into a relaxed state easily. Even facing off against an agitated patient. Right now, calm was not even remotely possible. I'd have to settle for sane instead.

"He's here," I guessed.

"We think so."

"I see." That's why he was still a suspect. "He did tell me he was going to visit," I pointed out.

"Hmm-mm," Maggie said.

"It can't be him," I muttered.

"Come on, doc," Maggie said cajolingly. "Is that the psychiatrist talking or the woman?"

I turned back to the potatoes and scrubbed one hard enough to gouge flesh off in the sink. My movements were jerky, and frustration made me breathe too fast. I watched as my knuckles turned whiter and whiter, while I gripped the vegetable in my fist.

I was on a rollercoaster, and I couldn't seem to get off. First I think it's him. Then I think it's not. And then Maggie confuses everything.

"We'll figure this out, Liv," Maggie said quietly. "It'll be OK."

"Is that the police officer talking or the woman?" I said.

"Touché," she whispered and scooped up her photos, walking out of the room.

I stared into the darkness gathering outside the window and wondered when this merry-go-round would stop. When this fairground attraction would slow down enough for me to think. To breathe. To just work it all out.

So many different suspects and still we couldn't figure out who had decided to stalk me. I knew so much about personality disorders. About mental illnesses and psychosis. I knew how stalkers behaved and how their patterns cycled. But I couldn't, for the life of me, work out who it was.

If it was David then what would he do next? First, a stalker will try to prove how much *they* love you. Then they progress to believing they can make *you* love them. And when that fails, they resort to death threats. *If I can't have you, nobody can.*

We'd made it to the death threats. Sure, he'd threatened Matt's life not mine.

The promise is broken. Your word is dead. Should he be?

But it all meant the same. My stalker had reached the end of the line. He could regress, that wasn't uncommon in such cases. And there was no way of knowing when he'd strike again, regression or not. But he'd progressed through enough stages now to warrant serious thought.

Hell, he'd warranted serious thought back when Detectives Pierce and Stone had sent me down here. Killing animals was a precursor to killing human beings. We all knew this.

But what promise had I broken? A doctor/patient promise? Or something more personal? Something else that only he perceived. He'd sent me flowers and cards in the beginning. Little trinkets and friendship bracelets. Told me I was beautiful and so very clever. Put me on a pedestal and then pulled me back down again afterwards.

The knife was cold. You never said it would be so cold. The blood was warm. You were right.

When had I ever discussed blood and knives with David? I shook my head.

My cell phone rang again, vibrating softly on the table top. I looked toward the doorway, but Maggie didn't come running. I doubted she'd left already; Maggie was my babysitter. But was she close enough to hear?

I stepped over to the table and picked the cell up, silencing the ring tone and staring at the screen. David again.

Was he really here? Had he come?

Damn it, he was my friend, first and foremost. He was my colleague, my business partner. I owed him at least that.

I swiped the call open and pressed the cell to my ear.

"Hello?"

"Hey, country bumpkin! You're not home."

So many feelings stormed through my body. Relief that he

sounded just like he usually did. Worry that he was indeed here in Twizel. Fear that he was chasing me down.

"Hey," I said, struggling to sound normal.

"Everything all right, Olivia?" he asked. "I thought I'd surprise you."

He'd done that.

"Although, I did hint I was coming to visit, didn't I?"

"Yes, you did," I managed.

"Well, surprise! I'm here, and you're not. Come on, floss." Floss. He'd called me that at uni. "Where are you? I'm famished. Let's grab some grub."

"Grub?" I said on a fragile laugh. "Since when do you call food 'grub'?"

"Duh," he said in exaggerated tones. "I am in Bumfuck Twizel."

"You sound different," I said.

"So do you," he replied. "Where are you, Olivia?" That was more demand.

I shouldn't have answered the phone. Just like Maggie had warned me not to. I shouldn't have opened up a dialogue. It only encouraged him.

"I'm out of town, David," I said, strictly not a lie. "You'll have to find your own accommodation for the night."

Silence. Then the staticky sound of wailing, as if in the distance.

"I can see why you'd move out," he muttered. "Damn place is as busy as Grafton."

I frowned at the floor, just as Maggie came in, crossed her arms over her chest, and stared me down.

"I've got to go," I said, but David didn't reply. I'm not sure he could hear me; the wailing had become more distinct. Sirens. They were police car sirens.

"Oh, holy shit," David muttered. "I, ah, have to go," he added. Then the line went dead.

A radio on the side of Maggie's hip beeped twice. Then a voice I recognised came out of the speaker.

"TZ1. Comms. 10-7. POI apprehended. Over."

"POI?" I said.

"Person of interest," Maggie replied steadily.

"Matt's arresting David."

Maggie sighed. I felt like crying.

This was what my life had come to. Betrayal from all sides.

CHAPTER 42

PUNCHING HIM WASN'T GOOD ENOUGH

MATT

He was good looking. If you went for that sort of thing. And I guess at one stage Liv did because she'd dated him. His hair was cut short and styled with some sort of product. His jaw was smoothly shaven as if he'd done so just before turning up on Liv's doorstep. His cologne was subtle not cloying. Expensive. And his clothes cost more than my monthly paycheque.

I hated him on sight.

"You want me to interview him?" Mac asked at my side. We were both standing outside the one interview room at the station. No two-way mirror here. We stared at the suspect - and damned if I'd call him anything else - through a small window high up on the door to the room.

"No."

Mac didn't say anything for a few seconds, but I knew he was bursting to.

Then, "It'd be good experience for Annmarie."

"Since when do you go out of your way for Annmarie?"

"She's my trainee," he argued, bristling.

I just grunted.

"Fine. Annmarie can observe. But you shouldn't lead on this."

I turned my head slowly and looked Mac hard in the eyes. He had his sunglasses on. It was night. We were inside. But the lights were bright. Mac suffered from photophobia. A concussion based injury from his youth. Not many people knew about it. He was cagey. Hell, Mac was a cagey bastard regardless. But the shades at night under bright lights was a dead giveaway.

He was having a bad day.

"Headache?" I asked.

His turn to grunt.

"Annmarie can sit in with me," I said.

"Fuck that."

I sighed. "I really don't have time to deal with your relationship issues with your trainee. Get your shit together, take a paracetamol, and watch through the door. Annmarie tags on this."

"Where's Maggie?"

"With Liv."

He sighed. "Dim the lights in there," he murmured, "and I can sit in. Or, you know, just stand at the back of the room and look threatening in my glasses."

I snorted. "This isn't a movie." I sighed. "Mac, just go get Annmarie."

He muttered under his breath and stormed off in the direction of the bullpen. I continued to watch David Jenkins.

He hadn't been driving a white car. Let alone a white WRX with underbody LED lights. And his hair, of course, was not purple. We needed to bring Derek Gribble in and put a notice out on the description of the car. Maggie had been checking up on the NZTA from Red Tussock, trying to locate a vehicle registered that matched. But boy racers weren't just a Twizel problem. There was a shitload of white WRX Subarus out there.

I stared at the stoic figure of Liv's business partner. At a man she had been intimate with and who could now be trying to harm her. And I tried to distance myself from the rage both thoughts caused. A few bars sounded out inside my head from my favourite song, but the words and tune failed to calm my nerves.

I was jumpy, agitated, and fucking riled. And about to step into an interview room with a rookie cop and a cat killing stalker after my woman.

Annmarie walked up, cautious but standing tall. She had more courage than Mac realised. Fuck, she needed big balls to deal with his shit every day.

"Constable," I said in greeting.

"Senior Sergeant," she replied.

"You won't need to say anything in there, just observe. And if I get off track, clear your throat or something."

"I've interviewed suspects before," she replied steadily.

"Yeah? At Porirua?" That's where the Royal New Zealand Police College was. They would have simulated interviews such as this in her training.

"No, sir. My father was a cop, remember?"

Yeah, I remembered. I nodded for her to go on.

"I helped him out on occasion."

"Before you qualified," I guessed.

She looked away. "I always knew I'd become a cop. He knew it, too."

I sighed and looked back in the room at the suspect. "I'm sure he taught you well, Constable."

"He did, sir," she said quietly. I was pretty sure Annmarie's natural state was not quiet. She might not have been a redhead like Liv, but there was something behind those piercing blue eyes that made you think she wanted to be.

"Let's do this," I muttered, unlocking the door and entering the room.

"I'd like a lawyer," Jenkins said before we'd even sat down. Fucking TV.

"Mr Jenkins, I'm Senior Sergeant Matt Drake. This is Constable Antil. We just want to talk."

"Am I under arrest?" he demanded as Annmarie and I took our seats.

"Not yet."

"Then either charge me or let me go." It wasn't unusual for a suspect, innocent or not, to come out on the offensive. But the more this guy did it, the more I wanted to plant my fist in his face.

"Just questions for now," I offered. "Nothing to worry about."

"You say that, but I saw the way your hands shook when you cuffed me, Senior Sergeant. Either you've got a neurodegenerative condition, or you're suffering from a lot of stress."

"Interesting diagnosis," I commented.

"Oh, that's not a diagnosis. That was an observation. You wouldn't like my diagnosis, should I make one."

"Is that a threat, Mr Jenkins?"

"I'd like a lawyer."

I sighed, tapping the folder I'd been carrying on the table top. I dropped it down, flipped it open, and fished out one of the photographs taken by Detective Sergeant Pierce.

I pushed the photo towards him.

"Do you recognise this?"

He stared down at the image of Liv's office wall; with the blown up picture of her outside her house covered in cat blood.

His eyes came up to mine, and he said nothing.

"What about this?" I asked, pulling a second photo out of the folder. This one of the picture of Liv and me at Smokey's.

"I've never seen that before in my life," he said, staring at the image as if he could make it move. Make it show him what we'd done. What we'd said. How we'd interacted with each other.

Jealousy was written all over his face. And then he schooled his features and slowly sat back in his chair.

"Lawyer," he said succinctly.

"You really want to go down that path?" I asked. He glared back. "This is Olivia Logan we're talking about. Your friend, business partner," I paused. "Ex-lover."

A slow smile curved his lips. Knowing and amused. Definitely amused.

"You don't like that, do you, Senior Sergeant?" he said. "I understand the shaking of the hands now. Not a neurological disease. Adrenaline dump. You were angry. You're angry now." He nodded towards my hands, gripping the folder too tightly. "I bet all you want to do is cross this table and throw a punch. Make me pay. Get rid of me, so you don't have competition."

"You're not competition."

"I've known Olivia a long time. Longer than you. I know what makes her tick. What makes her laugh. What makes her drink too much gin."

I stared at him, wanting nothing more than to do exactly what he'd predicted. I could feel the ache in my knuckles from the impending hit. Smell the scent of blood as it splattered.

David Jenkins started laughing. It grew in volume and mirth. His whole body shook, and he wiped at his eyes, dramatically.

"Poor, poor country copper," he whispered. "She is so far out of your league, and you haven't even realised it. Wake up! It's called slumming it, Senior Sergeant. Every once in a while, a woman feels the need to get down and dirty with a blue collar cock. Something about the lack of inhibitions. But they soon wake up. Olivia will wake up, too."

"You have a very poor opinion of women, Mr Jenkins. I'm thinking a poor opinion of Olivia, as well."

He said nothing, just stared. There was something not quite right about David Jenkins. Hell, if Liv were here right now, I'd bet my stake in Red Tussock she'd profile him, and he'd match our perp.

"Why are you here in Twizel, Mr Jenkins?" I asked.

"Visiting an old friend. Trying to cheer her up. She's been feeling a bit down having to stay here."

Every fibre in my body wanted to strike. I leant forward. Jenkins smirked.

Mac's loud knock on the door made my heart lurch. I turned and glared at my senior constable.

"Word, sir?" he said, acting it up for the suspect. I nodded, pushed up from my seat, and gathered the folder and photos.

"Hang tight, Mr Jenkins. We're not done."

"Law-y-er," he said, annunciating each syllable slowly.

I didn't reply, just moved toward the door. Annmarie hot on my tail. Just as I pushed it open fully to step through, Annmarie turned around and looked Jenkins in the eye.

Then said, "Do you like dogs, Mr Jenkins? Bitches?"

What the fuck?

He blinked. "I'm a cat person," he said, shaking his head, bemused.

Annmarie nodded, then walked out the door, three pairs of male eyes on the confident swing of her hips.

The lock clicked shut behind us as I crossed my arms over my chest and stared her down.

"What the hell was that?"

"Vulgarity from the good little policewoman who remained silent during the entirety of the interview throws them," she said, matter-of-factly. "Nine times out of ten they answer with their gut. Knee jerk reaction type of thing."

"Who are you and what have you done with Annmarie?" Mac asked.

I ignored him. "And the point here, Constable?" I asked. "That man is psychotic. I don't need Liv's psychology degree to see that."

"Maybe," Annmarie said. "But he likes cats."

"Cats?" Mac pressed.

I saw what she was getting at.

"Nice try, Annmarie," I offered, not unkindly. "But a person can kill things they like. It's called passion."

She lowered her head and glowered at the ground, a flush rising up her cheeks.

Great. Now I was taking out my adrenaline dumped anger on the staff.

Annmarie looked up at me and said, "But do stalkers?"

She had me there. Passionate crimes were opportunist crimes.

I looked back in the room and stared at Jenkins. Who stared back with a soft smile.

Punching him wasn't good enough.

But I wasn't entirely sure he deserved to die.

CHAPTER 43

THEN LIGHTS OUT

LIV

THE LANDLINE RINGING ROUSED ME FROM MY SNOOZE ON THE couch. Maggie blinked open her eyes and stretched in the armchair opposite. The wall mounted clock ticked away loudly, somehow managing to compete with the shrill ringing of the phone.

"You getting that or me?" Maggie asked on a yawn.

The only people who used the landline were Joshua and Catherine. And that was to phone out. Everyone else used cell phones to stay in touch. The guest cottage was low tech, but obviously, according to Mrs Drake, landlines didn't count.

I stood up and crossed the room, lifting the handset up.

"Red Tussock Guest House," I said into the device.

"Hello, Red Tussock Guest House," a male's cheery voice greeted. "This is your neighbour at Craggy Range to the west. Name's Devon McIntyre. Would Matt be about?"

"Ah, he's not here right now, Mr McIntyre. Can I take a message?"

"You alone, love?" he asked. I stilled. Maggie sat forward and frowned at me.

I covered the mouthpiece and said, "Devon McIntyre at Craggy Range Station asking for Matt."

Her eyebrows rose, and she pushed up off the seat. Holding her hand out for the phone, she said, "I know him."

She didn't reassure me, and I liked that about Maggie. She knew as well as me that this could be something else. Someone pretending to be a friendly neighbour.

"Devon," she said into the phone a second later. "Maggie Blackmore. What can I do for you?"

I moved closer and pressed my ear to the back of the phone. Maggie didn't object.

"You sure do get around, Sergeant," he drawled. "Had enough of your boyfriend yet? Ready to try out a real man?"

Maggie smiled, her whole body relaxing. I hadn't realised it had been so tight. Clearly, McIntyre had passed some sort of test. I didn't move away, though. He'd phoned here for Matt, and I wanted to know why.

"Not yet, Devon. But you're top of my list should I change my mind," Maggie said.

"Woman's prerogative," McIntyre said. Maggie smiled. "Listen," he went on immediately, all joviality gone from his voice. "I couldn't get hold of Matt on his cell."

"He's busy," Maggie hedged. "What's up?"

"I heard he was staying at the guest house. You know I can see it from my place?"

"I didn't," Maggie offered, apparently wanting McIntyre to get to the point.

"Just come home from a volunteer call out, and I spotted some lights where they shouldn't be."

"What sort of lights?" Maggie asked slowly. She also instinctively reached for her gun on her hip.

A chill raced down my spine, and I darted my eyes around the lounge. Checking the windows. Straining my ears. Trying to listen for sounds.

But McIntyre started talking again.

"Damnedest thing," he said. "Not only were they where they shouldn't be. But they were blue."

"Blue," Maggie said, her hand twitching. "Where were they exactly, Devon?"

"Behind the guest house. Down the old access way used for sectors six through nine. Now, I know those Drake boys don't use that particular road anymore, there's a better one coming in from sector five. Hell, last I heard it was all grown over. So, whoever is out there is likely to get their car stuck. But Maggie," he said. "Someone *is* out there, and they're heading towards the back of the guest cottage."

"How long have we got?'

"Minutes, sweetheart. I'll call 111."

"You do that," Maggie agreed. "We'll head out."

"Where to?" McIntyre asked.

"The homestead. It's close to here and Luke's at home."

"Once I've got ahold of your colleagues, I'll come up from behind along that old track."

"Don't do anything stupid, McIntyre," Maggie growled. "We'll be gone in sixty seconds as it is."

"Maggie," he said, chuckling. "I'm the local fire chief. I know how to swing a big axe."

"Devon," Maggie groaned just as the sound of glass breaking reached our ears. "Damn it," she muttered. "You're sweet talking's cost us. They're here."

She placed the phone down on the cradle quietly and lifted a finger to her lips.

"The girls," I whispered.

"I know," she mouthed back, worry etched across her wide-eyed face.

She crouch-walked over to the hallway, placing her back against the wall. Her gun was out. Determination stared out of her eyes. She signalled for me to get down. I lowered myself to a crouch beside the sofa, but I didn't move behind it as her nodded head advised.

She waited a second, maybe two, and then rounded the corner into the hallway out of sight.

My heart pounded. I could feel the rattle of my ribs. A buzzing had started up in my ears. I strained to hear any sound from the back of the house. From where the twins were sleeping. No noise sounded out and the longer it took for something to happen, the more agitated I became.

I practised a few breathing exercises to contain the effect of the adrenaline surging through my veins. Slowing my breaths down helped, but my heart rate only lowered a fraction.

If anything happened to Rachel or Dani...

I looked around the lounge frantically for a weapon of my own. Plastic chess pieces sat out on the coffee table where Maggie and I had attempted to pass the time. A couple of hardback books leant against dogeared paperbacks behind me on the shelf, along with various stacked boardgames. A Rubik's Cube, its sides a mismatch of primary colours, was closest, so I picked it up. The corners were pointy, but hardly lethal. Still, I clutched it like a lifeline.

Then I crawled toward the doorway, trying to make no sound.

The lack of noise coming from where the glass had shattered was a good thing, I thought. Maybe an animal had made something fall over outside, and it had hit the window in the bathroom, breaking it. Maybe we'd laugh about this around a coffee in the kitchen in half an hour.

Maybe the blue lights McIntyre had seen were something else. Something unexplainable. A mystery. Not what my whirring brain was trying to tell me they were.

I paused at the doorway, listening, breathing through my mouth. No sounds. Nothing. So I stepped out like Maggie had stepped out. Rounding the corner, Rubik's Cube up like she'd held up her gun. Double handed, elbows locked. Face hard.

Something moved.

Fabric covered my mouth.

I dropped the Rubik's Cube, my fingers scrabbling, nails biting into skin.

A sharp breath. A hard grip around my waist. Then teeth bit into my ear, making me cry out.

Crying out meant I breathed in. And within seconds sounds distorted. Lights flickered.

And a sickly sweet smelling scent drifted down my nasal passage directly to my lungs.

One deep breath and the world faded.

The last thing I saw was a splash of colour.

Purple, my numbed brain told me. Purple not blue, but it was bad enough.

Then lights out.

CHAPTER 44

OOH RAH

MATT

I stared down at the Rubik's Cube on the hardwood floor, my blood pumping.

"I was checking on the girls," Maggie said, sounding strained.

But then everything sounded strained right now.

"I'm so sorry, Matt," she said earnestly. "The front door was locked, but he picked it. Fucking picked it while I was checking out the broken glass."

"A distraction," Mac offered. "Needed you away from the target long enough to pounce."

"The target has a name," I growled.

"Sorry," Mac mumbled.

I shook my head to clear it. "Did you see anything?" I asked Maggie.

"Just the rock on the floor in the bathroom. No lights outside. Once I'd checked the girls and the back of the house, and then found Liv was gone and the front door open, I went outside and spotted the cut wires to the security lights. If he acted alone, he moved fucking fast."

"He wasn't alone," I said. "More than one set of footprints in the gardens." They'd looked inside the girls' bedroom.

My hand came up and covered my mouth. Bile surged up my throat. I swallowed thickly.

"The old access way to sectors six through nine," Maggie said, drawing my attention. "They used that to get near the house. Devon McIntyre was going to track them from his place. He might know more."

I pulled my cell out, but the call went to voicemail when I dialled Devon's phone number.

"Annmarie and I'll head out onto the state highway," Mac said. "See if there's any indication of them having made it back out."

I nodded.

"We'll get her back, Matt," he promised. A promise he knew damn well he shouldn't have made. He looked toward his recruit, a silent communication shared between them, and then they walked out. Mac's ute started up, and he gunned it, headlights sweeping across the front of the house.

"I'll call Luke," Maggie said after the light faded. "Let him know what's happened."

I nodded again, staring at the fucking Rubik's Cube on the floor.

She'd picked it up. Tried to use it as a weapon. And failed. I reached down and gingerly lifted the puzzle off the floor, finger and thumb holding the edges. There was no sign of it having met flesh. And I was sure the only fingerprints I'd find on it were Liv's and whoever else had last picked it up and not solved it.

I brought it to my nose and closed my eyes at the faint scent of chemicals coming from it. Chloroform. They'd knocked her out.

My hand fisted around the Cube and then I threw it. A pointy corner embedded itself into the drywall across the lounge. Maggie stopped talking into her phone and blinked at me. I stormed past her and went towards the girls.

They were awake; I could tell. Pretending to be asleep. Little chests rising and falling too swiftly under their covers.

"Hey," I said, turning on the bedside lamp. A soft yellow glow infused the room. "It's all right. I'm here."

Nothing. Just silence. I struggled to contain my emotions. To stop the rage, that was building up inside. My fingers tingled. My neck and shoulders ached. I could hear my teeth as they ground against each other, pain sparking along my jaw.

"Everything's gonna be OK," I said with such effort I wasn't sure if it cost me something. Something from deep down inside. As if the attempt to rein in my wildly raging emotions required a part of my soul to carry out.

"Where's Liv?" Dani asked.

I couldn't answer. I couldn't fucking lie to my kid. But I also couldn't scare her either. I just sat there, like a fucking imbecile. A delinquent father who'd allowed their mother to get hurt.

Liv wasn't their mother, but she could be. She wanted to be. I wanted her to be. They'd already lost one, and now I'd let another fall into danger.

Anger, like I'd never experienced, rose up my gullet, until the need to scream almost won out. My hand fisted Dani's duvet cover. Sweat ran down my spine. I was breathing too damn fast.

"Count them, Daddy," Rachel said. "We can help."

They both sat up, Rachel even climbing out of her bed, little knobbly knees knocking as she crossed the rug to place a small hand on my shoulder. Dani shifted, scurrying along the bed until she could cup my other one as well

"One-popsicle. Two-popsicle. Three-popsicle," Dani said, the words themselves belying the seriousness of her little voice.

"No, Daddy," Rachel scolded. "You hold it while Dani counts."

"One-popsicle. Two-popsicle. Three-popsicle."

"Now, slowly breath out while she counts again," Rachel ordered.

"One-popsicle. Two-popsicle..." I started to smile. Then I started to cry. Silent tears, but still. I reached for both my girls and pulled them into my arms, holding them carefully against my chest.

"I'm OK," I said. "I'm fine." I was so far from fine, but it didn't matter. I had two beautiful, precious daughters, who were going to be all right. And one gorgeous woman I was in love with, who I was damn well going to get back in one piece before sun-up.

Promises. They tell you not to make them in Police College. To the public. To the family of a victim.

But they never said anything about making them to yourself.

"I've got work to do, baby-girls," I said. "But thank you, so much. You're going to make very good doctors one day."

"Just like Liv," Rachel said, smiling broadly. She'd lost a tooth, I noticed. When had she lost a tooth?

I looked toward Dani who offered me a grin. Full set of chompers.

"I love you both so much," I said, voice scratchy.

"We know, Daddy," Dani said.

"Just wanted to say it," I rasped.

"Go get Liv," Rachel ordered.

"Tell her," Dani added.

"Tell her what?" I asked.

The girls looked at each other and then looked at me; identical looks of incredulity on their faces.

"The same thing, silly," Rachel scolded.

"That you love her, too," Dani explained.

"Cheeky monkeys," I growled, going in for the best tickle spots.

Squeals sounded out just as fast feet clattered into the room. I looked over a giggling Dani to Mum.

"We came as soon as we heard," she said breathlessly.

"Where do you need us?" Luke asked over her shoulder.

"Zach and Justin are on their bikes," Dad advised from behind him. "Waiting for the signal."

I gave my girls one last hug, as Mum moved in to replace me, and stood up.

OK, showtime.

"Zach goes north to sector six, approaching from that direction," I said. "Justin heads directly across to the old road, following their tracks. Luke," I added, coming abreast of my oldest brother, "get ahold of Devon McIntyre. Find out what he knows and where he is."

"On it," he said, spinning on his feet and starting to issue orders to Zach and Justin who were standing at the front door.

I looked at my father, for a second allowing all the fear and rage to show.

"Go get her, son," he said quietly, but no less proudly. He clapped me on the back. "You were made for this. Those bastards don't know who they're up against. Forged in fire," he growled. "Battle-hardened in a storm. No one messes with Red Tussock."

"*Ooh-rah*," my brothers said as if they were damn Marines.

I let out a shaky breath of air, so thankful for my family. We could do this. We could get Liv back in one piece.

But if David Jenkins was still in custody at Twizel Police Station, who the hell was pulling the boy racers' strings?

CHAPTER 45

AND THEN SILENCE

LIV

BICKERING FILTERED IN THROUGH MY FOGGY BRAIN. THE urgent, frantic words distorted for several seconds. My neck hurt. My ear hurt. It hurt to breathe. I kept my breaths shallow and tired to open my eyes. Nothing registered, but despite the pounding in my earlobe, I could hear perfectly.

"I told you this was a stupid idea!" a male voice said somewhere in front of me.

"Not like we had much choice," another male voice grumbled from beside me.

"Shut up and get out and push, you dickheads!" yet another male voice - that made three - this one, though, seemed familiar.

"Why should we push? Why not you?"

"Because, duh! I'm driving."

"Yeah, well, you're the one who drove us into this ditch!"

"It's not a fucking ditch, you moron! It's a clump of grass, stuck under my fucking car. And if it's knocked the LEDs off, I'll go fucking mental."

"Not like you're not fucking mental already."

"Jeez! Just get out and push already or we'll still be sitting here when the senior sergeant finds us."

I sucked in a breath of air at Matt's title. Clarity slow to return, but the fog was lifting.

A door opened, the fresh scent of farm pastures met my stinging nose, and someone muttered, "Rather the senior sergeant than that other fucking psycho."

My bound hands landed on the soft fabric of a car seat between my thighs. I blinked my eyes, my head spinning, the lights on the car's dashboard wavering slightly, and then slowly the driver came into focus.

Purple mohawk and a nose ring.

"Gribble," I slur-mumbled.

"Shit!" he exclaimed, jumping in his seat. "You're meant to be out for the count."

I blinked several more times, tears threatening to run down my cheeks, and then his pale face came into focus.

"What are you doing?" I asked.

"What am I doing?" he repeated back to me.

Nothing made sense. Derek Gribble was a young guy with too much testosterone and a penchant for flirting. He had not appeared psychotic in the slightest to me.

"Why am I here, Gribble?" I asked.

"Just go back to sleep, S6o," he muttered, revving the engine of the car.

"It's stuck!" a voice announced at the driver's window. Wide blue eyes met mine. "Fuck, she's looking at me. Should she be looking at me? What if she tells someone who I am?"

"You think it really matters now?" Gribble asked dryly. I didn't know he had it in him to be sarcastic.

"But she's looking at me!" Then to me, "Stop looking at me!"

"What's your name?" I asked.

"Now she's asking me my name!" the young guy said. He couldn't have been much older than twenty. The same age as

Gribble at a guess. Probably been friends since high school, got into mischief together over at Lake Ruataniwha growing up. Raced their souped-up cars against each other as soon as they got their driver's licenses. Progressed to killing cats and stalking psychiatrists.

Nope. Still didn't make any sense.

"Did David make you do this?" I asked.

"I can hear motorbikes," the third guy announced, also staring into the car directly at me. "We need to go."

"Leave the car?" the guy standing beside Gribble's window suggested.

"Would you leave your car if it was the one stuck here?" Gribble demanded.

"Come on," the third guy said, returning to the rear of the vehicle to give it another shove.

The second guy just kept staring at me. "Should we dose her again?"

Gribble turned around in his seat and looked me in the eye. "You gonna behave, S60?"

I was sitting in the rear of the car behind the front passenger seat. My seatbelt had been secured, my hands tied, my legs still a little shaky. I could have attempted to make a run for it. I probably would have accomplished a few metres as well. But three strapping young men on a mission didn't improve my odds.

"What are you doing, Gribble?" I repeated. No, my only shot was to reason with them. "You're not going to get away with this," I said. "Those motorbikes you heard?" I looked at the guy still standing at the driver's side door. His face was growing whiter by the second. "They were probably the Drake brothers. Mounting up, about to come after you. You think Matt Drake will let this lie? You think he hasn't already figured out you're involved?"

"He doesn't know nothing," the guy leaning in the window said.

"He doesn't know *anything*," I automatically corrected. Argh! I was grammar nazi-ing my kidnappers. I shook my head, attempting to get the last vestiges of whatever they'd 'dosed' me with to clear from my hazy mind.

I sucked in a deep breath, black spots appearing before my eyes, and tried to still my racing heartbeat.

"Gribble," I said. "This isn't like you."

"How do you know what I'm like?" he asked.

"I know things," I said, feeling tired all of a sudden. "I'm a good judge of character."

He snorted. "Teaching mute kids make you something special?"

"I'm a doctor," I said without preamble. "A psychiatrist. And I'm telling you now, Gribble; you don't fit the profile."

"What profile?" the guy standing outside said.

"A stalker's profile. A cat killer's profile. An abductor's profile. Someone's put you up to this."

"Fucking hell," the guy outside said. "Cat killer?"

"Shut up, Tyrone," Gribble muttered. "Just push the damn car. Those bikes are getting closer."

Gribble gave me one last perturbed look and revved the engine when the men outside grunted as they pushed. The car tyres skidded. Mud flew up in an arc alongside the car, and then the vehicle fish-tailed as it sprang free from whatever had trapped it.

"Finally," Gribble muttered.

"Don't do this," I murmured. "You take me away from Red Tussock, there's no going back. You can still make this right," I promised. "Matt will listen to reason. But if you do this..."

"Shut the fuck up," Tyrone said as he slid into the backseat, and then he reached out and punched me on the side of my jaw.

Pain like I'd never felt before shot up to the top of my skull, and then settled deep inside my jaw as I cupped it.

I made a sound, Gribble swore blue murder, and then the third guy started yelling as well. My head spun, nausea welled up inside my gut; it would serve these imbeciles right if I puked all over their 'ride'. Tears blurred my eyes, but I could still see the headlights driving towards us.

Panic warred with relief as I contemplated what fresh hell could be arriving. It wasn't coming from the guest house, that, I think, was to the east of here. It wasn't coming from farther up the old road we were on. But towards us, from where I could only assume was Gribble's escape out of here.

Gribble may not have fit the profile of my stalker, but that didn't mean being cornered wouldn't make him lash out. His friend, Tyrone, had just proved how fired up and scared these boys were. My reasoning with them had been threat enough requiring a swift punch to silence.

What would this new threat make these boys do?

The car skidded to a stop a few metres away, and someone got out of the driver's side door. It was hard to tell what the vehicle was, but the headlights seemed high off the ground, and the brief shadow of the person getting out as the dashboard lights lit him up seemed large.

"Who the fuck is that?" Tyrone asked, peering through the front seats.

"Is it the senior sergeant?" the third still nameless guy asked.

"Nah," Gribble said, making the two boys with him relax marginally. "That's the fire chief."

"Mr McIntyre?" Tyrone asked.

It hit me then, how young these boys were. They might be men in age, by law, but they were still country boys at heart, who'd been raised in a small town and called everyone by their title. Mr McIntyre. Ms Ruka. Senior Sergeant Drake.

What the hell had they got themselves into?

"You boys step on out of the car," Mr McIntyre said. I was guessing this was Devon McIntyre, from Craggy Range Station next door to Red Tussock. "Come on now; you've had your fun."

Gribble revved his engine.

"What are we gonna do?" Tyrone asked, his voice very close to a whine now.

"Don't be an idiot, Derek Gribble," McIntyre called out. "Do you really want me to tell your mum what you've been up to?"

Gribble leant out of his window and yelled, "Back away, Mr McIntyre. I don't want to hurt you."

I held my breath, and then thought, to hell with this and reached for my door.

Tyrone yelled something and slammed his body into mine, the guy in the front passenger seat squeaked and turned around to help. Gribble shouted out a war cry. And then we were lurching forward, the souped-up Subaru engine making a high pitched roar, the tyres spinning, mud flying, headlights shining right into Devon McIntyre's eyes.

He stood his ground. Legs spread wide; arms crossed over broad chest, determination like a pit bull staring Gribble down.

It was a poor excuse for a game of chicken. Everyone knows young men with too much testosterone, poor limbic control, and pre-frontal-cortex shutdowns don't think wisely when put under extreme pressure. Add in a ton and a half of car and one resolute farmer, and you've got an imbalance that rivals teenage hormones.

"No!" I cried out, as Tyrone cuffed me a second time on the side of my head. Gribble kept yelling his war cry; hands battered at me as I battered futilely back, and the sound of a body hitting a bumper filled the air.

Glass crunched, the car shuddered, a thud and thump followed.

And then silence. Inside the car and out, as we tore out of Red Tussock.

CHAPTER 46

FEELING PANICKED

MATT

I was breathless by the time I made it to Justin's side. The headlights of Devon's ute and Justin's motorbike flooded the area with a harsh white light. But I didn't need illumination to know this was bad.

"The ambulance is coming," Justin said, holding Devon's blood-soaked hand in his trembling one. His knees were dug deep into the dirt beside Devon's twisted and broken body as if my brother had run here from dismounting his bike, and thrown himself to the ground beside our friend. Dirt splattered his jeans; mud coated his arms. His face was pure white.

I rubbed a hand over my mouth, noticing my fingers were trembling as well, and took the final steps necessary to reach their sides.

"Devon," I said, his name a sharp breath of air that hurt my lungs.

He offered up a blood coated toothy smile and said on a splutter, "Fucking shits."

"Don't talk," Justin remonstrated.

"Fucking WRX on farm roads," Devon added. Blood dribbled out of the side of his lips. "Not so pristine now, eh?"

I sank to my knees on the other side of Devon's body from Justin, not sure if I should touch him, reassure him, or like my brother, tell him to shut up and conserve his energy. His arm on this side was broken. Open fracture, the bone poking out of torn flesh. My eyes catalogued the oblique angle of his left shin, the swelling of his right thigh, the uneven lean to his hips.

Blood matted his hair, little shards of safety glass embedded in his forehead. His nose was crooked. A rattled breath of air shook his chest, his face grimacing. The ground was wet, soaking into my trousers. I was unsure if it was mud or something else.

"You bloody idiot," I said, my heart aching. "Why the hell didn't you jump put of the way?"

Justin shot me an accusatory glare, but Devon just chuckled; a gurgling sound that acted as both death rattle and laughter.

"No hyped up boy racer is gonna scare me."

"Jesus," Justin muttered, barely keeping his shit together.

But a calmness settled over me.

"They won't get away with this, Devon," I vowed.

"They had her," he whispered, his words hard to hear in amongst the harsh effort required to breathe. "Three of 'em, Matt. Had your woman."

"I know who they are," I growled.

"Gribble's car," the fucking idiot said, trying to give me intel before he passed out. Before he passed completely.

"I know," I said. "They'll pay for taking her and for this."

"Always knew," Devon said, sucking in air and failing miserably. "You'd sort your shit out."

"Devon," I said, reaching for his shoulder, gripping it as hard as I dared.

His eyes turned glassy. Justin made a hitched sound. Noises and scents disappeared. Just this.

Just this moment on a back road of Red Tussock, impotently watching someone I knew as they died.

"Can't see," he whispered.

"We're here," both Justin and I said. God this hurt.

"Tell Luke," he started, then coughed up blood. "Tell him," more blood. And Justin's tears.

I couldn't cry. Not yet. Not with Liv out there and Gribble and his gang at large. I couldn't give in to the pain. Not yet.

"Tell Luke," Devon tried again. Both Justin and I leant closer.

"Tell him what?" Justin asked, gripping Devon's hand too tightly. Devon didn't feel a thing.

"Tell him my wool is better."

He smiled. Blood pooled. A rumble unlike anything I'd ever heard rattled up his chest.

Then Devon McIntyre of Craggy Range Station, my neighbour, my friend, the local fire chief for the volunteer fire service, died. Right there. In front of us. On our land.

Justin choked out a sound and stumbled backwards, his eyes too wide, his face too pale, and then he leant over and retched.

I knelt in the mud and blood feeling stunned. Feeling wrecked. Feeling panicked.

If Derek Gribble could do this, what would he do to Liv?

CHAPTER 47

THIS IS TWIZEL

LIV

"Oh, fuck! Oh, fuck! Oh, fuck! You hit him!"

"You fucking knocked me, and I couldn't turn the steering wheel in time."

"You hit him! You hit him! You hit him! This is bad!"

"I fucking know, all right! You fucking made me do it!"

"I did not make you do it. You're the one fucking driving."

"You fell against me," Gribble wailed, the car fishtailing in the dirt. "What the fuck were you doing?"

"Helping Ty!"

"I didn't need your fucking help, Trent!"

"She was halfway out the door!" Trent yelled back. "You almost lost her!"

"Shut up!" Gribble screamed. "Just shut up! Oh fuck," he said, sounding shattered.

I blinked back stars, bile churning in my stomach. My head was beyond painful. My cheek was already swelling. I couldn't see out of my right eye.

"She's not escaping now," Tyrone said matter-of-factly.

"You're fucking psychotic," Gribble snarled.

"Well, we all know you're not, according to the good doc here," Ty hissed. "But then, you just killed a man. I ain't done that yet."

"He might be all right," Gribble answered, not sounding convinced.

"He hit the windshield," Trent pointed out, nodding toward the shattered dent in the centre of the glass. "Then bounced off the roof. I watched him land hard out the back."

"Must have gone ten metres," Tyrone said.

"Twenty," Trent helpfully supplied.

"Shut up!" Gribble growled. "There's a car ahead."

"Fuck," both Tyrone and Trent muttered.

"Cop car," Gribble announced, making my heart leap into my chest.

"What do we do?" Trent asked.

"Fang it," Tyrone suggested.

"Wish you were fucking driving," Gribble muttered.

"Pull over, and we'll swap," Tyrone dryly said. I blinked back spots and stared out at the dark landscape that flashed by. The moon hung large in the night sky, stars twinkling all around it. A fine night to die.

I swallowed back more bile. I couldn't think of Devon McIntyre right now. I could barely think as it was. I struggled to focus, struggled to see what hazards were set up in front of us.

"They'll have road spikes," I said, my words slurring slightly.

"What?" Gribble asked.

"Fuck, she's right. Road spikes," Tyrone snarled. "Jump the kerb."

"There's no fucking kerb in the country, you fucking psychotic piece of shit!" Gribble yelled.

"Don't shoot the messenger!"

"What fucking messenger? What fucking message?" Gribble was losing it. I giggled.

"What's funny, doc?" Tyrone asked, pressing his scowling face up into mine in what had to be a clear threat.

"Concussion," I slur-muttered.

"Shit," Trent said. "Now you've gone and done it. She was meant to be unharmed."

"You think it matters now?" Tyrone demanded. "We're about to be arrested."

"Not if I can help it," Gribble muttered, and downshifted the car.

Blue and red lights flashed lazily up ahead, becoming more distinct the closer we got to them. Trent gripped the oh-shit handle above his head with two hands. Tyrone muttered something under his breath; I think it might have been a prayer.

And then we were somehow airborne, and two dark figures were throwing themselves to the ground beneath us, as blue flashing underbody lights lit up a police ute while it stood sentinel at the end of the road. The exhaust hit. A bang and crash sounded out. The WRX hit the ground on two wheels, rocking precariously.

And then with a screech from all four tyres and a further war cry from Gribble, the car righted itself and shot off down the road.

"Fucking A!" Trent yelled.

"Aced it!" Tyrone shouted, thumping Gribble on the shoulder.

"Pigs don't know who they're dealing with," Trent added, sounding inordinately pleased with himself.

I snorted. Rolling my head back on the headrest, pressing my still bound hands against the throbbing in my skull.

"What?" Gribble asked, looking at me in the rearview mirror.

"They know exactly who you are, boys," I said.

"Doesn't matter," Tyrone announced. "Gribble can outrace the best of 'em."

All one big happy team now they'd outfoxed the cops.

I smiled. It hurt.

"This is Twizel," I said. "You've nowhere to hide."

CHAPTER 48

HE'D BEEN MY FRIEND

MATT

"Oh, God," Justin said, wiping his mouth. His whole body was trembling. He shook his head as if shaking it would make the grisly vision before him disappear. "Fuck!" he shouted, tipping his face up to the stars.

I sat there quietly while anger bubbled up and rage swirled around, and fury burned a hole inside my heart.

Justin finished shouting and looked back down at Devon's body, his hands on his hips, a scowl on his face, a darkness I'd never seen in my loveable brother marring his pale blue eyes.

Another head shake. Anger warring with confusion crossing his brow. Then his troubled eyes turned to me.

"Derek Gribble," he said, sounding stunned. "He's practically just a kid. Why would he do this?"

I let out a long breath of air. I'd already thought on the matter, and it boiled down to this; Derek Gribble was a coward. He worked a dead-end job, owed a shit-tonne of money on his car, and had lived his entire life in Twizel.

It didn't take a genius to realise he'd been bought and then manipulated, perhaps scared into doing someone's bidding.

David Jenkins? Or someone else? Who was that tourist?

I shook my head and pushed up to my feet, running a hand through my hair and then realising it was covered in blood. I grimaced. Justin turned away, staring out over the pastures toward Red Tussock.

We're not new to death. Farming can be brutal. Being a country copper, you see it all. But this type of death? It would be with Justin forever. Justin who prays to Buddha, recycles like there's no tomorrow, and talks about 'paying it forward.'

My radio crackled, Mac's gruff voice coming over the airwaves. I couldn't quite catch what he was saying. But I knew where he would be. I looked down at Devon one last time and then looked at my brother.

"Go," Justin said. "I'll wait for the ambulance. Make sure he's taken care of."

I lifted my radio up off my shirt, tipped my head down and said into it, "Stand by." Then crossed the small space between us and wrapped Justin up in my arms.

He slapped my back. I slapped his, roughed up his hair, muttered something under my breath that may or may not have been "I love you." Then turned and walked to Devon's ute.

Mine was back at the guest house, and Justin had come on the bike. And Devon, fucking Devon, wouldn't mind.

I cleared my throat as I slipped into the driver's seat, spotting the keys still in the ignition. He'd turned the car off, leaving the headlights on to illuminate him. No doubt jumping out of the vehicle as soon as he saw Liv in the WRX.

He'd tried to stop them from taking her. He'd tried to stand up to a car.

"Bloody idiot," I growled turning the key. Pretending it wasn't tears stinging my eyes.

Devon McIntyre had been a constant in my life since before I could remember. His family just as much a part of this land as the Drakes. He'd always been nice to Missy. Never teased her like some of the others did in school. Always smiled at her, greeted her, included her.

He came to our wedding.

He attended the christening of the twins.

He helped pull up Missy's mangled body from the wreckage.

He drank a glass of whisky with me at Smokey's afterwards. Never said a word. Just leant against the bar and kept me company. Devon McIntyre who'd talk the leg off a ewe and then sell her wool out from under her.

He'd been my friend. And I'd miss him.

But, right now, I had more important things to do than grieve. I'd grieved once before at the wrong time. I wasn't going to do it again. Two beautiful girls were waiting for me to bring home their teacher. Their... mother.

Because that's what Liv was to Rachel and Dani. Not Missy. But someone new they could love and trust. Someone new they could expect to be there. Liv hadn't run when things had got bad. She hadn't sought to save herself.

She'd stayed. Because she'd promised two little girls that she'd be there for them, that she'd carry their hurt, share their load, be the dragon when they needed it and the hugger when it was called for.

And Liv was mine, too. I knew that now as if she was a part of me. Deeply ingrained. Essential to life. Mine. Whoever was pulling Derek Gribble's strings, who'd been stalking Liv and escalating their behaviour, whoever it was, I was coming.

I was coming for my woman, for my kids' new mother. I was coming, and I wouldn't stop until they'd paid.

CHAPTER 49

WE'D GOT IT SO WRONG

LIV

THE CAR RATTLED AS IT ROLLED THROUGH THE CENTRE OF town. The muffler, no doubt, scraping along the roadway sending sparks up into the air behind us. Every time Gribble changed gear, the car didn't so much hiss as whine. It limped down Main Street, passed the Musterer's Hut, the Shearing Shed, and the Smoking Salmon.

I looked out of the window at the souvenir shop and wondered if the cameras were picking this up, images of a shattered WRX cruising down the main drag of Twizel. I pressed my still bound hands to the window, pushed my face up as far as I could, hoping Alicia Parsons would be able to recognise me.

"Sit back," Tyrone growled, hauling me backwards into my seat by a firm grip on my shoulder. I let out a burst of air when my shoulders hit the seat, then sucked it in again when my head hit the headrest.

I hurt. All over. Inside and out. My face was swollen, my eye was shut, my jaw ached, my heart broken.

Had David orchestrated all of this?

"Who made you do this?" I asked the car at large.

"No one made us do anything," Trent said.

"Shut up," Tyrone growled. To him or me, it was hard to guess.

"Did you even know me before I came here?" I asked.

"Why would we know you?" Trent offered.

"Shut up!" Tyrone shouted.

I bit my lip and stared out of the window. There was a crack running down the side of it. Not as big as the windscreen 'dent' but enough to fracture my view.

"Your car is broken," I murmured.

"Don't remind me," Gribble grumbled back.

"It'll cost a lot to fix it," I offered.

"Might as well ditch it now and claim insurance."

"Will insurance cover this?" I asked, genuinely surprised that the boy thought he'd get away with everything that had happened tonight and then be compensated for it.

"You mean will it cover a hit and run?" Gribble growled.

Tyrone muttered something under his breath, but Trent turned in his seat and smiled. It seemed so out of place, considering.

"*Our* insurance will cover it," he said. He seemed sure of that fact. But from what I knew of insurance companies, Gribble would be out of pocket on this.

Out of pocket and arrested.

I almost asked where the nearest prison to Twizel was. I had no idea. Christchurch?

The battered car continued its inexorable rattle down Main Street. No one rushed out of Smokey's to see what was causing the racket. And no movement at the souvenir shop led me to believe the cameras were unmanned for the night. I was on my own. Surrounded by malfunctioning young adults. Heading towards a confrontation I had tried my best to avoid.

I'd moved down to Twizel to get away from my stalker. I'd left everything I knew and started again. I might have fallen for Red Tussock, for two damaged girls and their equally as damaged father, but I'd come here to escape.

And now I was trapped. Tied up and battered. Shattered as much as Gribble's Subaru.

Had I known this would happen would I have chosen to leave?

I'm not a coward. I don't believe in hiding. I'd tried it Detective Sergeant Pierce's way. I'd tried it Matt's way.

Now I was going to do it my way.

"Who is it?" I demanded, sitting up straight in my seat.

Gribble caught the change in my demeanour, his eyes rising from scanning the street to the rearview mirror.

"You'll find out soon enough," he said, then looked away.

If it was David, it would hurt. No denying. But if it was David, then I had a connection already established with him. A way to reach him. A way to help.

And if it was a yet unidentified patient, then I'd think on my feet. I could do it. I had an excellent memory. I could recall consultations and profiles I'd made decades ago. I'd treat them like any returning patient; carefully, openly, supportively. Remission is not something to be ashamed of.

But when the WRX finally made it to a darkened alley, out of sight of the main road and any late night drinkers at Smokey's, I realised my mistake.

Because the person waiting wasn't David. It wasn't a patient I'd treated before, either.

It was a stranger. Or more precisely, someone I'd met but didn't yet know well.

"Hello, Dr Logan," Helen Cameron said as she stood on the back steps of the library.

Purple hair, I thought. We'd got it so wrong.

Who the hell was Helen Cameron to me?

CHAPTER 50

I HADN'T SEEN THAT ONE COMING

MATT

"God knows how they did it," Mac said, straining to tighten the nut on his wheel, "but they slashed our tyre as they went airborne, *Dukes of Hazard* style."

"The *General Lee* has nothing on boy racers," Annmarie muttered.

You've got to be kidding me. "So, we lost them," I said, staring hard at the back of Mac's bent head.

"Car took off towards town," Mac replied smoothly as if he couldn't feel the heated stare I was drilling his glasses wearing arse with.

"Town's a big area to get lost in," I replied, pulling out my cell phone.

Mac snorted. "Those dickheads aren't bright enough to bypass Main Street." He stood up and dusted down his trousers, giving the new tyre one last look before turning to me.

"Alicia Parsons," we both said together.

My turn to snort as I lifted the phone to my ear.

Strangely a calm had settled over me. They had Liv. They were taking her to whoever had started all of this. Part of me was frantic.

Another part of me was just AWOL; that part of me that constantly thought of how bad things could get. But the biggest part of me was already calculating how to combat this. Who to pull in. What assets to use. How best to resolve this and rescue Liv.

"Senior Sergeant," Alicia Parsons greeted down the line.

"I'm getting her back," I said. I wasn't sure if that was to her or me, but it was said with conviction.

"I know you are," the souvenir shop owner replied steadily.

It hadn't crossed my mind that Alicia wouldn't have known what was happening. Somehow that woman, either through her extensive network of CCTV cameras or just from some sort of strange sixth sense, knew exactly what was going on in our township.

It was creepy. But creepy I could use.

"Are you going to help me?" I demanded.

"When have I not?"

That didn't deserve an answer.

"Gribble's WRX. Have you seen it?"

"What did you do to it, Senior Sergeant?" she asked. "That boy's pride and joy, a complete wreck."

"You've seen it," I concluded.

"I know you have a temper," Alicia went on smoothly, "but a baseball bat to the windscreen was tempestuous even for you."

"It wasn't a bat." There were places her cameras didn't reach. "He killed Devon McIntyre," I said bluntly. "Ran him down and didn't stop."

Silence.

For once I'd managed to shut Alicia Parsons up.

It was a hollow victory.

"Ms Parsons?" I called.

"I liked Devon," she said eventually.

"Everyone liked Devon," I replied steadily.

"Yes," she said, not sounding at all like her upper-class self. I realised then that the prim and proper Brit had a heart beneath the houndstooth and Laura Ashley.

"Have you seen Derek Gribble's car?" I asked again.

"Yes," she repeated. "I've seen it."

Pulling teeth, that's what this was. But I'd let Alicia have this one. She was as much affected by Devon's death as we all were.

"Where is it, Alicia?" I pressed, going for a more personal approach. She deserved it. She'd shown her true colours.

Devon was one of ours, and she grieved.

"The library," Alicia Parsons said. "He's taken her to the library, Senior Sergeant."

The library? And then it clicked. Purple hair.

Motherfucker. I hadn't seen that one coming.

Who the hell was Helen Cameron to Liv?

CHAPTER 51

THAT'S WHO SHE WAS TO ME

LIV

The library seemed so different now that I was here under duress. My wrists chaffed where the plastic ties Gribble had used rubbed them. My fingers were starting to tingle; I wriggled them as much as I could, but it was looking grim for my circulation. My head hurt, my eyes hurt, my stomach was roiling.

Who on earth was Helen Cameron to me?

"Take a seat, Doctor," the librarian said, walking across to the front desk without a care in the world.

Tyrone pulled out a chair from a table on the end of a stack and spun it around to face the checkout area. I sat gingerly, studying my stalker, trying to find something to work with here.

"Would you like a cup of tea?" she asked. "No wait, you prefer coffee. Milk no sugar." She smiled at me as if we were friends. As if her knowing how I take my coffee made us bosom buddies.

I swallowed and nodded my head.

Gribble and his mates loitered off to the side, not talking, barely moving, their eyes darting from me - the prisoner - to Helen - their puppet master. I wasn't sure which one of us they feared the most.

Helen produced two cups of steaming coffee from the small

office behind the desk and walked out to hand one to me. I lifted my bound hands and took the cup, unsure if I wanted to drink it. She'd had Gribble drug me. There could be anything in this mug.

"Drink up," she said, taking a sip of her own as if to encourage me.

I offered a small smile and brought the cup to my lips, sniffing. It smelled like coffee. It looked like coffee. I pretended to drink.

Helen smiled; it was knowing.

I took in her short hair; so purple. Her violet eyes, noting the tell-tale edges of contacts on her sclera. Her smile widened at my perusal. She ran a hand over her shirt and rested it at her waist, cocking her hip jauntily.

"I knew we'd get along," she said excitedly.

Time to earn my paycheque.

"Why did you think that?" I asked, pretending to drink the coffee again. Sooner or later I'd have to dispose of it; this charade had a limited expiry.

"You don't see it?" She seemed disappointed. Then quickly her demeanour changed. "Of course you don't; you've been brainwashed. What were they thinking sending you down here?"

It would have been easy to believe the mood swings, but the emotions did not reach her eyes. Tone of voice is the most natural human character to alter. Most people take that as their cue to a person's state of mind.

I'm not most people. Helen Cameron did not feel emotion like the rest of us. She was incapable of it. Why? I didn't yet know. But the librarian was a classic psychopath. This connection she sought with me was entirely superficial.

But fabricated or not, she believed it. She believed we had a connection; one I had to use.

"It's good that I was sent here," I offered. Helen tilted her head to the side and studied me. She was good at this; she'd had practice. How long had Matt said she'd lived here? It didn't matter; it had been long enough for her to perfect her charm. "We would never have met face to face," I finished.

She smiled. "But I've seen you before, Doctor. I've watched you often."

I kept my face impassive, but inside I frowned.

"I would have remembered meeting you," I said.

Her smile widened. "I remember the first time I saw you. You made everyone around you brighten. I hadn't expected to see that, not after what had happened. But there you were, making a difference. Brightening his life."

Whose life?

I didn't get to ask; Helen was on a roll. "And then, of course, I just had to get to know you better. I suspect it's the same for everyone. Matt Drake didn't stand a chance."

I didn't like her bringing up Matt's name.

"I think you read too much into my allure."

"Allure, that's the word. You are alluring. I've seen it so many times. Even your neighbours in George Street are drawn to you." My home address. "Taking photos without them becoming aware was difficult." She'd been there.

Of course she had. The picture on my office wall.

"How often did you travel to Auckland?" I asked.

"Once a month. Everyone thought I was attending LIANZ meetings. I did go to one once when it happened to be held in Auckland. But all the others in Wellington and Christchurch and Hamilton and Dunedin, I just pretended to attend them. Instead, I attended to you."

The locals would believe that, too. What head librarian - especially one in charge of such a progressive and singular library - wouldn't attend Library and Information Association of New Zealand meetings?

"A good cover," I offered, treading carefully.

"It was, wasn't it? My brother would have been proud. He always told me I was so smart." She had a brother; it was significant. But she'd moved on before I could get her to open up. "And then you turned up here. It was easy, really. Making sure those idiotic detectives in Auckland noted Matt Drake's advert in the Otago Times. One quick call to CIB regarding a wanted notice on an escaped prisoner, and they started buying up the local rags. Matt did the rest.

"Of course," she went on, "I had expected the police to be a little more circumspect. I'd hoped they had improved their skills in the intervening years. But they're just as incompetent as ever. No surprises there."

She lacked respect for the police; undoubtedly because she had a criminal record. Antisocial Personality Disorder manifested in different ways for different patients. But Helen had already shown much of their traits in her actions to date. Increasingly risky behaviour. Conducting herself in a manner that is unpleasant or uncomfortable for others. Impulsive. Aggressive. She'd fit the profile to a T.

Including, I was picking, a criminal record.

"When did you first encounter the police?" I asked.

"Ten years ago," she said. "But I don't want to talk about that."

"What do you want to talk about?"

"Us, of course. You're here now. With me. He can't have you."

"Who, Matt?" I asked steadily.

"Yes, Matt. The senior sergeant. If you only knew how screwed up he is. He killed her, you know. He might as well have. She was a lost soul, and he was too concerned about the job to notice. I saw them together."

She was losing me. She was flitting from one subject to the next. Typical ASPD. Bored too quickly.

"They thought they could hide from me," she went on. "But I know a thing or two about hiding."

"Because you've been hiding here?" I guessed.

"Yes, you understand. You came here to hide, too." She laughed. It was chilling. "But you walked right into the trap. They did, too, you know. And the senior sergeant was too busy to see."

"Who did, Helen?"

Her smile turned sultry. "I like you saying my name like that."

I didn't offer an argument. I was treading on very thin ice here.

Helen Cameron was psychotic, suffered from ASPD, and had demonstrated time and again, a level of aggression that chilled me.

She walked closer, her body lithe; graceful and seductive. She reached the chair I was sitting on; I had to work hard not to draw back and show my fear. Her hand came up and cupped my cheek as she crouched down to look me in the eye. In such a short amount of time, she'd become familiar to me. I recognised her eyes, even if the colour wasn't real. The tilt of her lips, the angle of her nose.

It puzzled me.

"You are so beautiful," she whispered. "Inside and out. He doesn't deserve you." Matt. She was fixated on Matt's relationship with me.

"I'm here with you," I pointed out.

"Yes. Yes, you are. But I'm not sure you want to be."

My heart offered up a sudden thump inside my chest. My throat became parchment dry. I licked my lips, and Helen's eyes darkened.

"Why me?" I said, my voice scratchy.

"Because you made him smile again."

"Who, Helen? Who did I make smile?"

"You don't know?" She seemed genuinely surprised. "But you're so clever," she added, as if to herself. Then to me, "Can't you see the resemblance?"

Standing there, no more than a foot from me, her hand still cupping my jaw, her face serene, I struggled to see what she wanted me to see.

I saw a stalker.

I saw a woman with ASPD.

I saw psychosis and a thin veneer covering impulsive-aggressive behaviour.

"Wait," she said, reaching up and removing her contacts. She blinked a few times to clear her vision and then looked down at me.

"Olivia," she said, lowering her voice, clipping my name in a way that was all too familiar to me.

My heart thudded, my chest tightened, my stomach dropped to my feet.

"You're dead," I whispered, stunned. "He thinks you're dead." Surely he did. Surely it hadn't been an act all these years.

"My little brother is not as bright as you and me," Helen Cameron said smugly.

Not Helen Cameron, I corrected; Marie Jenkins. The sister who David had been grieving.

That's who she was to me.

CHAPTER 52

BUT NOT FAST ENOUGH

MATT

Bloody hell! She was David Jenkins' sister. I was guessing from Liv's reaction, the *dead* sister. The one Liv had said had committed suicide while they'd been at university.

I looked at the end of the stack opposite, towards Mac; his eyes met mine, putting it all together.

We'd snuck in the back entrance to the library. Gribble's banged up car was parked out the back, next to a brand new, mud splattered, white WRX which we believed belonged to Helen Cameron. Alicia's cameras had spotted Liv in the rear seat of Gribble's Subaru as it rounded the library building.

We'd known she was here; it was just a matter of getting her out now.

Mac crouched at the end of one stack, Annmarie at the end of another. Maggie beside me. I'd made Luke and Zach wait outside, ostensibly because they weren't cops. In reality for cover. I wanted no one escaping.

Justin, of course, was still with Devon.

Devon.

I pushed all thoughts of wringing Derek Gribble's neck from my mind and concentrated on Liv.

Her hands were bound by plastic ties, the hard edges digging into flesh, her fingers were white; bad circulation at a guess. Her back was straight, though, and her eyes bright. Well, one eye was, the other was swollen shut, and didn't that just make me want to rage?

I sucked in a slow breath of air and attempted a few of Liv's breathing exercises. Hell if I knew if they worked, but Dani and Rachel swore by them. A few deep breaths later and I was able to catalogue the rest of Liv's health.

She looked tough. Ready for anything; which considering her hands were tied, and she'd been roughed up a bit, seemed disconnected from reality. But, damn, I was proud.

She questioned, no *engaged*, Helen, as if she meant every word. Her focus solely on her patient, her voice caring but firm. Helen for her part was enamoured.

But then, we already knew the stalker had the hots for Olivia Logan.

Helen Fucking Cameron. I'd shared drinks with the woman at Smokey's. I'd welcomed her onto Red Tussock land every Easter for the Fair. I'd borrowed books, sought her aid in finding information I couldn't quite get on the Net. I'd trusted her with my children.

How could you think you knew someone and really you didn't know them at all?

Story of my life. The thought only reminded me of Missy.

"David," Liv was saying. "You're Marie."

"Yes," Helen said, smiling. Something was off about that smile. My gut roiled, making acid surge up my gullet.

"Does he know?" Liv sounded hurt. I wasn't sure it was an act; this was real. She still doubted her business partner.

"He was a much better person consumed in grief."

"You wanted him to grieve you?" Liv asked.

"I wanted him to feel. He never felt a damn thing growing up. Always so contained. Always so well put together. He knew what he would become. He knew how to get there. But not once did he want it like he wanted it after I faked my death."

"You must love him very much," Liv guessed, and how she got that out of what Helen had just said, I did not know.

"He was my little brother. Little brothers are supposed to look up to you, aren't they? Well, he looked up to me after I was dead."

"He mourned you," Liv corrected.

"With more feeling than he'd shown me while I was alive."

This was one fucked up family. David Jenkins was as psychotic as his sister. But where one had thrown that psychosis into his work, the other had started stalking, killed cats, and drugged a psychiatrist.

Both of them should rot in prison as far as I was concerned.

"Marie," Liv said.

"Don't call me that. I'm Helen now."

"You prefer Helen? Why?"

"Helen has her shit together."

"But Marie is who makes David feel."

Helen Cameron cocked her head to the side and studied Liv. I did *not* like her looking at my woman in that fashion. I glanced across at Mac and gave the signal. Time to surround our boy racers, and get ourselves into position to end this. Mac nodded his head, turned and gave the signal to Annmarie, and then with one check down their stacks, they moved off to make their way to the other side of the library.

It would take them a few moments to get into position. I returned my attention to the scene in the middle of the library.

"Marie dead is what makes him feel," Helen finally countered. "No. I am no longer that pathetic wimp of a girl. Now I command my brother's attention."

"He doesn't even know you're alive," Liv pointed out.

"But that's the point! Have you not been listening?" The increase in volume of her words had my hackles rising. I steadied myself, ready to launch.

But Liv handled it like a pro. I was so damn proud.

"Then we'd better make sure he doesn't see you," she said quickly. "You do know he's here? In Twizel."

"Idiot brother, coming to your rescue."

"He wouldn't have done that before," Liv said smoothly. "But you made him feel. You fixed him."

I doubted that was a psychiatric term Liv used often.

"Yes, I did, didn't I?"

"A job well done, Helen."

Helen offered Liv an arched brow. "You're psychoanalysing me."

"It's what I do." No hesitation at all.

"You think I'm mad."

"I think I could help you." Of course she did. This was Liv. She'd spent her adult life helping people like Helen Cameron. She wouldn't think otherwise now when faced with her own mortality.

Maybe Liv wasn't aware of the risk she was in. My heart beat too quickly.

Shifting uneasily, I tried to spot Mac and Annmarie across the library. The shadows were thin on the ground, but no face peered around the end of the stack opposite me. *Come on!*

"I don't need your help," Helen said.

"Then what do you want from me?"

Liv. Fuck. She'd be great in hostage negotiations. But was hopeless with her own safety. Don't make the psycho say it. Giving Helen focus right now seemed counterintuitive.

"I'm not sure," Helen said slowly. "I wanted to make you see like I made David see."

"That you're worthy of attention? Worthy of more?" Liv pressed.

"Yes! Yes! You made him so happy. You helped him concentrate on his career. You even stuck by him."

"And you want that from me?"

"Yes." Surer now, less excitable. "You'll like me like you like David. But I'm more clever than David is. I'm more your type."

"David is my friend," Liv said.

"David masturbates to the thought of you every day in his office."

Fucking hell. "He has one of your t-shirts from college there. He wraps it around his dick and moans your name when he comes."

I didn't know how to breathe anymore.

"Oh," Liv said. "That's flattering." Flattering?

"Flattering?" Helen echoed. "He masturbated in your office." Liv winced. "When he found the picture I'd left."

Holy fucking shit.

"Did he?" Liv said steadily. "And how do you know this?"

"Because I left a camera there."

CIB Auckland hadn't found a camera in Liv's office, and that place had been searched with a fine toothed comb.

"I think the police would have found one when they searched," Liv pointed out, calling Helen's bluff expertly.

"I didn't leave one in your office, Olivia. I left one on my brother. On his cufflink. On his ties. On his laptop."

Pierce and Stone wouldn't have searched David Jenkins.

"Stupid idiot didn't realise the message was for him and not you. He stood there, looking at the picture of you covered in blood, and stroked himself to completion. Caught it all on film. I can show you it sometime."

I grimaced, a bad taste on my tongue.

"That's why you went back for his laptop," Liv guessed. My clever, clever woman. Able to reason it all out without batting an eyelash. "You took the files to cover your tracks."

"I took the files because the cops suspected David." I nodded my head. Pierce had told me that's why he'd sent Liv down here; a contained environment, only they and David Jenkins knew. They were calling him out. "It confused the detectives for a while. Confused your senior sergeant, as well."

"You didn't even know Callum Wilkes," Liv surmised.

Helen smiled. There was absolutely no emotion in it.

"The police are so easily led, Olivia. So easily controlled if you know how."

Liv lifted her chin and stared Helen in the eye.

"You don't look worried," Helen commented mildly.

"Should I be?" Liv demanded. Damn, my woman was on fire. My eyes were drawn immediately to her flame-red hair.

"Not for yourself, darling," Helen purred. "But for your lover? Yes."

Liv went to stand up. Helen took two steps toward her and slapped her cheek so hard Liv spun in the air, and with a teeth-jarring splat, landed face down on the unforgiving floor. One booted foot settled into Liv's back.

It all happened so fast; I hadn't even sucked in a breath of air.

And then Helen growled, "Now, Tyrone."

And the stacks started to topple over, one after the other after the other. Making Maggie and I scramble to get out of the way.

But not fast enough.

CHAPTER 53

AND DEFINITELY NOT AFTER

LIV

"You're a bit of a disappointment," Helen said in my ear as I struggled to get out from under her body.

Noise ricocheted off the high ceilings, bouncing off the four walls; row upon row of massive stacks plummeting to the wooden floors. The sound was deafening, but I could still hear the lack of emotion in Helen's voice. The dead tone. That fateful certainty.

"I think you've failed to understand my messages to you," she said conversationally. Her knee pressed harder into my spine. "My love notes, so to speak." I forced my still-bound hands up under my chin and attempted to rise an inch.

A firm grip settled in my hair, and my bruised cheek smashed into wood. Tears streamed out of my eyes, running down the side of my nose, trickling into the corner of my mouth. I spluttered.

"Such a disappointment," Helen said steadily. "I realised we weren't on the same page when you kissed the senior sergeant. Right outside the Jasmine Thai. Right after I'd paid handsomely for a picture of your deception inside Smokey's."

Jesus. Had she hired the tourist to take that shot? I was sure she hadn't been there; in Smokey's Tavern. Who else could she have used? The pharmacist?

It didn't matter. Not with Helen's hand in my hair, forcing my face into submission on the ground.

"Get off me," I growled.

"*Tsk, tsk,*" she purred. "You *are* feisty. I can see why he'd fuck you. I'd fuck you. I might even do it, yet." Her free hand landed between my thighs, rubbing roughly. I gritted my teeth and kicked up with my heel, landing a blow to her elbow. Her hand flew out and then immediately cuffed me on the side of my head.

I grunted out a sound, lost in amongst the clatter of falling books and flesh on flesh slaps. Were Tyrone and Gribble fighting? I couldn't see a rescue coming from that quarter, so I just renewed my efforts to buck Helen off my back.

"It's no use, you know," she said, leaning down to lick my earlobe. I tried for a headbutt, but her grip was too sure, and I failed. "I own them. They'll deal with your lover and his useless sidekicks, and then clean up this mess afterwards."

"You don't own anyone," I growled against the floor. I was pretty sure the number of penises drawn on the side of the library was Gribble's way of telling Helen to fuck off.

The one on the side of my flat, I was thinking, was his way of telling us to join the dots.

Shame we hadn't until it was too late.

"Oh, you're so sweet. So innocent. David has kept you sheltered. I knew he would. I trusted him. *He* trusted you. But you couldn't help letting him down, could you?"

I continued to struggle, but I was tiring. She might have been short, but Helen Cameron was all muscle. A boulder sitting on my back.

"Why did you dump him?" Helen asked, hot breath against my tear dampened cheek.

"That was years ago," I panted beneath her.

"When you dumped him, I thought he'd dump you back. But he

didn't. He just started to wank off while he listened to your voice on his answer machine. His nose in that damn t-shirt. It must have lost your scent years ago, but the idiot kept on wrapping it around his dick to get himself off."

She was pathologically psychotic. Aggression poured off her. The only emotion I was sure she actually felt. She wasn't concerned about me dumping David when we were back in university. She wasn't even worried about him... masturbating to thoughts of me.

No, Helen Cameron was angered that I'd broken a promise.

I've dated since David, but not seriously. I've never shared a home with someone before Matt.

The promise is broken. Your word is dead. Should he be?

I searched the fallen stacks, my vision limited. The dust of disturbed reading also made the air thick and hard to see through. But I saw the shadows shift. And I caught the flash of purple. As it was Helen anchoring me to the floor, I knew that flash had to belong to Gribble.

And then I saw Matt throw a punch.

My heart skittered to a halt. My eyes brimmed with further tears. Helen started to laugh.

"You think he can beat a twenty-year-old? Matt's no spring chicken," she said. "And the boys have been practising. It was part of the deal."

"What deal?" The more she talked, the more distracted she'd be. My eyes tracked Matt's progress for as long as he stayed in my line of sight and then it was just sounds, and Helen and me.

"Their cars for their cooperation. Young bucks are so easily bought, aren't they? Show them a flashy vehicle, add in a few modifications, and they're yours."

I felt like vomiting. Panting, trying to fight when there was simply no energy left to do so, I turned my head as far as she'd let me and glared in her eyes.

"They sure have a strange way of showing their appreciation," I said, flashing teeth in a smile. "Penises. Do you think they were trying to tell you something?"

The hit to my head was immobilising. But then, I wasn't exactly going anywhere right then.

I registered Helen's weight lifting off me, then the pull on my hair as she tugged me up onto my shaking legs. Metal flashed. A knife, my numbed brain told me.

The knife was cold. You never said it would be so cold. The blood was warm. You were right.

The message she'd left on my picture in my office. For David. Not me.

Part of me grieved for the children they must have once been. David never talked about his childhood. Refused to. He'd distract with talk of his sister's sudden death. I should have seen it. I'm paid to see it. I'm good at what I do, but I missed that.

How could I have put it all together? Marie was meant to be dead. I was missing part of the equation.

Two kids, both psychotic, both registering on the ASPD spectrum.

Nausea welled in my gut, frustration at myself warring with empathy for them. And then Helen flipped the knife in her hand as if it was a toy. The same knife she'd used to kill the cat?

Something snapped inside me. My eyes darted to the floor. Books and pieces of metal shelving lay scattered across it. One piece right there by my foot.

I stomped on the end hard. It sprang up in the air in front of me. My hands, still fucking bound, were tied in front of me, too. So, I simply gripped the shelving, swung with all my might and hit Helen Cameron on the side of her head.

And then I was running, and Maggie was shouting, and someone had started a fire in the corner. Gribble raged, and Matt swung a fist at his face and then I was in Maggie's arms, and she was trying to lead me from the room, but Tyrone stood there. Blocking our path.

"Tyrone," I said, panting. "It's over."

He scowled, fisted his hands, and then took a menacing step toward us.

Maggie pulled her gun. Tyrone didn't even see it. And then we were hit hard from the side, both of us tumbling, as Trent went sailing past.

"She's using you!" I yelled as chaos surrounded. Mac appeared in the middle of the melee. Annmarie threw a punch as if she wasn't petite and usually quiet. While Maggie crawled one way and I crawled the other, until we were out of harm's way but separated. I stared across the expanse between me and the gun-slinging police officer, frantic, panicked, too many stimuli. Flashes of light. Bursts of sound. My body overloaded as I futilely tried to settle myself.

It wasn't working. Nothing was working. Lights. Noise. Heartache.

I sucked in a breath. Started muttering to myself. The words somehow became a song: Rachel Platten's 'This Is My Fight Song.' Singing always worked for Matt. I had to try.

"What are you doing?" Matt suddenly said from beside me.

Joy like I'd never felt welled up in my chest. I wanted to hug him. I wanted to kiss him.

Instead, I said, "Singing a song to help calm me down." I shrugged and held my breath, heart pounding.

He just stared at me as if I was mad. Maybe I was. Maybe we were mad together.

"A song with the word 'fight' in it?" he queried, keeping an eye on the 'fight scene' still unravelling all around us.

Hmmm. He had a point.

"What do you sing?" I asked, aware this was all a little surreal. But I was breathing again. Slowly. Surely.

Matt, though, didn't seem in a hurry to reenter the fray. Mac and Annmarie and Maggie seemed to have that all under control. I noticed then, that Luke and Zach had also entered the library, and were rounding up the boy racers.

I searched for Helen; saw her out cold on the floor. The shelving unit I'd used to get free of her discarded to the side. Nauseatingly, there was a little bit of blood on the edge of it. I swallowed.

Matt gripped my chin, turned my face toward him. Away from the scene unfolding.

That's why he was here, I realised; talking not acting. Giving me time to catch up.

At that moment, I couldn't have loved him more.

He offered a grimace and then said, "For starters, I sing it in my head." I waited. Right then, I couldn't have moved an inch. Matt knew. He stroked my jaw softly and lowered his voice and said, "The Exponents. 'Even Though I'm Blue.'"

In the middle of what seemed like a war zone, at the culmination of months and months of fear, Matt Drake gave me a part of himself. A part I was sure he hadn't given another soul. He gave me his song. The one he uses to calm himself down, centre himself when the world is swirling around his head. The one he's had to use so often over the past year.

It was a gift. A treasure. One I accepted with care and the gravity the situation demanded.

Thankfully, I was familiar with the song. I started singing it softly to myself. It was a good song. An appropriate one for a man who dressed in blue. And it worked. The room quietened. The lights seemed less harsh. All that was left was just Matt.

"Can I borrow it?" I asked.

"Have at it, doll," he drawled. "Although it *will* take on a whole new meaning when you sing it."

I stopped singing and met his unshuttered gaze. Matt wore his heart on his sleeve, I realised. For everyone to see. Helen Cameron had seen it and not liked it. I saw it and fell completely.

This man who had appeared in my life so unexpectedly certainly knew how to make me feel.

I felt things, then, that I had never felt before; loved; wanted; desired. Matt Drake stole my heart, right then and there, on the library floor. Such courage to love again. Such a big heart full of love to give.

I was unsure if I could *ever* say goodbye to him. Not before he'd told me his fight song.

And definitely not after.

Matt Drake had the biggest heart in the world and he'd given it to me. I reached up and cupped his cheek, my hands awkward because of the ties still binding them. He closed his eyes, leant his face against my palm, breathed deeply.

And welcomed us both home for eternity.

EPILOGUE

MATT

ONE WEEK LATER

It was at times like these that I realised life was unpredictable. Uncontrollable even. We're just holding on by the seat of our pants, hoping we won't get thrown off the merry-go-round. Hoping it won't hurt when we hit the ground hard.

It had hurt when I hit the ground after Missy. It had hurt again when I realised how absent I'd been in my daughters' lives. It had hurt for the third time when Helen Cameron admitted under psychiatric assessment that she'd played a part in Missy falling into Marinkovich's arms.

I'd fucked up; I knew it. I hadn't been there for Missy. I hadn't been what she'd needed. But then Missy hadn't been what I had needed either. In then end, Missy chose her path, despite having been manipulated by an aggressive psychotic with antisocial personality disorder; a woman who had faked her own death.

Helen Cameron, or as her legal records stated, Marie Jenkins, had twisted Missy's loneliness into something truly ugly. And right when Missy had realised she'd become someone she didn't recognise,

Helen had twisted Marinkovich's own psychotic tendencies into a desire to kill if he couldn't possess.

Missy had been trying to leave him. But Helen had already flicked the switch on Marinkovich to make him commit murder.

Thank fuck he'd drawn the line at Missy.

I glanced across the room to Rachel and Dani. Playing with a subdued Rory and Jerome McIntyre; who were mourning their Uncle Devon. I ran a hand over my mouth, trying to hold the emotion in, trying to accept that another good person had been lost to the machinations of the town librarian.

It was hard. So many deaths. So much heartache. Would we ever recover?

"Senior Sergeant," Alan Bennet greeted softly off to my side. He dropped the 't' again, but his French was as subdued as this event.

"Bennet," I said, watching Liv wrap Rachel up in a hug, as Dani chased after a screaming Rory. I didn't think it was anything I needed to get involved with. Kids will be kids, and Liv was a natural with them. She'd have Rachel smiling again in no time and entering back into the fray with her friends.

"You 'ave had a busy time of it," the pharmacist said.

"We all have," I commented mildly.

"It was unexpected. The librarian," he clarified.

"Was it?" I asked. Alan Bennet had been inside Smokey's when the photo of Liv and I had been taken on Helen's order. He'd even been talking to the tourist who we suspected had taken the photo for Helen.

How much had Alan Bennet known of what was happening in our town?

"For a certainty," the Frenchman said. "But all has turned out for the best, *non*?"

I looked toward Devon's family and thought of the funeral we'd just attended. So similar to Missy's and yet so different. The entire town had turned out for Devon. They had also turned out for Missy. But whereas they'd whispered behind closed hands of what my wife had been caught doing, they only had grand words and fond memories of Devon.

I let out a slow breath of air. Missy. Strangely, despite evidence to the contrary, she didn't consume my thoughts so much anymore.

"The man you are looking for," Alan murmured. "He is still in town."

"The tourist?" I asked.

"Yes. He is keeping a low profile, but I would not think he has finished his business here just yet."

"And what business do you think he has in Twizel?" I demanded.

Alan smiled; an enigmatic smile, one that often accompanied his Gallic shrug.

"How should I know, Senior Sergeant?" he murmured, nodding his head in farewell and wandering off into the crowd of mourners.

That man was hiding a secret the size of Canterbury, but I couldn't help thinking his intel was sound. Just what the hell had Alan Bennet been before he became a chemist?

Liv walked up then, the twins laughing together - all differences mended - making the boys even crack a few smiles.

"Children are so resilient," Liv said as she slipped an arm over mine. My hand came down on top of hers instantly, as if to trap her there. But I was gradually beginning to realise that Liv had no intention of leaving.

Her business partner was soon to become her ex-business partner, something Liv grieved but didn't allow too much ingress. In fact, she'd said to me only that morning that she was looking for a new place to set up her offices down here.

Twizel might not be a large town, but it sure as hell needed a psychiatrist.

"Have they talked to you about what happened?" I asked, entwining my fingers in hers, wanting nothing more than to pull her away from this crowd.

Somehow sneaking off for a quickie at a wake didn't seem appropriate.

And then I pictured Devon McIntyre in my mind. He would have offered a wink, distracted the busybodies, and thumped me on the back as I dragged Liv by.

I smiled. Liv blinked up at me but chose to answer my question instead.

"They've started talking about that day."

That day. When my life had changed.

I'd thought at the time, and for a long time afterwards, that my life had been torn apart.

I'd been wrong.

It *had* changed, no denying. But without that heartache, I wouldn't have found true love.

"What did they say?" I whispered, pulling her closer, unable to stop myself wrapping her up in my arms. My nose buried in all that glorious riot of red. I inhaled deeply and felt my heartbeat settle. There was no ache there anymore, only a burst of something I had come to realise was absolute love.

How could you live so long and not experience this kind of emotion? How could loving someone like I loved Liv make all other emotions pale in comparison?

I'd had my fair share of turmoil; a storm I'd had to battle and damn near lost. But standing here with Liv, at what was undoubtedly one of the saddest events I'd had to attend recently, and all I could feel was the sun on my face and the heat of her body and the promise of another bright day full of love.

"He told them, on Mount Cook Road, that he was sorry," Liv said, drawing me back to my daughters' recoveries. "That sometimes things just happened."

"He was there."

We'd suspected it. We'd concluded that it had been him who'd killed Missy. He'd said enough at the end for us to join the dots. Helen Cameron had added weight to the supposition. But to hear proof?

"How accurate do you think their memory is?" I asked.

Liv looked out across the room to where the girls were playing; two Monster High dolls clasped in their little hands dressed up just like their beloved Liv. I smiled. No, I grinned like a fucking lunatic. They were loud. Boisterous. Playing with complete feeling. Yelling at the boys as they turned their noses up at the dolls. Hearing such beautiful noise coming from my beautiful children had me clearing my throat past a lump that had formed.

Not so mute now, eh?

"Does it matter?" Liv asked.

Liv did that a lot, I thought; answered a question with another question. I smiled. I'd come to realise that when she did that, Liv was protecting me. Or pushing me to see something from another angle.

Did it matter? Liv would take care of them. They were healing. They loved Missy. They missed her. But they knew they were safe and cared for and loved.

Life can be hard. It can be a hell on earth, but if you're strong enough, you can fight the flames and come out singed not scorched. Rachel and Dani were strong enough. They also had a dragon in their corner who doused the flames with her fiery heart.

I looked down at the woman who had changed everything. Who had saved me from myself. Who had saved my girls.

"I love you," I said. Not exactly poetry. But it was the truth. Pure and simple. Straight from the heart.

"I love you, too," Liv offered with a soft smile.

I could have sworn I heard Devon chuckle, and then mutter under his breath, "Jeez, Drake. Get a fucking room."

I decided I'd take my friend's advice. Life was for the living. To be seized at every opportunity. I was determined I'd grasp Liv to my chest, hold her carefully against my heart, and count my blessings.

Life was extraordinary. A miracle we shouldn't pass up.

Life was for the living. I chuckled to myself. Life was for Liv.